CLAY

P.C. ROGERS

To every woman who ever believed that being thrown away or abandoned was their identity. And to all the good men who possess the strength to pluck treasures from ashes, clean them up, and let them shine.

To the immediate and extended family that made me and raised me, and the lineage that designed me to be too stubborn to quit on anyone or anything.

To David, my own good man for enduring the muse. And to God who binds us.

Also, to Mom for passing to me the writing gene which cannot be revoked and for lighting the spark at an early age so I could see to share all these stories.

My dearest children:
Be the hero.
Be the treasure.

All I have I invest in you. Good, bad, success and mistake.
You have all of me. You have shared my hardest journey, and
my life. And you make that something great. And your
greatness will endure long after me.

-CHAPTER ONE-

Kelli Christi leaned against the door jam of the trailer home entrance. Her two small children ran and toddled about the echoing space, making shrill noises and laughing at each other. They dodged the stacks of boxes, bags, and large pieces of worn furniture strewn about. Their red hair glowed like fire in the morning sunlight that streamed in through the windows.

They were so innocent and unaware. Kelli fought back the urge to break down and cry. She had rented the decrepit trailer just last night and she felt a crushing sense of failure for moving them into it. But she had no other option.

"It's only temporary." She assured herself quietly. "Only a few months." She told the despair inside herself.

Her coppery eyes drifted exhaustedly around the space. The walls were clean. The usual printed trailer-style wall paper had been freshly painted an off white color; as had all the trim. The floors were a simple brown vinyl, embossed with a wood grain pattern, and it spread through all the living area.

The place smelled like paint and despair. Sunny despair. At least the windows were big and south facing.

She slid her hands down her face and refused to look at anything more. Luckily she wasn't forced to since the landlord walked up behind her. He squinted into the morning sun and reached up to her.

"Missus Christi, here are..."

"Miss." Kelli corrected him, dryly.

"Miss, of course. I'm sorry." He held out his weathered hand, "Here are the spare keys. I had the locks reset for you. There aren't any kids in the park, I'm afraid." He nodded towards her son and daughter who stared at him motionless and wide eyed from behind a stack of boxes, "Mostly rig workers these days. But, they're quiet for the most part. The sheriff knows the lot well, so don't hesitate to call if you ever feel the need."

"You don't live on the premises?" She had reluctantly rented the place because the old man felt fatherly and safe. It was a silly notion, she knew him no more than any of the other men in the town. But the thought of him not being there at all did feel abandoning to her raw emotions. It certainly didn't help that the police were familiar with the place"No. I live north of town. I have a fella in the first trailer who takes care of emergencies for me. Broken pipes, backed up toilets, that sorta thing. His name is Howard." He stepped down, thumbing over his shoulder.

Kelli nodded, logging the name in her mind.

"You all have a good time here. Don't forget rent is due on the first, and late by the fourth. I file eviction papers with the county after that." He tipped his weathered hat and strode away as if she might never see him again.

Kelli watched his tan Chevy pickup drive down the broken road through the center of the trailer park. Just ahead of him the moving truck that had brought all her things lumbered away. Not that her things were many. The vehicles rounded the corner simultaneously, and suddenly they were alone.

She didn't know what time it was. But, they had left the house after nine o'clock, the moving van trailing behind. Calculations raced through her mind as she tried to estimate the amount of time it took to drive to their new town. She added the time it had taken the men to unload everything from the truck. It had to be after noon, though she wasn't sure. She didn't even own a clock, not even a cell phone that could tell her the time.

Timothy had taken everything in the divorce.

Just like that her mind reached the t rail-head of a path she dreaded to follow. She blinked hard and snapped herself out of it.

Her daughter Ruby clutched the last half of a pop-tart in her sticky hands, still unmoving in the quiet place. Her younger brother Joshua protectively held his bottle in the crook of his fat baby arm. They stared at her wide-eyed, waiting for a cue, some indication of what to do next. Kelli's heart ached for them and their new-found insecurities.

"Come on babies. It's nap time."

She scooped up the baby and took the toddler by the hand, leading them down the narrow hall to the empty back bedroom. As if she could fool any of them, including herself that is was theirs, or normal. Or home, for that matter.

The room she took them to was the larger of the two bedrooms. Though neither were really big enough for much more than a double bed and a small dresser. Kelli had neither, so they were certainly spacious now.

"I want my bed." Ruby whined sleepily.

Joshua laid his head quietly on Kelli's shoulder. Her stomach hurt from the knots it'd been in for the last two weeks. Her shoulders throbbed from the weight of her world crashing down on them. Even this simple statement tore her apart like wild animals. She felt so powerless and alone. It was entirely overwhelming. Kelli denied herself the luxury of despair in the moment. Her kids needed her to take charge. *She* needed herself to take charge.

"Mommy will get you a bed, Honey. But right now we get to camp out. Come on, we'll make a tent."

She set the baby on floor and proceeded to tear open some garbage bags, searching through the bedding packed inside. She yanked out a few sheets from the second bag, one of which she poked through the naked curtain rod brackets to cover the window. She stepped out to the living area and dragged in the dining room chairs and tossed the other sheet over them. Under it she made a mat of blankets and pillows. Finally she crawled in and beckoned her children.

"See? This is fun. We're like Indians in a teepee." She persuaded them. Ruby crawled in obediently, but her face showed uncertainty. She was only three but Kelli knew she was trying to please her; trying to do the right thing. Trying to be as grown up as mommy.

"We don't have to paint our faces though, Mommy." She hunkered down beside Kelli.

Joshua toddled in and threw himself full force against Kelli's head. Smashing her nose. "Momma!" He exclaimed, pointing at the fabric ceiling above them.

"Sleep with us, Mommy, please?" Ruby begged quietly as Kelli moved to leave the room.

"Sure, Baby." Kelli climbed back into the tent.

She lay on the blankets between the kids and waited quietly for them to fall asleep. She thought of the only things on her mind.

Two weeks ago she had been Mrs. Nevins. Two weeks ago she had a pretty house in a new neighborhood. She had what she had convinced herself was a devoted, loving husband. A man she'd been in love with since high school, married to for over seven years.

But, two weeks ago she'd opened her front door in the middle of a warm and sunny spring day to find a police officer holding a stack of papers. His voice was still audible in her mind.

"Ma'am? I hate to do this. You're being served with divorce papers."

The deputy had been young and nervous, he had even left the door to his cruiser open when he walked up the wide path to the door. And his voice cracked a little when he said "divorce papers".

"I... I don't understand?" Kelli had taken the papers mindlessly, "My husband is at work. He's only been gone a few hours."

"Sorry, Ma'am." The officer whispered. "Sometimes men just don't like to do this part of it. The county sometimes has us drop them off to verify they've been received."

"I think you've got the wrong house." She said, immediately offering them back to him, "I love my husband. He's a good man. We have two children."

"Good men don't divorce their wives with no warning." He had held up the stack of papers and pointed to the name and address on the first line, "Kelli Ann Nevins, four twenty- four Valley Road, Bismark, North Dakota."

A wave of cold sweat had sent her reeling, and she stumbled for the bottom stair, just inside the door. The officer stepped in to help her sit without falling. She remembered the clicking of the things hanging from his belt and the creak of the leather it was made of. He laid the pile on her lap.

"I am so sorry, Mrs. Nevins." He said, his voice had been genuinely tight with emotion.

Kelli looked at the packet of papers. She had quickly skimmed through the words on the first page and flipped through the dozen others behind it.

"Miss. Miss Christi." She said quietly in response a few minutes later.

"Ma'am?" The officer asked.

"My maiden name. Apparently I am not to be missus any longer." She had heard the baby stir from his morning nap in his room upstairs and stood to dismiss the officer.

"Uh, there's more. He's also filed an eviction notice. You have thirty days." He handed her the pink slip of paper. "But Ma'am, there is no way the court will uphold this. The divorce isn't finished and likely you're on the mortgage. Also you've got little one's living here with you..."

It had all unfolded like a nightmare she couldn't wake from. She shook the memory away; let the current reality set back in. But as she lay in their new home, between her groggy children, the officer's visit still haunted her. She had still not cried. There hadn't been time.

Tim had not come home that day, instead he called her after the kid's bedtime to "discuss" the terms he had outlined in the papers. He explained that he had been seeing a woman from work for some years now, he claimed he didn't love Kelli anymore and the other woman wanted to marry. It was a cliché and she was stuck living it. He wasn't overly interested in seeing the children. He wasn't able to provide her with alimony, and the best he could do for child support was to sell their house and offer her half the money. However, homes moved comparatively slow in Bismark, unlike the western part of the state where the oil boom was, and until it sold he had nothing to offer her.

He also warned her that he was no longer willing to make payments on the mortgage for her to live there, since his new woman insisted they have a place of their own together. He and this new lover felt it would be best for her and the kids to move out. After all, she was not on the mortgage and if the home foreclosed she'd get no money at all. It had to sell, both of them needed it. It had made sense at the time, it'd been so rational, but when she looked back on it now she couldn't seem to remember why.

She could take him to court for money, but they would insist on him having visitation rights. As it sat he was offering her a clean break. Honestly, she felt it was merciful. He had become so foreign in the blink of an eye. The thought of him having access to their children while in the company of some other woman was more than she could handle.

She had agreed to the terms and they listed the house that next day. She moved out as soon as she was able to. Her parents had sent her some money, even her old grandfather had caught wind of the dealings and mailed her a check for some small amount. It had all been just enough for her to pay for the move and secure the trailer. She couldn't afford first, last and security on a normal home- let alone the monthly rent of a real place. Housing was expensive because of the North Dakota oil boom and the aged trailer was only 300 a month. It wasn't in the worst part of town, but it wasn't in a part she felt entirely comfortable in either.

Kelli had lined up some work there in town, that's what had forced her hand to move here. She would be collecting blood specimens from different doctor's offices and dropping them off at the local hospital's lab. It required only a high school education and a legal vehicle. Two things she actually had left from her former life. It only paid minimum wage plus mileage, though. But she was certain she wouldn't need to leave the kids with anyone else. She planned to bring them along with her and lock them in the car while she made her pick ups and deliveries. She hoped it would work since she had no other option.

Child care was too expensive even if she had wanted it. She knew it was a foolish plan, but she couldn't bear to think any further yet. Especially since she didn't know what she'd do come summer when it was too hot to sit in a locked car. Kelli pushed the uncertainty from her mind, praying that some how these looming problems would spontaneously solve themselves.

With the kids finally asleep she crept from the tent and silently closed their bedroom door. In the combined kitchen and living space she surveyed the various stacks of boxes and bags.

She'd had to sell almost everything that was left her in an attempt to collect enough money for the move, and still she'd had to take money from family. She kept a loveseat, but sold the sofa. They were the set from the basement rec room. Tim had insisted on keeping the nice new set in their formal living room upstairs. Kelli imagined his new woman had fancied them, and for the sake of her nerves hadn't argued.

Tim had even insisted on keeping the crib they had used for Ruby, the same one Joshua was still in. He contended that since it had belonged to him as a baby that his parents should have it back for sentimental reasons. All that was left was Ruby's twin bed. Tim had also seen fit to keep their king size bedroom suite. She hadn't argued with him, didn't risk upsetting the delicate balancing act of their divorce, but it had felt as if not only she but even their children were of no consequence to him.

"Just as well," Kelli mused to herself as she thought about their old bed, "it would never have fit."

She set to work unpacking the kitchen supplies. Tim's lucky lady must have come equipped with her own, since Kelli had been allowed to keep all that she had. It was comical that almost all their boxes contained cookware. She piled the kitchen boxes on the small island that denoted the kitchen boundary and set to unpacking them.

The insides of the cabinets had recently been painted the same white as the walls, but she washed them out anyway with some bleach water before stacking the pots and pans and different utensils in them. She found space for the cups and the flatware. And for the plates and bowls. She discovered the fridge was turned off, but after turning it on and finishing unpacking the kitchen it still had not turned on or produced any cold air. She was pulling it away from the wall to check that it was plugged in when someone beat heavily on the door.

Her heart lurched about in her chest and she dreaded looking to see who it was. Tim was not a violent person; he was a coward. But she still felt raw and insecure. His behavior had been so entirely unprecedented lately and it left her feeling as if the whole world was out to get her. As a consequence her anxiety levels were through the roof.

She paced to the door and stood on tip-toes to look through the small diamond shaped window at its top. A bearded man in filthy clothes stood on the steps outside. She cracked the door open a few inches and eyeballed him.

"You're parked in my spot." He growled.

For a fraction of a second his face flicked with uncertainty before resuming its scowl. Clearly he had expected rig workers to answer the door, not a woman. His thick, oil stained, finger pointed to her little white Honda parked beside the trailer.

"That's where the landlord told me to park." She stated, trying not to sound overly defensive.

"Don't care much who told you to park where, woman." The man's face was also blackened with filth and mud, except for a white band of skin where the strap from a hard hat had crossed his forehead. "Can't get my truck into my drive when you're parked there." His eyes were blood shot and his appearance was haggard. He smelled like the railroad outside her trailer, but despite the rough edges and growling voice his eyes spoke kindly, betraying him.

Kelli felt ill though. She couldn't stand any type of confrontation at the moment. There was no where else to park. Her trailer was the last on the road, which ended immediately by her trailer in a string of cement dividers with "stop!" spray painted in red across them. The space between her trailer and what was apparently this neighbor's was rutted with four side- by-side tire marks. Clearly two parking spaces.

"There's two parking spaces there. There's a parking space right next to my car." She pointed at the opening.

The man made a low growling sound in his throat and stuck his thumb over his shoulder. "Bessie don't fit in a single parking spot. And I was living here first." A large pickup with duel back tires and extended mirrors loomed behind him.

"I have no where else to park."

"Those car seats in that car? You got kid's living here?" He sighed heavily as he said the last part.

Kelli remained defensively silent.

"Look. I sleep all day 'cause I work all night. I can't have a bunch of screaming little monsters keeping me up. You keep your children quiet and I'll park on the drive." He spit a wad of tobacco over the side of the steps, "Deal?"

She wanted to say something; to do something in defense of herself and her kids, but her brain was numb. Instead she nodded without saying anything and shut the door.

Kelli wanted to cry. She wanted her mother. Or her father. Anyone really. A friend, a cousin. She'd settle for her old familiar mailman. But she had no one, and no phone to call anyone even if she did.

Her parents were divorced, neither had the lifestyle or space for her. Beside that there was the fact that they both had moved far south years ago. But just hearing someone tell her she could do it would be enough. Both her parents had come to dislike her ex, but her dad especially. He always had comforting things to say. She'd get a phone with her first paycheck, she promised herself, and call them.

It didn't take longer than an hour to get the kitchen unpacked and put away. She broke down the boxes and stacked them inside another box beside the door. In the living room area she shoved the loveseat under the windows and used one of the two end tables to place the small tube TV on. It had Mickey Mouse ears and only analog reception on it so it couldn't even pick up local stations. It had been in the kids' playroom at one time. But it did play the kids' DVDs, which she had kept all of. The other end table set beside the loveseat and that completed the living room.

The remaining boxes were sentimental items and toys. She carried the toys to the second bedroom and dumped them into a pile on the floor of the empty room. The bathroom was between the two bedrooms and offered a linen closet the size of a flower box. She rolled up their bath towels and stuffed them in it, and sat out their few toiletry items in the tub and on the sink. Everything else would have to wait to find their new places.

She had just finished and sat down on the loveseat when the bedroom door opened and both kids came out rubbing their eyes. They stumbled the short distance to her and clambered up on her lap. Both stared into space, as if trying to reconcile themselves to the new surroundings.

"Did you sleep?" She asked quietly, pulling them to her. They snuggled against her without answering.

"Are you hungry?" Neither said anything.

"Are you still sleepy?" Kelli tried to get a response.

Finally Ruby pushed the hair from her face and spoke, "Mommy?"

"Mm?"

"Where is daddy?" Her voice was so small. Sometimes Kelli forgot just how young three really was.

"Daddy is..." She struggled to find an acceptable answer, but Ruby interrupted her.

"Why do we have to live here now?"

Kelli sighed. She hugged them both tight against her and kissed their heads, "I don't know, Honey. I don't know where daddy is or what got into him. I don't know why we have to live here now. I don't know why things are like this. But I do know we are okay. We will be just fine. We got a job, we got a house. And, right now we will go get some food. Okay?"

Ruby nodded.

Kelli left them on the small sofa and gathered up their shoes and jackets and then returned to dress them. It was still early spring and the afternoons were chilly. Especially as nighttime came on.

Her back ached as she bent and strained to buckle them into their respective child seats in the back seat of the small car a moment later. All of her ached. But nothing half so much as her heart.

She drove around town looking for a decent grocery store. Dixson was still new to her. The extent of their new neighborhood was slowly setting in as Kelli drove past the empty storefronts and gas stations with bars on the windows. They were entirely out of their element, and she lamented inside over how unsettled she felt.

At the last mile, just before giving up, she found a super store just beyond town. The area was full of shopping centers and strip malls, the type of shopping she was used to. It hadn't taken long to fill a grocery cart with various food stuffs when Ruby suddenly announced at full volume that she was about to pee her pants. They were already in the middle of the checkout line. Kelli had the cart mostly emptied on the conveyor belt.

"You have to wait, Honey." She said absently, trying to unload everything in the small space left by the person ahead of her.

"I can't Mommy!" The little girl held her crotch and danced in desperation. Her red hair bobbing with her.

Kelli cursed under her breath. She hadn't been thinking straight at all. She had forgotten to have Ruby pee before leaving home. Kelli grabbed her hand and threw the baby onto her hip.

"We have a potty emergency, I promise I'll be *right back*." She said to the cashier. She had interrupted the conversation she was having with the customer ahead of her. Kelli couldn't wait for an answer, she ran with the kids to the bathroom and helped Ruby, between her little dances, onto the toilet.

She balanced the baby and helped the little girl wash her hands and also managed to wash her own. She helped her back into her jacket and grabbed her hand and ran back to the checkout isle. It hadn't taken long. Kelli stood dumbfounded at the end of the checkout counter. It was the same cashier, but the items on the belt were not hers. She'd only been gone less than three minutes, she was certain, but her cart was nowhere in sight.

"Where are my things?" She implored the cashier. "There were frozen items, they were re-shopped." She said without skipping a beat between scanning items.

"I wasn't gone more than a couple minutes, can't you stop the person who's putting it all back?"

"Sorry ma'am. Store policy. We can't leave frozen food out, it has to be re-shopped immediately." She barely even looked up from her work. The woman she was helping looked at Kelli as if she were a leper and scooted away slightly.

Kelli's blood boiled. So much so that she thought for sure that her head would explode from the pressure of her heartbeat. She gathered up her children again and ran in the direction of the food department. In the frozen section she searched for an employee pushing her reclaimed cart, but the isles were empty of workers. She doubled back through the entire grocery store looking. Finally she gave up and grabbed a new cart, starting the whole agonizing process over again.

Eventually she made it through the checkout aisle and out to the car. The day was rapidly coming to a close. They had been gone for nearly five hours and accomplished little more than spending ten dollars in gas and over one hundred on groceries.

"I'm hungry." Ruby cried as Kelli buckled her into her seat.

"Okay Baby, I'll get you some food." Kelli buckled Joshua in his seat before rummaging through the food for something to suffice for their dinners. She gave them each a spoon full of peanut butter, some applesauce in a little pouch and a cheese stick. After they finally finished their foods she gave them each a cup of cheese crackers.

At last she fell into her seat, started the engine and began the drive home. Awaiting her there was the process of getting the children and the food inside before putting it all away. Joshua desperately needed a diaper change and Ruby had peanut butter all over her hair and fingers, which Kelli found she had then used to draw a smiley face on the back of the front seat. Her head pounded when she saw it. Kelli's back ached still. Her stomach was in an even tighter knot than it had been yet. This was what one single, benign, outing took out of her. How was she going to survive work and daily life as a single parent?

Her very sanity seemed to be coming unhinged with the world around her and that sensation was magnified when she had taken a wrong turn on the way home; certain she had come that way originally. Eventually she had found their road and turned into the trailer court, but she couldn't reconcile how she'd gotten lost in the first place.

Kelli hauled the kids into the bathroom and scrubbed them up. She answered their questions and made jokes to ease their troubles. She brushed their teeth and fished out pajamas for them. Half an hour later, in the dark of their new bedroom, she crashed with them in their tent.

"Where is daddy?" Ruby asked again. "I don't know."

"Well, when will you know then?" Ruby propped herself up on her elbows. Her big brown eyes were wide and her perfect red lips were pushed into a very serious pout.

Kelli felt a burning dislike for Tim. She had been grossly betrayed and cast aside as though she were entirely valueless. She had wasted her best years on him; ruined her perfect female body birthing his children. Not that she regretted having the children one iota, she only began to wish it had been with someone who appreciated all that meant. Here she was alone, fending for her young like some animal in the savage wild. Her body scarred and ravaged by gravity for having birthed them and sustained them. Who could ever want her now? Who would ever want her children as his own? Even their own father sent them away. She wanted to breed the same contempt and angst in the kids as she felt, but something inside her wouldn't allow it. Inside she knew it was like losing something too great to ever have back – dignity.

"Daddy found a different...life, Ruby." She spoke slowly, choosing her words carefully, "Some times people do wrong things, and it hurts us, but we love them anyway. Daddy is being bad. But he loves you, and I love you, and we get to have our own different life now, too. It will be fun, you'll see." She pulled everything she had left inside her soul to sound convincing.

Ruby remained skeptical.

"This house is not fun." She whispered.

Kelli chuckled. "I am not having much fun in it either. We'll find a funner place soon. We'll just pretend its a nice hotel."

Ruby thought about that for a few seconds and then nodded slowly; satisfied. She laid her head down on her pillow and snuggled against her baby brother who had climbed over Kelli while they were talking. Kelli kissed them both and hugged them close before slipping out of the room to carry the groceries in.

She felt so lost and alone standing on the steps outside the trailer. But she stuffed defeat and despair down into the dark corners of her mind, one more time, and hopped down the stairs. The day wasn't done yet, and there wasn't time for pity, or pain.

The night was cold and crisp as she popped open the trunk and reached in for the bags there. A fuzzy layer of spring frost was growing across the white paint of the car. It reminded her of sweet confectioners glazing. Which reminded her that she hadn't eaten yet that day. She decided she'd have a bowl of cereal once she got the groceries put away.

Inside Kelli laid the pile of bags on the island and turned the thermostat up against the chill outside. She put the dry goods in the cabinets that she had left empty for that purpose, laying the bags of cold food near the fridge as she came across them. Suddenly she had a sinking feeling. She whipped the fridge door open, remembering that when she had turned it on earlier it had never kicked on. It hadn't even turned on when she checked it some time later. Sure enough the inside of the appliance was still warmer than the house.

She trotted over to the door and looked down the park drive at the trailer the landlord had indicated was Howard's. There were no lights on. She grabbed her keys to lock the house and walked the short distance to his trailer quickly, huddled against the cold.

There were only ten trailers in the park. Five on each side of the road. They were old, most of them from the '70's and were tan and dark brown. Some had decks and porches. Others, like hers, had only fiberglass steps leading up to the door, they thumped like drum skins when people climbed them.

All of it seemed even dingier and more hopeless in the monochromatic dark. Howard's trailer was like hers also: narrow and short, looking more like a contractor's office on a job site than a home.

She took the four steps two at a time and rapped on the closed door. No one moved inside. She knocked again, this time calling out his name, to no avail. She looked around, there was no vehicle parked in the driveway and she couldn't remember if there had been one there at all that day.

Kelli gave up and retreated back to her own trailer. She walked slowly, noticing the dilapidated cars sitting outside her neighbor's homes. The broken gravel drives; the busted cement walkways. The missing pieces of siding and skirting on the trailers. The ugly old polyester curtains pulled haphazardly across their dark windows. Everything smelled cold and dusty and was tinged with oil from the railroad.

At the end of their park drive, past the cement barricade, was the wide, stinking, railway. Beyond that was the main drag of town. Cars slipped by there in a slow but steady stream past the broken buildings and empty storefronts. Sounds of people coughing and laughing loud in the neighborhoods around the trailer park sounded sinister and hollow. Car doors opening and front door slamming echoed through the place, rattling the tin siding and making it hum. The grit and gravel under her feet crunched and added to the noise. All of it was colored in sad sepia tones, muddied and browned by winter and the setting of the sun. And she was alone in it, for all the noise and stimulation of her senses there wasn't another human being in sight.

Like a terrible, invisible, supernova the universe around her closed in. This was her life. A single mother, below the poverty line, living in a trailer in a town she'd only ever driven through. Utterly alone. She reached her steps and collapsed.

All the tears she'd been bottling up through the previous weeks unleashed in a torrent. She covered her face with her hands and tried in vain to quiet herself. But the more she tried the more she choked noisily on her sobs and found herself reeling and gasping for air. She cried until she thought she might throw up from the force of it.

Suddenly her neighbor's porch light flicked on and the door tore open. The dirty bearded man stuck his head out and glared at her, squinting into the dark. He slammed the door shut, but opened it again a moment later, stuffing his arms into his dirty canvas jacket. He stamped forcefully across his small porch and down the wooden steps. Kelli tried to stop crying, but even his walking was as menacing as her life had become.

The closer he came the harder she cried. He opened the back cab door of his truck as he made his way, pulling out a tool box and a large aerosol can. He lumbered over to her and sat the collection on the bottom step, just below her feet. She hiccuped and stared at him. He pulled a pack of chewing tobacco from his coat pocket and stuffed some in his mouth.

His nose whistled a little as he chewed it. For a few breaths he just stared at her, his eyes level.

"Where's your man?" He asked around the mouthful.

"He left me. I'm divorced." She said, the syllables broken by hiccups and sucks of air.

His mouth pushed up towards his nose before falling again and making smacking noises. He stood in thoughtful consideration for a few moments. A screen door whined somewhere behind them before slapping shut.

"Fridge not working?" He finally said, spitting juice like a grasshopper onto the driveway.

Kelli nodded quietly, but started crying again instantly.

"Woman. Keeping me up. Move then, outta the way." He didn't wait for her to react, or even respond, he just shoved his way past her, grabbing up his tool box and mumbling, "Damn fridge never did work," as he went.

Kelli followed him inside silently. Her hands hung limp by her side and she still breathed in shudders as she watched him. He wore a brown canvas jacket over his red plaid shirt. His beard was graying, and although it was not particularly long it was still stained around his mouth from tobacco and other things. He wore a camouflage hat and his gray hair stuck out from underneath it in tufts. His skin, what little there was to be seen, was reddened by sun and weather and wrinkly in places like his neck and the backs of his hands.

The toolbox clanked a little as he sat it down and hiked up his pants. For a few seconds he chewed the tobacco in his mouth and just stared at the appliance. Finally, he sighed and pulled the refrigerator out of its cubby, reached behind it deftly, and unplugged it before turning it around.

"What's your name?" Kelli asked, after clearing her throat and blowing her nose in a napkin.

"Scruggs. Marty. I go by either." He fiddled with his toolbox, using a fat black-stained index finger to push bits of things around before selecting whatever it was he was searching for.

"I'm Kelli. Ruby's my daughter, Joshua is the baby." She offered, trying to sound friendly.

He fitted a small hose attached to the can he'd brought in onto the small tool from his box which he then affixed some place on the back of the appliance. "Don't much care who you are. Darn women always needing something. Making noise. *Crying*. Nothing I can't stand worse than a crying woman." He pulled the can off, dropped the metal piece back into the tool box and pushed himself up, his knees cracking with the effort.

"I didn't mean to cry so loud." She finally stammered.

Marty only made a "humph" sound in reply as he pushed the fridge back, plugged it in, and shoved it the rest of the way in place. It hummed happily, tinkling with cold sounds.

"Thank you." She looked around for something to give him out of appreciation. But she didn't even have a coffee maker.

He stood up straight, holding the empty can in one hand and the tool box in the other. He stared at her with a look she couldn't quite understand. It wasn't hate or disdain, but it wasn't exactly friendly either.

"I don't have anything to offer you. We just don't have anything. I could make you a cup of tea." She looked at her hands, "It's raspberry flavored, though."

"I don't drink tea." The last word sounded funny as it stumbled across his mustache.

He gripped the tool box a little tighter; his hand made a squeaky sound and he looked around the empty place. Again she couldn't quite read him. He wasn't judging the space but he didn't seem to approve of any of it either. He just looked at it all... slowly.

"I don't drink fruity tea." He reiterated, "You just stop crying so darn loud, okay?"

Marty stuffed the can under his arm and opened the door, letting himself out. His big truck fired up outside and he pulled away in it. The entire park seemed to follow as the minutes passed, until it was entirely empty.

Kelli looked at the little face clock she had bought a few hours earlier. She had been careful to set it while in the store. It was twenty to midnight. She told herself to calm down, and was able to only because the gruff kindness of a stranger made the world seem a little less hostile.

She stuffed the, now warm, food into the fridge and threw the empty plastic bags under the sink. She saved one and hung it from a drawer knob. The ache inside her pulled tight again; they didn't even own a trash can. But they did own bowls and spoons. And cereal.

She stuffed her feet under her and curled up on the

sofa, tepid cereal in hand. She pushed play on the little TV's remote. Dumbo came on.

For the shortest of moments she imagined she was five years old. Mom and dad were asleep in their bedroom down the hall. She sat in the early morning dim and watched a cartoon; playing with some toys. All was right with the world. Bad things were a mystery. Scary things were only shadows on the bedroom wall. Everything was easy and simple.

But that moment faded quickly. It was all at once replaced by the strange sick feeling of a foreign place and exhaustion. Her stomach hurt from eating, but not quite as bad as it had from not eating. There was no winning.

A little later she shoved the twin mattress that was leaning in the hall into the small bedroom and laid it on the floor by the pile of toys. Kelli fished a blanket and pillow from the kid's tent and fell onto the little bed.

One day done. There was no way of counting how many remained. Or where they ended.

-CHAPTER TWO-

The first month or more had gone by smooth enough. Kelli had been right in assuming it would work for the kids to ride with her while she picked up samples and dropped them off at the lab. Thankfully she found that at almost every stop there was always a group of nurses on break, smoking, by the back doors she had to use. It hadn't taken long for her and the kids to be noticed and the short version of her story to circulate. As the weather began to warm she was able to leave the car unlocked and the windows open under the watchful eye of different nurses without worrying that the children would over heat or be stolen.

She had eventually even made enough money to buy a cell phone and open a checking and savings account. Their savings had grown already to two hundred dollars. It wouldn't be long until she'd have enough for a proper apartment. It was a thought that energized her on her bad days.

Kelli had decided to make do with what they had to help further their cause. But they needed another bed and she refused to buy a used mattress for her or the kids. She had found a furniture store with a layaway program that was selling a reasonably priced pull out sofa. It seemed like a logical choice- the loveseat was too small for two people to sit on comfortably and it was threadbare and falling apart. She'd be able to pay it off with the next paycheck and use it as a bed for herself, leaving the smaller bedroom as a playroom for now. Some day, later, she'd buy herself a bed.

The trailer park was beginning to make sense to her now, also. Howard, who was supposed to be in charge of maintenance and general tasks around the place, was usually not home. Like the others in the park he worked nights. Unlike the others at the park he predated the oil rigs and wells and so he worked at a factory instead. He spent his off time sleeping or at the bar on the other side of the railroad past the concrete barricade. Everyone else worked for the oil boom that had recently hit up north in the state. Most of the trailers housed teams of men, about four per home. They slept all day, except Sunday. Which they generally spent, for the most part, in each others' yards working on vehicles, sitting in lawn chairs and talking loudly about oil rigs, vehicles and especially women. The fear factor of it all was wearing off. She avoided contact with the lot of them and for the most part they left her and the kids alone.

Marty was the only one she had any sort of interactions with. Initially she had tried to be pleasant and smile or wave at whoever happened to be out, but learned that it was best to ignore them. She was like a lamb before wolves. Because the nature of oil work drew more men than women the demographic of the region had shifted. Just being female made her interesting and the men lewd.

One of the younger rig workers had hopped up from his lawn chair one Sunday afternoon and hooted loudly at her as she bent over to buckle the kids into the car. She had turned just in time to see Marty chuck a full beer can directly into the boy's head from across the drive.

"Darn kids making so much damn noise. Shut up, you!" He yelled as the twenty-something man-child rubbed his head and sucked on the broken beer can dejectedly.

Marty hadn't made eye contact with her during the episode, instead he quietly picked another beer from his ice- filled cooler, replaced his dirty feet on the porch railing and pretended to doze. As a result she had not interacted with anyone at all in Dixson beyond the nurses who handed her their coolers filled with bloody vials. She had yet to make any friends. There just never seemed to be any time. She'd given up on keeping friendships years ago, and now the thought of forging new ones seemed as foreign as dating.

It never dawned on her just how alone she had always been. She plugged on alone, for now, mostly because it was easier that way. She'd have been lonesome if she stopped to think about it. Luckily there was hardly time.

It was Saturday that day. Spring was in full force and there was no longer the threat of frost or snow squalls. The days were creeping up into the high 60's regularly. Kelli had discovered only the day before that long ago someone had planted hyacinths and crocuses along the front of the trailer. They were growing in gravel and pieces of broken blacktop that had been shoved into the old garden bed by snow plows. But they were growing just the same. It was particularly pleasant out so she stuck the kids' shoes on them, stuffed their arms into jackets and turned them lose in the drive in front of the trailer while she cleaned out the tiny garden bed.

The air smelled warm with spring and wet growing things. And despite the ever moving traffic a little way beyond the barrier the sound of happy migrating birds was warming the air. The kids hopped and skipped and played with each other on the blacktop and gravel near the trailer. Joshua would be turning two soon and was beginning to muster his way through different words. Today's word was rock. Every few minutes he brought Kelli a fist full of them and proclaimed their identity at full volume.

The sun warmed her back as she weeded out the grass and bits of roadway from the strip of growing flowers. Eventually she uncovered more bulbs that had been thwarted in their growth, but were desperately trying to push up green sprouts anyway. Kelli thought they looked like daffodils and tulips. They had grown into such massive clumps at some point that they were choking themselves. She walked around her trailer looking for some place to relocate some, but she found nowhere suitable. She did, however, spot a pair of overturned terracotta pots sitting along the backside of Marty's trailer.

Certainly they weren't his; he was only living there because the oil company paid for the trailer. They had to have been left by the previous tenant; someone who wanted to make home and not just live in the place. She couldn't imagine the grumpy old man ever keeping any potted plants. Or any living thing besides himself, for that matter.

Kelli quickly trespassed into his yard and snatched them up. She never had been able to repay him for saving her groceries and solving her fridge problem. It was also hard for her to believe that the cat-calling young oilman was simply annoying him that day, since others had yelled at different times over other things and he'd never thrown beer cans at them. She suspected he was not as gruff and miserable as he appeared to be. It was hard not to be somewhat fond of him. After all, he'd saved her groceries without her asking.

She located a small patch of dirt along the side of her trailer and after a layer of rocks she filled them with it. Next she pulled apart some of the unruly bulbs and tucked them into the moist dirt. To add some appeal, to the otherwise empty looking pot, she transplanted some of the flowering hyacinths and crocuses into them. The pots were sparse, but they smelled sweet and fresh when they were finished. She placed one on the second step of her trailer and carefully slid the other under the railing of Marty's porch, near his door.

Kelli herded the kids inside and fed them lunch. She checked from time to time for movement at her neighbor's house. He had left a couple hours earlier, but he was never gone long when he wasn't at work. He would surely be pulling in shortly, and she had her ears perked for the sound of his truck. It was almost like a game. She wanted to see his reaction to fit together the pieces of his personality. If he was irritated by the gift she'd be fairly sure he was just a grumpy old man that hated everything. If not, well, he at least wasn't a threat.

The kids were colored with jelly and smelled of peanut butter when they hopped down from their chairs. Joshua had brought his sippy cup with him from the table, and it was also sticky. Their gummy fingers sought her out and smeared against her skin and clothes as they climbed on the sofa where she sat.

"Sticky!" Joshua exclaimed proudly, holding out one of his fat hands as flat as he could manage to uncurl it from the drying jelly.

"Yes, you are sticky. Let's wash up and get ready for a nap." They both came willingly with her to the bathroom.

Kelli was grateful that they both still napped, it gave her some quiet time to herself whenever they were home. She was also glad for the days off when they could stretch out and get a good rest at the house instead of crumpled up in their car seats while she was working. They watched her with big brown eyes that were weary and solemn as she ran the water.

She worried about them as she wiped them off with the warm washcloth. Was she making the right choice bringing them with her while she worked? She feared leaving them with a stranger, it was greater than the worry of not having enough money. Somehow she had the idea that being homeless, huddled together in an alley, was less frightening than a stranger having access to them eight hours a day. They couldn't go on like this forever, though; she saw that.

At some point Kelli knew she'd have to let go a little. For their sake she'd have to take that perceived risk. She'd make friends soon. She'd find someone to stay home in the trailer with them. A friendly church going grandmother, with a mile long list of references and no medical conditions. And no other commitments. That shouldn't be too hard to find, she assured herself mockingly.

Kelli had moved the twin mattresses into the kids' bedroom, she had bought a couple foam mattress toppers from the store and stacked them under a sheet on the box spring. It provided them with two beds while they waited for the new sofa. The kid's were still so small that they had more than enough room on the makeshift box spring bed. And she was able to stretch out on the little mattress to sleep. She learned after the first night that it was nearly impossible for her to sleep alone. Ruby had become so fond of their tent that after shoving their mattress into the corner to keep Joshua from rolling off of it Kelli had tacked a sheet to the wall and tucked it under the long side of the bed. And so they all slept together in the same room, her on one mattress, and them under their lean-to tent.

Her sleepy babies piled into the tent and she crawled in after them, tucking them under their fuzzy blanket and running her fingers through their silky red hair soothingly.

"I love you mommy." Ruby said sleepily.

It felt like balm to her heart, though it broke at the same time. She wanted to give them everything. And felt entirely limited to give them anything.

"I love you too, Ruby." Kelli croaked, holding in tears. She kissed her son, "Mommy loves you too, buddy." She rumpled his hair a little.

As she sneaked out and closed their bedroom door she heard the rumbling of a pick-up truck pulling in next door. Kelli ran silently on her tiptoes to the window at the door and peeked out. But it wasn't Marty.

It was a young man in a muddy four-door truck. He crawled out of the vehicle painfully slow and lumbered to the deck railing where he paused to breathe. His face was swollen and bruised and his dusty brown hair was stuck in different directions with medical tape and dried blood. He stood up straight and smoothed out his wrinkled flannel shirt before shuffling his cowboy boots farther up the driveway to Marty's porch stairs. He paused another moment there, his hand on the ribs under one arm. At length he heaved himself up the porch steps, pulling himself up with his good arm. He stopped again at the top of the steps. But this time it was to stare at the pot of flowers by the door. After a still moment he scratched his head slowly and went on.

He must have known Marty, and known that since his truck was gone he wouldn't be home. He eased his slim figure into Marty's lawn chair and gingerly placed his boots on the porch railing and waited without even knocking.

Kelli left her post at the door and poured herself a glass of milk, and waited. Her curiosity was piqued. She wanted to see Marty's reaction to the flower pot, but was also interested in what he'd think about the pummeled young man sitting on his porch. She'd wait for however long it took to catch his response at discovering them both. It was more excitement and fun than she'd had in a long while.

Her world had for many years now revolved around her children. She had had no real hobbies while with Tim. The highlight of her life had been his daily homecoming and grocery shopping day. He worked late hours, although now she realized he wasn't *working* all those hours. So she was mostly home-bound and alone. Only when she stopped to look back on that time did she recognize the loneliness she'd been made to endure.

They had moved to Bismark from Michigan when he got his corporate job. It had been shortly after high school and their wedding. Aside from a few casual friends, Timothy had been her life. After she found she was pregnant with Ruby Tim worked even more. He was always concerned about money, or what he perceived to be the lack thereof. Ruby had been a happy distraction for Kelli, though.

Her free time, and self, vanished shortly before Ruby's first birthday. Kelli had found herself unexpectedly pregnant again. Suddenly there was no time for her to even exist anymore. Let alone foster friendships or hobbies.

She had entirely forgotten how to have fun. It wasn't that the kids were not enjoyable, but the mounting stress of what she realized now had been single parenting, even then, stole all of her time. And so figuring Marty out had become a sort of entertainment she had not entirely expected to invent. But she felt strangely free to, and since he was the only person in the area she had any interaction with he became her target.

She could have set a clock by him. He came home every morning at eleven, and left for work every night shortly before midnight. He dozed in the sun on his day off and drank beer. Although he never appeared drunk, it was impossible to imagine he wasn't somewhat adversely affected by the drink due to the sheer number consumed. Kelli had never once seen him bring groceries into his trailer, either, which was curious, he obviously didn't cook for himself. She finished the glass of milk and placed it in the sink and peeked again out the window at Marty's trailer. It was after noon and Marty still wasn't home.

The beaten up visitor on his porch was the first person she'd seen, besides herself, attempt to interact with Marty. The people in the trailer court didn't interact with him much either. Marty was their foreman. They lived and worked together yet not a single one ever ventured over to his trailer. He didn't seem so horrible whenever she'd had exchanges with him. But then, who really wanted to spend their down time with their boss?

She wondered if his visitor was also an employee of

the oil company. She imagined him having been beaten in a bar brawl. By the looks of him it must have been a whole team of men that worked him over. He was thin looking, but not willowy by any means. He looked like most of the prairie men did in that area; tall and lean. Likely little more than bones, muscle and skin. His face wasn't bearded, like Marty's was, and most of the other men in the park. And his clothes were clean. Even his dark blue jeans looked crisp and new. His boots were dusty and worn though. She decided he must be wearing his good clothes for the occasion. Which meant it must be a fairly important meeting with her neighbor.

Curiouser and curiouser. The waiting game continued.

Finally, at a few minutes before one, she heard the unmistakable rumble of Marty's beat up old dually pulling down the park drive and she ran to her door. His visitor didn't bother to stand, although he slipped his feet down off the railing and sat up a little straighter.

The sun glimmered off the car windows outside, and through the cool glass of her door she could hear the same birds from earlier singing over the sound of constant traffic. Marty, carrying his lunchbox, strode up the drive and climbed the stairs without so much as glancing at the man sitting on the porch. The younger man moved his feet as Marty lumbered past purposefully. Marty stopped in his tracks just outside his door, staring down at the pot of flowers Kelli had left. He turned and looked straight at her in the door window and she ducked down so fast she gasped.

She chuckled to herself over it as she caught her breath and calmed down. She stood back up on her tiptoes and looked back over at the trailer. The pot remained by the door, as did the stranger in the lawn chair. Neither had been moved, but the trailer door was shut fast. Kelli gave up and stretched out on the couch. The kid's usually slept for over two hours; she had plenty of time to rest and plenty of need for it.

Kelli dozed off almost immediately. She dreamed of her former life. Her heart swelled as she stood in the kitchen making dinner and heard the front door open. Her love was home, her Timothy. He'd come home early because he'd missed her. The children were playing upstairs in their rooms and she ran from the kitchen to greet him with a kiss.

As she rounded the opening into the hallway her heart skipped a beat; Tim was on fire, standing like a dead man just inside the door. His suit was melting away with pieces of his flesh. Bones grasped his briefcase where his hands should have been. The air was so thick with the stench of burning skin she couldn't catch her breath. Her heart pounded in her head until her teeth ached. Timothy glared at her, reached for her pleadingly, as if begging her to help him. But as she stepped closer he lunged out possessively, his burning hand of melted flesh and bone grasping blindly. His fingers slashed like razors into her chest.

Through the immobilizing pain her head screamed at her: the house would burn because of him and the children were out of her sight. They'd all be consumed. And yet she was cemented in place, only able to silently endure the pain of Tim's hand. No matter how hard she screamed no noise was produced.

She sat up with a gasp. Sleep was not going to happen this day. It took a few minutes to recognize the real world and acknowledge that the dream was over. The trailer around her was still quiet. She'd only been asleep less than an hour.

The place was depressing. The white walls, with their bumpy pattern and strips of flat plastic, were still empty. She hadn't even spent money on curtains. She didn't really plan on it either, but they couldn't live forever with sheets tacked over the openings. Blinds were cheap and she had bought some recently and meant to put them up. But she had no tools to install them. Maybe

Marty would lend her some...

Something had to be done. The place was plain and dispiriting, and she was creeped out by her dream. She needed to be busy.

Kelli tiptoed again to the door and peeked out at Marty's trailer. The strange man with the broken face was still sitting in the same lawn chair, his feet propped back up on the railing. The door was closed still and Marty was nowhere in sight.

She bit her lip while she judged the situation. It seemed presumptuous to just show up with her hand out, but she had no one else to turn to, either. They owned almost nothing, so there were no messes to clean. If the dishes were done there wasn't any housework. They had no cable and she was bored with watching children's cartoons. She didn't even have a book. A n d s he'd even put a roast in the crock pot that morning, so there was no supper to make.

Finally she gave in. She pulled a jacket on and slipped through the door barefoot. As she crossed the narrow driveways the man in the chair looked up from where he was, having dozed off.

"Hi." She said quietly as she reached the stairs.

"Hey." The stranger said slowly, glancing her over as though he were in a dream still.

The backs of her legs cringed sympathetically as she looked at him. His brown hair was matted with blood in places where it had oozed out from under a patch of first aid tape on the side of his head. His right eye was purple and swollen shut. There was a gash on his cheek bone under it, which was stitched and taped together. His open eye was brown and solemnly looked at her with a painful grimace as he sat up a little.

"Is Marty home?" She asked.

He stared at her with his glassy looking good eye for a moment, as though trying to remember.

"Sure is." He said finally. He still hadn't taken his legs down from the porch railing, so she couldn't walk past him. They stared at each other in silence for an agonizing few moments.

"Did you win the fight?" She said finally, pointing at his face.

"Fight?" He looked at her quizzically.

"You look pretty beat up."

"Oh, right." He chuckled slowly. He sounded drunk. "It was a draw I guess."

His left hand was tucked under his open flannel jacket, between his right arm and ribcage. He pulled it out and dropped his feet to the floor, leaned forward and offered his hand. She reached up the few stairs and shook it. The rough callouses on his palm scratched her soft hands, but his grip was hot and strong.

"Clayton. You can call me Clay." There was a pale line across his forehead where his hat should have sat, and he wore an enormous silver and gold belt buckle on his jeans which was barely visible through his open coat. It had no image, just words she didn't take the time to read.

"Kelli." She smiled softly and pulled her hand away.

Something about him seemed familiar, though it was for no good reason. He wasn't quite right, either. He nearly fell forward as she let go of him. He stamped his boots and caught himself, winching as he stuffed his hand back into his jacket.

He started to speak again but the door swung open and Marty poked his head out.

"Can't sleep when you're being so damn loud." He growled.

Clay didn't bother looking at him, he just tucked his chin into his chest and grew silent again, a mischievous grin on his lips. Kelli considered him for a fraction of a second but looked past to Marty.

"Marty, can I borrow some tools? I need to hang some blinds, but I don't even own a screw driver."

He narrowed his eyes at her, still poking just his head out the door. He muttered under his breath before slamming it shut again. The walls of his trailer rattled. Clay made no eye contact with her, just closed his bruised eyes and hunkered down, as if the sounds hurt his head. The door flew open again in a flash and Marty clamored out, his work boots untied. Clay winced as he shied away, making more room. Marty sneered at him angrily and kicked the chair leg on his way by. The jarring effect made Clay gasp and twist his face, clutching all the harder at his side. Kelli stepped back as he stomped down the stairs.

"I guess I don't really need the tools right now, Marty. I can do it later. It's just the kids are napping and there's not much to do over..."

"Darn woman. Like a stray cat." He muttered at her. He shuffled his untied boots along the driveway past Clay's truck and to his own, his pants sagging around his waist and under his gut.

Marty rummaged through the back seat of the truck and produced a black plastic case which housed a cordless drill and various bits and presented it to her.

"Thanks." She said, taking it meekly. "I didn't mean to bother you."

He only grunted at her and waved his hand over his head as he shuffled back to his porch. She stood at the end of the drive and watched the two men interact. Clay leaned out of the way once more, Marty snarled and kicked the chair again. Clay grimaced. Kelli tiptoed away, her bare feet quite chilled.

She shut the door quietly so as to not wake the children and after throwing her jacket on the floor beside it stood on tiptoes again to peer out the window.

There was no measuring her curiosity. And there was no obvious way to solve the question of why Clay was on Marty's porch. Or why Marty seemed to dislike him so much yet let him stay. She gave up and set to installing the mini-blinds.

Kelli's body ached as she set to work. The stress of having to think of, remember, and do everything for three people while their world crumbled around her was taking its toll. She was like a child at the beach, frantically racing to build the walls of her sand castle even as the waves tore them down. During the week she seemed to never stop. She was thankful that her work didn't involve much standing or physical activity. The driving was nice, with the added bonus that it provided them a chance to familiarize themselves with the local area. She'd become pretty good at navigating the whole of Dixson's business districts and the outlying areas. But it was an unfair exchange for the exhaustion she suffered for it.

Dixson was a little too big to be called a town, and a little too small to be considered a city. Big box stores had made an appearance though, so it was on the verge of growing. Most of the town was just old and tired with rings of new growth surrounding it. She lived in the worst part of town. It wasn't high in crime or anything, it was just run down and deserted. Sad looking. But it was beginning to fill up again. Mostly with male oil workers.

The oil boom had trickled down workers and vacancies for housing were near impossible to find. Kelli had begun to feel hopeless about their housing situation. There seemed no way to get her kids out of the trailer unless they moved to another town, but the thought of saving up the thousands of dollars it would take to do that seemed daunting. It'd certainly take her a year, if not more. And that was while they spent that time living like destitute people. Her kids would need clothes come summer. What they had they were already outgrowing and she didn't have much set aside for the warm season. Even her own clothes were wearing out quickly.

She climbed up on a kitchen chair and set to work fastening the plastic brackets that held the blinds to the plastic window frames. These windows were southern facing, but since she was the last trailer in the park they looked directly over the sooty rail road. The stench of oil and tar and coal always filled the air. It was magnified when the wind happened to pick up from the east. It made the whole house smell industrial, like an acrid repair garage. Today, at least, the smells of spring were mostly overpowering it, aided greatly by a shift in the wind. But it had years ago sunk into the fibers of the press-board walls, and while standing so close to the them she could detect that faint pungent scent.

Kelli hung the final blind and stepped down to work the string, lowering them and then spinning the rod to close the slats on the dreary view. The light was pleasant, she told herself, but something inside her broke. It was like dressing a corpse and ignoring the death.

The house Tim had bought for her was a dream home compared to this trailer. She had had rich roman blinds in her living room, and sheer gauzy white curtains. Her walls had been venetian plaster and painted a creamy white color. She had had gleaming hardwood floors and a pretty area rug that sat under her carved wood and over-stuffed sofa and loveseat. There had even been a little gas fireplace in the dining room and massive mantle and fireplace in the living room.

Long before they had kids, when she was still working, she had collected paintings of peaceful scenery. She had lined shelves with pictures of her and Tim from their high school years as boyfriend and girlfriend. Pictures of their wedding and then of their children were scattered everywhere, making it pleasant. Her house even used to smell of wood polish and citrus, never oil and coal.

She looked around the blank white trailer and the beaten saggy loveseat with all its brown stains from different foods and drinks the kids had covered it in. That was all that provided any color in the space. That and the comical red and yellow Micky Mouse television. Her insides ached; she'd never again have that beautiful house. She felt that life fall away from her like the last dead leaf from a naked tree.

She wanted and needed a break. She wanted to rest. Not just sleep, but rest. Her mind was worried constantly and she doubted her ability to raise the kids. It plagued her. Ruby would be school age summer after next. How could she send her to school from a ratty old trailer? She'd never even seen a school bus anywhere near their trailer park. Unless children were hiding somewhere near the park Ruby would have no nearby friends.

Her children would be considered poor. Their peers would consider them trash. What were their chances; their options in life? What about Joshua? Everyone knew the effects of an absent father on boys. They took it especially hard. Who would her kids manage to associate themselves with? Sure, as

small children no one would notice, but by middle school they'd be labeled, sorted, grouped. She finally broke down and cried over it. She had nothing. She had nothing to give them. No opportunities, no hope. How would they even afford to go to college? She wanted something more for her kids, so they'd never be cast out unprepared like she had been.

A new thought she'd never considered stifled her tears. What if they didn't even make it that far? What if one of them got sick instead of starting school? They had no insurance, how could she pay those bills? What if *she* was sick or injured and couldn't work? They'd be homeless. They really would have nothing. The state might take her children from her if they truly were homeless. Fear prickled her scalp and made her stomach churn.

"Please God. Please don't let it get any worse. Please don't take my babies from me. Don't do that to them." She cried quietly into the space, her hands stretched up towards the ceiling, her fists clenched.

"What are you doing mommy?" Ruby suddenly appeared at the end of the hall, rubbing the sleep from her eyes.

Kelli startled. "Hanging blinds." She croaked, her throat sore and raspy. She wiped her tears before Ruby could notice them and scooped her up for a hug.

"Mommy has to take some tools back to Mister Marty." Kelli explained to the little girl as she sat her on the sofa and turned on the television for her. "I'll be right back. If brother wakes up just go sit with him until I come back. I am just right outside; I can hear you yell for me." Ruby nodded sleepily and snuggled on the sofa anticipating her cartoon.

Kelli packed the drill and bits back into their plastic case and ran outside quickly without her jacket. Clay was still on the porch, except he was dead asleep this time. She decided to try putting the tools back in Marty's truck instead. But upon jogging to it realized it was locked tight. She glanced at the sleeping man on the porch again. She could step over his low slung legs, or leave the tools on the porch; shove them under his legs. She chose the latter. As she retreated to her trailer she could hear her cell phone ringing inside.

Chaos greeted her. Joshua had woken up and was crying for having been abandoned by his sister. Ruby was crying on the sofa because her brother was crying.

She answered her phone without looking to see who it was.

"Hello?" She uttered breathlessly, racing to sooth and quiet both children.

"Hey Sugar, its me." Tim's voice rasped on the other line.

Kelli felt instantaneously nauseous. "Oh. Hi Tim." She muttered.

"What's my babies crying for? Lemme talk to them."

"Nah. They're okay. They just woke up a little grumpy."

"Got some good news." He chimed, his voice sickly sweet.

"Oh?" Kelli just wanted to hang up the phone. Her afternoon had been depressing enough already.

"We got a solid offer on the house today. The realtor just called me. We should have a contract by Monday."

"Oh good!" Kelli's heart leaped. She feared they'd some how never be able to sell the house, certainly not after less than two months on the market. "This is the best news ever, Tim."

"I just need your address and I'll overnight you the contract to sign. It'll be there Tuesday."

She excitedly recited their new address to him before saying good bye and hanging up. Kelli drew Ruby and Joshua tight against her and snuggled them animatedly, giggling with them, though they didn't know why. She glanced at the clock; it was still another two hours until dinner time.

"Let's go look for a new house!" She sang to the kids, "Want to take a drive and look for pretty houses?"

Joshua babbled in reply, and Ruby jumped up and down on the sofa screeching "Yesssss!".

So she suited them up and carried them outside to the car. Kelli buckled the kids in their car seats and carefully backed the car out the narrow drive after eyeing Clay over one more time. Even through the swollen injuries and mysterious exchanges between him and Marty she was strangely drawn to him. He had pleasantness about him that she couldn't quite pin down. She wished she had a reason to know him, but it was a fleeting thought soon replaced by the press of real life.

-CHAPTER THREE-

Kelli did some quick math in her head as she drove them around. They had listed the house for $200,000. They'd bought it years ago for $154,000. They owed about 130,000 on it. So if all went right she should get between 30,000 and 35,000 dollars. And she might get more if Tim would do the right thing and include more than just her half as extra child support. It wouldn't be enough to buy anything outright. But with the job and the money down she might be able to get them into something small. Something reasonable. In a decent part of town, or just outside of it.

Kelli and the kids spent a couple hours driving around looking at houses with "for sale" signs in their yards. She even stopped and picked up a real estate magazine. The prices of things were disappointing. She could buy another trailer outright for the amount she expected to get from the sale of their house. There was nothing she'd be willing to live in that was listed under $120,000. She could do it on her own, she assured herself. Some how.

After driving by a dozen places she realized it was only possible if she could get a bigger lump sum for the down payment. She wouldn't have to mortgage so much and her payments would be tolerable. But that was only if Tim would give her a little more than her half of the $200,000 sale.

There were two places that encouraged her. The first was a townhouse near a Walmart. It wasn't ideal, but the area was clean and it had conveniences like a pool and shopping. The other was a small craftsman style home in an older neighborhood. It said it was only two bedrooms, and it did look very tiny, but it was only

$80,000. With her job and credit her payments would be about the same as rent was. She'd never have picked them under other circumstances, but they were the best of her available options to buy and it would be hers. No one could take it from her, or send them away from it. The tiniest seedlings of hope sprang up in her heart. Maybe it would all come together after all.

The sun was low when they returned. She eased her car back into her little driveway, surprised to find Clay was still rooted on the porch where she had left him. Except he had donned a broad rimmed cowboy hat while she was away. He was asleep still. He held his side with one hand, and a pill bottle in the other. She felt satisfied that one little mystery had solved itself; no wonder he'd seemed so off; he was on pain killers.

Kelli had a moment to consider the scene before a car pulled up behind her. She looked in her rear view mirror and almost vomited. Her hands shook as she turned up the radio and opened her door, leaving the children.

In his silver Toyota SUV sat Timothy, grinning sheepishly. She closed her car door and faced him, knees wobbling. The love of her life; the only man she'd ever loved; ever known; ever been with. The same one that had spurned her away, abandoned their children and taken a new lover. Her head swirled with conflicting emotions. As much as she wanted to hate him, she couldn't. Not really. What she felt besides aching betrayal was the desire for him to take it all away.

His ruddy complexion stood in contrast to his blonde hair. Tim was not at all tall, but he was thick and muscular. Although the closer they got to their thirties the rounder he'd started looking; that sedentary job that paid so well wasn't doing much for his midsection. He popped open his door and hopped out.

"What are you doing here, Tim?" She said, trying to sound confident and disgusted.

He sauntered up to her the same way he always had since they were teenagers. "Hey, Babe. Listen, Sweetheart. I know I can't possibly expect you to forgive me, but I need you to know that I made a horrible mistake." He reached out and took her hands in his firm, smooth, grasp. Before she could make herself jerk away he raised them up and kissed the backs of her fingers.

"Tim, I..."

"Shh. I know you're mad, Baby. But I couldn't help myself. I had to come straight away and tell you."

"You really shouldn't be here." She said a little too loud, her voice was stern and it shocked her. Kelli pulled her hands away from him. "I really think you should just go. We can talk this over later. On the phone."

Her insides swam at the sight of him. She wanted to leap into his arms and beg him to rescue her. She wanted to beat him furiously with her fists until he fell to the damp ground. And then she wanted to kick him. She loved and loathed him simultaneously and the conflicting forces created a dizzying vortex within her. She spoke on auto-pilot. Saying all the things she knew she ought to.

He opened his mouth to speak, reached for her face to hold it in his hands. But he was cut short by the children screaming. Even muffled by the vehicle their high pitched voices rang clear and true.

"Daddy! Daddy!" Ruby shouted with all her strength, twisted around in her seat to catch a tiny glimpse out the back window, "Daddy's here!"

Joshua couldn't see but he screamed "Daaaaah!" Just as loud, his kicking feet and thrashing about shook the entire car.

Tim left her and ran to them, throwing open the door he reached in and pulled Ruby free from her seat. She latched on and nearly strangled him.

"Here I am, Baby!" Tim sang to her.

Kelli went around and turned Joshua loose. He ran and grabbed tight to Tim's leg. He seated himself on the top of his foot and Tim dragged him to the trailer that way. Following Kelli he alighted the steps and deposited the wiggling, excited mass of kids inside. But then he stood still, looking remorsefully around the space. Kelli was sickeningly ashamed, yet also proud that he should see what she and the kids had been made to endure because of his selfish idiocy.

"Don't go daddy!" Ruby clung to his shirt, her lips quivering. Joshua was already crying, unable to express himself well at his little age.

Tim looked at Kelli. Her heart melted at the sight of her kids. They deserved better. They deserved to believe that their father loved them, and to see it in his eyes and feel it in his arms.

"Daddy came to stay for dinner, and to read you a bedtime story!" She chimed in, trying to sound happy for their sakes.

"Come and see our tent Daddy!" Ruby hopped up and down, she grabbed his thick index finger and coaxed him along, nearly leaning horizontally against his weight.

Tim's wide smile flashed at Kelli, and his green eyes sparkled. And just like that her defenses crumbled. She didn't exactly feel like he was home, but it did feel good to have a familiar person there with her. Joshua chased them down the short hallway, pushing the backs of Tim's knees. Kelli was cautious, and skeptical...

But maybe this was an answer to her prayers.

She pulled dishes from the cabinet and laid them on the counter. Four. It felt right. It felt normal.

She opened the steaming crockpot and pushed the contents around, everything fell apart perfectly. She cut up

Ruby and Joshua's meat, potatoes and carrots. She

44

heaped each of the same onto a man-sized plate for Tim. Her stomach was in knots and the very last thing she wanted to do was eat, but she put some food on her own plate just for the sake of it. She'd lost so much weight because of the stress of the last month. It was part of the reason her clothes were wearing out. She'd dropped all her baby fat, and more. Everything clung like tents to her ever shrinking frame.

Kelli set the plates around the table. She'd been forced to scoot two of the four chairs nearer to one end so she could reach the kids while they ate, but since Tim was there she centered all four chairs neatly. There was nothing but juice and milk in the fridge, so she poured two glasses of milk for the children and water for her and Tim. She didn't even have ice cube trays, so they'd have to drink it at tap temperature.

"Dinner's ready!" She called from the kitchen, carrying the four cups to the table.

In the back bedroom she heard his thick voice talking low, peppered with the high, excited voices of their children. They seemed to be making no progress towards the table, so she ventured back in search of them. She found all three piled up under the little sheet tent on the kid's make-shift bed. Her own bare mattress was across the room, unmade. It cried out in lonely desperation at her. As if betraying her with tales of all the sleepless tear-filled nights she'd endured on it. Certainly Tim would know if he only looked at it.

"Its dinner time, guys. Come on." She said, throwing her blankets in order a little.

"We don't wanna eat dinner." Ruby announced.

"No, Momma!" Joshua called, suddenly stringing audible words together.

Tim crawled out, clutching them both in his thick arms. "Come on, I smell something good in the kitchen! One, two, three, GO!" He shouted, and the two children tore out of the room excitedly.

Tim chucked her under the chin as he walked past, and stole a quick kiss. It was so natural and familiar that she didn't even have a chance to defend herself against it.

At the table Ruby talked around mouthfuls of food about their adventures in the car while Kelli worked; about their neighbor Marty; about the flowers and the various pebbles she'd discovered in the driveway that day. Joshua babbled along with her, telling his own incoherent stories. Tim listened intently to their every word. Kelli couldn't remember a time when they'd shared a similar meal. She couldn't even remember the last time he'd stolen a kiss from her, or flashed that impish grin she'd loved as a school girl. It was like a dream, and she was too tired and too worn down to fight it.

They laughed and played, working together to clean up after the meal. The kids stood on chairs pulled up to the sink and played in the sudsy water while Tim washed up the dishes. Kelli dried each piece and carefully put them in their places. Her heart felt like bursting.

Standing behind them, leaning on the kitchen island, they were the picture of all she had longed for all those years when Tim had seemed inexplicably distant and busy. It was as if they had been tested by fire and she had found perfection on the other side. As if maybe it would be okay. Finally. Maybe the fearful hell of this foreign life was over. Tim could rescue them from it because he'd finally begun to come to his senses.

Timothy excused himself after the dishes were done and slipped out to his SUV. Kelli watched from the window as he glanced at his cell phone eagerly, but threw it back onto the seat where it had been, almost instantly. Kelli turned away from the window but not before she noticed that Clay was still sitting in the lawn chair on Marty's porch, watching Tim from under the low brim of his hat. He reminded her of a cat watching a bird; irritated and curious. Obviously he intended to sleep on the porch and didn't enjoy being kept up by car doors.

As she looked away her mind questioned Tim's need to check his phone. Perhaps he was waiting for a call from the realtor, she assured herself. But were they really selling the house now that he was back? Maybe he'd want to start over some where new. A new job. New house. New life. But he'd never done anything new as long as she'd known him. She shook her head and ignored it. It was his phone, he could make his own phone calls. What mattered was here and now. Time with him would tell her all she needed to know, surely.

They spent the minutes before putting the kids to sleep talking more and laughing as the sun set around the trailer. Tim told the kids fantastic tales about monsters and knights, Indians and cowboys and heroes and damsels in distress. They were enthralled, obviously living out some tiny childhood dream of being the center of their daddy's attention. It melted her heart to see them, wide eyed, laying with their chins in their hands on the floor in the living room. They hung on every word and every motion Tim had.

Finally, an hour past bedtime, Kelli forced them to brush their teeth and get into their little bed. She kissed Ruby and Joshua, rocked them tenderly in her arms before laying them under their little tent and covering them with their fuzzy blanket. Tim crawled in too and snuggled them. For lack of space she left the three of them to themselves and retreated to the main living area.

Kelli took a minute to sweep the linoleum floor that stretched through the whole space. Tim was silent in the bedroom, as were the children. With one chore done and still no sign of him she decided to take the time to wipe down the bathroom and sort the two loads of laundry that had piled up there. Afterward she stalked around the place for a few minutes before giving up and turning off the lights for the evening; except for the fixture in the stove vent, which cast a cool white light through the living area. Finally she settled onto the couch and waited another fifteen minutes before Tim finally emerged from the darkened room.

He sat down beside her and put his arm across the back of her shoulders along the sofa. He smelled good. Familiar. Like cologne and coffee. They sat in silence. She couldn't quite bear to look at him. He didn't seem to be interested in looking at her either. Finally he cleared his throat.

"This place is awful, Kelli." He confessed finally.

She nodded silently in reply. Unable and unwilling to voice her opinions on it. Doing so might unleash all the dreadful bitterness she'd stored up.

"I am so sorry I did this to you. I really truly am." His voice was smooth and soft.

It had been the voice that had comforted her through all life's storms for so many years. Through all the turmoil of late adolescence, through all the drama of their fledgling relationship. Through their adult years together. She hadn't realized how much she'd missed that voice in his absence.

His sharp green eyes, always tight and penetrating, pierced her skin wherever they happened to fall. His nose was long but not too long, and it had a rough bump on it at the top from a sports injury their first year in high school together. Tim was handsome. The only flaw his body possessed was his short stature for a man, and the softness his muscles had been cloaked in over the years behind a desk. Bleach blond hair tousled over his head and his long side burns flared into a tightly groomed beard he had kept for years now. No one could resist his devilish smile and she felt powerless against his gaze now, too. He knew her inside and out, and the sense of ownership his knowing eyes conveyed made her stomach flutter despite the rage of memories her thoughts swirled with.

Kelli ventured a cautious sideways glance at him. She tried to control her emotions, but just the sight of his eyes, pleading for forgiveness, and his down-turned mouth made her cry. She wept for having lost him; for having been utterly heartbroken and betrayed by him. For having been so bitterly alone through so many of their years together; for having wasted years thinking she was something important to him when she wasn't. For having wasted her love on him, and yet, even now, for desperately wanting him to love her. Needing him to somehow validate her self worth and value as a woman, as a human being.

He drew her close against him, smoothing the hair from her face and tucking it carefully behind her ear as she regained her composure. "I am so sorry, Baby." He whispered, kissing her head. He pulled her face up to his and kissed her passionately. His hot hands on her skin melting her heart. "I am so very sorry I hurt you."

She could feel his pulse quicken, and her own breathing eventually sped up to match his own as he urgently kissed her neck and shoulders.

"Oh Tim!" She cried, "Its been so awful. I've been so alone." He traced all the well-known paths of her curves, sliding his hands under her clothes, leading her down the same familiar path she'd known her whole sexual life.

"I am so sorry, Kelli."

"I've been so scared." She managed to whimper through the swirling confusion in her brain.

What was she doing? This man had betrayed her most ultimately. He'd abandoned her and his own children. He'd lied. He'd seduced another woman with these same hands, this same body, that he tempted her with now. Yet she wanted him and needed him. She wanted something familiar, something she recognized. She needed the comfort of something she knew. She wanted reconciliation. She wanted back what she'd lost;

what had been stolen from her.

And so when he pulled her onto the bare floor she found herself not only relenting but willing to participate. She made no attempt to stop him, or slow him. She had no argument or grudge. Only the aching, broken, need to be loved. And she wanted familiarity. His thick and heavy hands; their quick jerking movements and tight grip. The smell and taste of his mouth. She gave up. Gave in. All without even trying to put up a fight. He was her husband, even if the paper he had given her said otherwise. Surely he truly loved her, despite it all.

Sometime later, sweaty and spent, they lounged together on the couch under a little throw-blanket. Her head rested on his shoulder and he petted her hair soothingly, the same way he always had whenever they sat this way.

"You'll stay the night then?" She asked tentatively.

He was silent for a minute. He inhaled deeply and let it out slowly. "Sure, if you say so."

"You could sleep on the couch, here." She suggested, before quickly adding, "I only have a little twin mattress."

"I guess that works." He shrugged and pressed her side against his a little.

"I don't have an extra pillow. You'll have to use a throw pillow."

"Okay."

She slipped off the sofa and gathered up her clothes, piece by piece. "I need to get ready for bed. The kids have been getting up pretty early in this new place. I don't get much sleep these days..." She trailed off, thinking of the past month as though it had been some horrible exile executed by mistake.

"Alright." He answered. His eyes looked guiltily at hers for a brief instant, but he blinked and smiled at her sweetly.

"I'm glad you're here." She said, near tears again.

"Yep." He said casually around a dashing half-smile.

She returned his smile and slipped down the hall to the bathroom. She took a moment to brush her teeth and pull her dark blonde hair up into a high ponytail so she could sleep without the long strands getting caught under her.

Suddenly she heard the trailer door open and close quietly. Were it not for the change of air pressure that sucked against the bathroom door she might not have noticed. She glanced out the tiny bathroom window at the driveway. Tim pulled his car door open and reached into the seat, pulling out his cell phone again. He seemed to be scrolling through messages or missed calls before he put the phone up to his ear. He was checking his voice mail. He hung up and dialed another number. Kelli strained to hear his voice beyond the glass, but couldn't make out anything he said.

After a few brief words he scowled and threw the phone back into the car and returned to the house just as silently as he had left it. Before she looked away from the miniscule window she noted Clay again; still on Marty's porch, illuminated by the naked bulb of the single porch light. His face had followed Tim back into the trailer before it seemed to look in her direction. The window was only big enough for her head to look through, but she stuffed a towel into its opening anyway, feeling as though she were suddenly on display.

They spent all day Sunday together. Tim made no mentions of leaving. They ate breakfast as a family. Kelli made pancakes, their favorite, as a treat. At their leisure they dressed the kids and headed out into the town. Clay was still unmoved, looking rather worn, having slept the whole night sitting in the rickety old lawn chair. Kelli eyed him curiously as Tim drove them away in her car. She was soon distracted by other things, though.

It was nice to be a family for the day. She couldn't remember the last time they'd gone anywhere together. Something that she'd strangely never thought of when they were together, she'd always been to busy just handling daily life.

He had insisted on paying off the c o u c h she had on layaway and paid the little extra to have it delivered that evening. He even offered to buy her a bargain priced queen size mattress set he noticed in the clearance section of the furniture store as they were leaving. Through it all she was forced to stamp down the tiny voice in the back of her head that kept reminding her that they were no longer husband and wife. She refused to hear it. She didn't want to.

She needed. Wanted.

Kelli slowly began to dare to hope that he might be serious. That he was really trying to repair their broken home. Even while they walked around the playground later in the day, the children playing excitedly around them, he offered his hand for her to hold. And it felt good; right.

Back home that late afternoon Tim ordered them all pizza to be delivered while they set about reorganizing the rooms around the incoming furniture. After paying the delivery boy and while they all munched happily on their little order-in treat he slipped out.

"I'll be back in a little bit, Sweetheart." He called to her, grabbing his car keys from the counter.

She watched him from the little diamond shaped window in the door as he climbed into the Toyota and again checked his phone. He made a quick call and seemed to talk heatedly for a few minutes before closing it again and throwing it back on the seat beside him. The tiny beaten voice in her head questioned the phone again. It wouldn't be silenced until she'd considered it. Who was he calling anyway? The other woman

What would become of them all tomorrow when the work day dawned? She'd have to talk to him about it, but some how she was afraid to bring it up. Afraid of what she knew the answer would be. Kelli shut the voice up in her head and crammed the questions back into their dark corner.

Tim was gone for over an hour before she heard his vehicle return. He hauled in bags and bags of groceries. So much food that her tiny fridge and freezer could hardly contain it, nor her overflowing cabinets. Most of the non- perishables had to be stacked in a pile on the counter by the fridge. She paused from unloading bag after bag and stepped to the door. Kelli glanced out at him bringing in the last bags. He paused to check his phone, before throwing it into his car and coming inside. Kelli also saw that Clay was not on the neighboring porch; his truck was gone. She slipped away before Tim noticed her.

He spilled in through the door, carrying the last of the items and a big grin. "That'll take care of those bare cabinets." He said cheerfully, laying the bags at her feet.

Ruby bounded over to him, followed by her little brother. "You're back again Daddy! I missed you!" She crooned. Joshua babbled a string of words which were only half in comprehensible English.

"Here I am! Who want's daddy to sleep over?" He directed it at them, but he looked at Kelli; cautious.

Her mind pricked and her heart and stomach both ached. She wanted to ask him outright what he was doing. What this was. What they were. But at the sight of her charmed and elated children she simply smiled and replied, "That sounds fun, doesn't it! Daddy gets to stay another night with us!"

The furniture had been delivered while Tim was out, and with bellies full of pizza they all worked to reorganize the two tiny bedrooms again. Kelly set up the twin mattress and the make-shift bed created by foam mattress toppers and the twin box spring as separate beds for the kids. One on one wall, one on the other. She also carefully pinned another sheet to the wall above the second bed, making a tent for each child. She arranged their toys pleasantly about the room, emptying the little second bedroom of everything except her boxes of clothes and the new mattress set. She had no sheets for her new bed, so she spread a thin blanket she had across it and tucked it in. It would do until she could buy some.

The living room now contained the two pieces of furniture. She had wanted to get rid of the old stained couch, but decided that maybe she could cover it instead. Technically she didn't need the new one anymore, since she had bought the pull out to use as her bed. But it was nice to have something new and decent looking. She promised herself she'd buy a slip cover for the old one in a color that would match or compliment the light suede material of the new couch.

She did own a small picture hanging hammer and a package of tiny nails for that purpose. And from the boxes of mementos she had stacked up in the larger of the two rooms she set about hanging photographs and little pieces of artwork. By bedtime the place looked more homey. The kids wandered around pointing at the pictures and ooing and awing. She even had enough to break up the bareness of their bedroom walls.

She had not been able to take all her decorations with her in the divorce, but she did take most of her favorite pieces. One of her very favorites was a big painting of a pastoral scene. It looked European. The view looked out from a forest of tall dark trees onto a sunlit pasture of manicured grass where a few fluffy sheep grazed beside a refined, shining, bay horse. She hung it in the living room above the new sofa, between the two windows. It dwarfed the space.

She also had plaques with tiny painted birds and swirling vines, three of them, in varying shades of brown and amber, the tiny birds were baby blue. She hung them in series down the hallway. The bright pictures from her old sitting room she hung about her bedroom. They were mostly burnt yellows and reds and included another large picture of a weathered, gray, shack of a ranch house in a field of blowing prairie grasses. Big billowing clouds floated by overhead and blotched the distant landscape with shade. She hung it at the head of the bed, which sat sadly on the floor without a frame. But it did add a lot to the room just having the pictures.

Following the previous nights routine they put the kids to bed before settling on the sofa. This time however Kelli was a little less interested in any advances Timothy might have considered making. Either he wasn't interested either, or he could tell she wasn't, because he didn't bother.

"Don't you work tomorrow?" She asked finally, after a few moments that felt awkward to her.

"Yeah." He said, considering his hands.

"That's a heck of a drive to make." She ventured when he remained silent.

"It's not so bad. I don't mind it." He forced a smile when he looked at her.

"Are you upset about something?"

"Nope, not at all." He pulled her against his side and hugged her around the shoulders with one arm, "But I was thinking that I can't handle another night on a sofa. Do you mind sharing that new bed I got you. For old time's sake?"

She looked at their feet kicked up on some boxes that served as a make-shift coffee table. Saw his hand around her arm out of the corner of her eye, reveled in the warmth of his body against her side. It would be nice to share a bed with someone other than a tangle of children who were all knees and elbows.

"Yeah, that'd be okay I think." She said and he

squeezed her in response. She rose to leave, "Speaking of, I was going to get ready for bed. I am exhausted. I leave for work early on Mondays."

"Alright. I'll be in in a minute."

In the other room, Kelli closed the bathroom door quietly and stood in front of the little white medicine cabinet on the tiny blank bathroom wall. A version of her stared back. A tired, older girl than she remembered. Her hazel eyes were circled darkly, and her mouth seemed creased from being turned down so often. But having Tim around did make her feel lighter, although it was stressful having so much unsaid between them. She hoped she'd have the courage to address things with him. Or that he'd explain himself more fully. Maybe in the quiet of the bedroom. Or perhaps first thing in the morning.

As she spread toothpaste on her toothbrush she heard the door open again. She peaked out the tiny window and watched as Tim opened his car door and checked his phone once more. He dialed a number and talked less animatedly than last time. This time his smile flashed and sparked before he hung up and came in quietly. She finished getting ready for bed and came out, glancing at him as she turned into the room. He sat in the same spot on the sofa, in the same position, his face blank. He looked up at her, but she pretended not to notice as the silence dragged on. Eventually she excused herself and went to bed.

For a long while there was no movement from the rest of the house. She laid in the foreign bed alone, looking at her familiar pictures in the dim light from the window. They made the room feel eerie in the dark, as though she were trapped in some alternate reality. At length Tim crept in. He eased himself into the bed and wrapped his arms around her under the blankets and pulled her to him. She looked at him, wondering what he was thinking inside those snapping green eyes. He kissed her neck and jaw, his hot breath and smooth fingers raised a field of goosebumps across her arms and legs. Her stomach did somersaults.

"You're like being home, Kelli." He crawled on top of her, smoothing his hands under her shoulders, holding her against his face as he kissed lines across her collar bones and chest. "No matter where a person goes, no matter what they do, or what happens, they always long to go home in the end."

She closed her eyes. The room was pulling and pushing against her like some unseen tide. He slipped her clothes off without her caring, and kicked his own off the bed. Still she kept her eyes closed. She imagined their old house. Her house. Imagined being a wife to the man she'd loved her whole life. Her first love. Raising a family with him, cherishing their two small children together. She thought of all their years together, their promises to each other before and on their wedding day. She remembered sitting in the attorneys office signing divorce papers, physically sick with despair. And she remembered being utterly and completely alone. Tim lay motionless beside her now, spent from his deeds.

In the silent dark the room swirled around her and she had the sense of drifting on a current, their bodies separated by miles in the inches between them. She woke up from her daze suddenly and he caught his breath when she spoke.

"Who was on the phone earlier?" She asked in a whisper.

"No one." He answered, far too quickly.

He pulled them together like spoons and slowly drifted to sleep, stopping her from talking to him further. Just like always, escaping her by leaving. Even if leaving was just falling asleep. Kelli listened to his breathing. She tried to ignore the unpleasantness as she closed her eyes and eased into a sound sleep. It took a little time, but she eventually managed.

Sometime later she was dreaming that a storm was rattling the tiny trailer. The windows and doors slapped against the paltry wood frame of the home. Great howling winds scoured the walls outside, threatening to tear them away entirely as it scratched the roof clear. The huge expanse of the sky above her churned with ugly green clouds. The sound of a car engine woke her up.

She sat up in the dark. Her hand instinctively swiped Tim's side of the bed, but she found it empty. "He's only left for work." She told herself, pulling a shirt over her head as she stumbled from the room. The clock on the kitchen wall read three A.M. Tim worked at nine. She slapped on the porch light and tore the door open, flying down the stairs as his tail lights retreated from the park. She ran as fast as she could to the road, and standing there in the cool dark night she screamed.

"Tim! Timothy!" Her voice echoed against the other trailers. Sobs raked her throat but she refused to let them out.

She was standing in her underwear and a shirt in the middle of the street, as her world crashed down around her for the second time in six weeks and she didn't care. She was trailer trash. Standing in her underclothes in the middle of the street seemed to pale in comparison to that reality. She'd been discarded again, just like that quiet screaming voice in her head had warned. Kelli dragged herself back to her steps. Movement on Marty's porch called her attention. Clay had returned. She'd not noticed his truck parked on the street. His boots slipped off the railing and he pushed his hat up from where it had rested over his eyes as he slept. She climbed the steps sideways, watching him.

Something in his gaze felt different. It wasn't a leer like she got from men on the street. It wasn't even the hungry look of ownership she recognized from Tim. It was softer. He made no motion to speak, he just watched her like a sentinel as she returned to the trailer and shut herself inside it.

On the kitchen island was a crude note scribbled on a paper plate in Tim's handwriting. "Sorry I hurt you so much baby. Everyone leaves home someday. I love you."

She felt like the world's biggest fool. She staggered over to the couch and collapsed into a pile of tears and sobs. It was probably a spat between him and his lover. The other woman had taken him back. Why else would he come to her? Why didn't he care if he hurt her? She was worthless. She was less than garbage. Kelli cried as silently as she possibly could. When there was nothing left she checked on the sleeping babies and carried herself back to bed and heaved some dry sobs into her pillow. As exhaustion pulled her into a fitful sleep she wondered achingly if she'd ever be good enough again. Or if she ever really had been in the first place. Her heart felt as empty as the quiet black void of the dreamless sleep that took over her conscious.

In a daze she managed to make it through work that day. S h e repeated the process through the next ten days, always on autopilot. Just barely aware. Her body ached like acid through every movement. No matter how many cups of coffee she stopped for her mind never cleared, and her back ached after pulling the kids in and out of the car repeatedly between job related stops. She gave up and bought them fast food for dinner, which she allowed the kids to eat in the restaurant before playing on the indoor playground.

"Where did daddy go?" Ruby asked for the fortieth time that day, pausing at Kelli's knees before running to play.

"He went home, Honey. I am sorry you missed him. Mommy didn't even hear him leave."

"Did you make him mad?" Ruby whispered it, pushing her own little face closer to Kelli.

She stared at the child a moment. Her fiery hair was inherited through Tim. Even the large round shape of her eyes was from his side of the family. Kelli had dark blonde hair that was nearly brown and coppery hazel eyes. Her children took after their father. His hair was very blonde and curly, but his mother and sisters' hair had been as red as strawberries. Even the texture was different. Her's had a slight wave in it, but the kids' curled wildly. She sighed. Who was she? Even her children were him.

"No, Baby. I didn't make him mad. Daddy wasn't mad. He has a different lady he lives with instead of us. He just likes her better some times. Daddy's head is broken, it doesn't work right. We'll be okay. I love you, and I love Joshua too." She hugged her, her energy utterly sapped. "Run, go play before we have to go home for bed."

"What about daddy?"

"Huh?" She chuffed frustratedly.

"Don't you love daddy too?" Her big eyes longed to hear her say it. Kelli knew she needed to know that her parents weren't at odds. She struggled to say the right thing, but failed.

"No, Honey. I don't love daddy. But, its okay. Run, go play." She turned her and shoved her in the direction of the playground, stopping the surge of temper that flared just below the surface.

Kelli stared at her phone while the kids played, contemplating who she might call to talk to. She tried her mother's number but it was busy. She tried her dad. It rang a few times before he finally answered.

"Yellow." The older man answered.

"Hey, Dad. It's me." Her voice wavered for a brief moment but she caught it.

"Hey, Kelster. Listen, I can't talk long, I have to run. Tonight is poker night and I have to be across town in twenty minutes." She could hear his shoes squeaking in the background as he paced around his apartment getting his things. "How are you and the kids doing?"

She sighed. There was no time to explain even part of the situation. "We're getting on great dad. How about you?" She lied.

"Not a day goes by that it doesn't burn me up knowing that piece of crap did this to you. I blame myself, Sweetie. I should have separated you two when you were still young and I had that ability. I just didn't know he'd turn out so worthless." He puffed into the phone as he moved about. His prickly gray beard rasped against the mouthpiece of the phone. He hated Tim, and never failed to mentioned it.

"It's not your fault, dad. Really, we're doing good."

"I'm glad, Kelli. Listen, I have to run. As soon as I am able to I'll send you a package with some things for the kids. Maybe even something for you, too, if you're good."

She smiled. At least it was comforting to hear his voice. "Alrighty, love you, Daddy."

"Love you, too, Pumpkin." The line went silent. Kelli was alone, and that sense crushed in around her from all directions.

She listened to the kids playing, out of sight in the swaying tangle of plastic tubes before her. They shrieked and giggled as they interacted with the other children within its colorful confines. Suddenly she remembered Tim's original call. The contract! Kelli couldn't believe she'd forgotten his promises of a sale contract for the house all these days! She whipped her phone open and dialed his number.

"Kelli?" His voice sounded irritated.

"Where's the contract?" She nearly growled into the mouthpiece.

"Contract?" He took a deep breath, "Oh, yeah."

"You damn liar."

"Oh, Kelli come on, its not that bad. The house was shown and some people were really interested in it. They'll probably write a contract eventually. They looked at it twice."

"You *lied* to me to get my address."

"I just wanted to see you. I just needed to know you and the kids were alright."

"I had sex with you, Tim. Twice. That was not my idea." She snipped quietly, her hand covering her mouth as she looked around to make sure no one was noticing her conversation, but the place was empty.

"Well you certainly didn't complain."

Kelli bit her lip as it quivered. She swallowed down a cry.

"If you ever show up again, Timothy, I will call the police."

"Oh, Baby come on. Don't be like that. Think of all the nice stuff we did! I bought you a bed! And some food. It wasn't all bad!"

"I mean it. I'll call the police." She hung up the phone before he could respond.

She set it on the table and buried her face in her hands. Her cell phone jingled on the table. Tim's number showed on the front. She ignored it. He called again. She turned it off.

She let the kids play until well past bedtime. It took her that long just to find the strength to consider even lifting her head. The sun set around the restaurant. Everything swam in slow motion around her as she sat in the hard plastic chair. Her back ached. Her head ached. Her stomach churned against itself. She felt as if she could fail to exist just from being so exhausted. The store had completely emptied, its big plate- glass windows were blackened by the missing the sun.

"We're tired mommy." Ruby whined, suddenly before her. Joshua held her hand, but clumsily attempted to climb Kelli's knees at the same time.

She scooped him up and rocked him against her. Ruby clambered up and curled up on what little was left of her lap. "I love you, Mommy." She whispered.

Kelli kissed their little red heads. "I love you, too, babies."

P. C. Rogers

-CHAPTER FOUR-

June was pleasant during the day and terrible at night. All day long thunder clouds piled up on the south western horizon and spilled out over Dixson in the night. Kelli grew more uneasy as the weeks passed. Their old house had included not only a basement but a separate safe room. It was tornado proof. Her trailer was merely a tasty hors d'oeuvres for a funnel cloud. Sleeplessness was really taking its toll on her, as she spent most nights sleeping lightly while listening to raging storms and the weather radio.

After weeks of forgetting she had finally invested in a belt after her pants reached the point of no return. She'd lost so much weight that they wouldn't stay on her on their own. She felt taut and pulled thin. The stress in her life kept mounting. Bills seemed endless; the kids' needs unlimited; the cost of food and electricity ever rising. Not to mention the stress of work.

Kelli was unsure how to keep the kids safe in the car in the heat when she had to run into the doctors offices and clinics to pick up the little blue coolers of samples. She had bought a copied key for the door locks, but it just felt instinctively wrong to lock the kids in a running vehicle. Her stomach turned knots as she rushed through her pick ups, unable to hurry the people in the offices and desperately wanting to. She feared someone would report her to child protective services, or that the police would notice them one day and accuse her of neglect. Often times she had to leave her post at the counters in the offices to run out and re-cool the car.

The last thing she wanted to do was put them in daycare, but as the days trickled from the calendar she was running out of options. It would mean applying for aid from the state, which was something she hated the idea of almost as much as being separate from her children all day. She knew she paid taxes that supported those programs, and though it hurt her pride to use them the biggest turn off was knowing she'd be labeled. And her children with her. She knew it was silly, and she shouldn't care. But the honest truth was that she *did* care. It felt like proof she was failing.

They had also gotten in the habit of eating out a lot for dinner. She hated it. Some days she was too exhausted to even pack them meals, and ended up buying them crappy food all day long. She often forgot to eat herself and feared she was becoming hypoglycemic. Often she found herself shaking and dizzy; suddenly weak and foggy. She'd have to pull over and buy a candy bar and wait for it to pass as she ate it. It was just so hard to find time to take care of herself. Everything was poured into keeping the trailer, her job, and the children. She felt herself shrinking into the oblivion of failure on every front.

Kelli pulled through the big puddle in her driveway that was nightly refilled by storms. It was Friday night. She'd let the kids play late at the fast food place again. It wasn't dark yet, but it was still well past their bedtimes. They'd passed out in the car as soon as she'd driven away from the restaurant. She noticed Clay on Marty's porch again. He'd been an inconstant figure there since he first appeared. Once Marty let him in, but only for a few minutes, and Clay left directly after. He didn't return for a few weeks, and she had assumed he was definitely gone.

She was still curious about him and Marty and their relationship- whatever it was. She hadn't ever had the chance to speak to Clay again, though part of her desperately wanted to. She'd just been too busy. Typically if he was on the porch he was asleep under his hat anyway and she didn't want to disturb him. Marty had been always holed up in his trailer, or asleep in the same lawn chair.

The night was humid and the sky was dark with a

new moon. She sighed as she opened her door and mustered the energy to unload the kids. Clay watched her from under his hat. She paused to take note of him and he flicked his hand at her, as if he were not certain she was looking at him but wanted to wave if she were. She smiled a half smile in reply before leaning into the back car door.

Kelli still hadn't even had time to make friends in town either, in fact she'd given up trying. She had thought about joining a church for the sake of meeting a friend or someone with something in common. Anything really. But every Sunday that rolled around she was barely able to pull herself out of bed, let alone get the three of them fed, dressed and ready for church on time. Depression seemed to be setting in. Her lack of caring about the pain, and her sick ability to embrace and even need it told her that. But she ignored it. She wouldn't be able to get treatment for anything anyway. And this certainly wasn't a time for emotional weakness.

She tucked the kids into bed and peeled her shoes and socks off and left them by the door. The house needed picking up but she was too exhausted. She talked herself into doing up the dishes and wiping down the kitchen counters. The rest would have to wait for tomorrow, if she managed to have the energy for it after hauling out the children and the laundry to the laundromat. Every piece of their clothing was dirty. Kelli had shamefully worn a shirt from earlier in the week to work that day.

Almost every moment of every day her mind ran across all the tasks left to accomplish before she could sit down, before she could sleep, before the weekend was over. Tonight was no different. Do the dishes, then collapse on the sofa. The hot soapy dish water threatened to lull her to sleep. She longed to take a bath, but that only reminded her that the bathroom desperately needed cleaning.

She sighed deeply. Her mind hurt from the

responsibility of thinking for three people and all the world around them, nonstop.

Kelli jumped at the sudden, unexpected, sound of knocking at the door. Her heart leaped into her throat wondering if it was Tim. She hadn't heard a word from him since their last conversation when she had hung up on him and refused to answer his calls. That had been a long while ago. Pulling a paper towel from the roll to dry her hands she mentally prepared herself. The cool metal door knob made her muscles clench in anticipation as she threw open the door, fully ready to give Timothy an earful.

Clay stood on the step instead.

"Hey." He said, a little nervously, holding the brim of his black cowboy hat in his hands limply.

She hadn't seen him up close in over a month. His face was not bruised anymore, and both his eyes were open wide. They were dark brown and pleasantly shaped. His hair was short and a mousy brown color. Clay was also much taller than she had realized. Tim was only a couple inches taller than her, maybe five foot eight inches, plus he was broad and thick. Clay was tall, and no where near as thick as Tim. Although his shoulders were wide and even through his collared shirt she could tell they were well muscled. He was also older looking than she'd realized at their first meeting, older than she was. She was turning twenty-seven this winter, but now that his face wasn't swollen and she was close enough to really see him she realized he had to be well into his thirties.

Kelli shook her head a little, rattling her thoughts. "Hi." She managed to squeak out.

She hadn't interacted with a man as a single woman in over a decade. At least not one in her age group. He didn't reply, just looked at her coolly in silence. His mouth had curled into a crooked little smile. His long legs were planted like pillars on her top step. It seemed to take him a while to come to himself.

"Can I come in?" He flicked his hat towards the kitchen beyond her, breaking the awkward silence he had created.

"Oh, jeez, yeah." She opened the door wider and stepped out of the way.

Clay kicked his boots on the lip of the door frame before he entered. Their heels made an official sounding noise as he crossed the hard floor to the table between the kitchen island and the living room sofas.

Kelli smoothed her hair and glanced down at her stained shirt. She danced around a little, unsure where to go next. She settled for the kitchen.

"Can I get you a drink? I have some lemonade made up... I think." She indicated the fridge and hoped there was indeed lemonade still inside.

"Sure, that sounds great." He set his hat on the table beside him and grinned. One of the teeth on the left side of his mouth was missing. An upper first molar. It wasn't noticeable until he smiled wide.

Kelli sighed inwardly with relief that there was lemonade left, and enough for two glasses. She poured them and carried them over to the table and sat down, handing Clay his.

"It's nice to have an evening without a thunderstorm." She said, making small talk.

"Yup. It gets old, especially after that tornado that ripped through town a few years ago."

"It keeps me up at night remembering it. Maybe its like lightning though. At least that's what I tell myself." She took a sip of her drink, "Maybe it won't strike the same place twice."

"Not for a few years I'd bet." He smiled again. His gaping bite was comical, and the weathered skin around his eyes crinkled warmly. He was handsome in a rugged, earthy, way. Not remarkable like Tim was, but the more she looked at him the more she found to her liking. Straight nose, thin lips, kind wide eyes.

They settled into another silence. Kelli was afraid to take a drink again, just the sound of her swallowing seemed to echo through the room. Clay looked around the space from his seat, pushing himself back a little in the chair before leaning back over the table again.

"Place looks nice." He finally ventured.

"No it doesn't." She said seriously. "Its a mess. I need to clean it. And it certainly was pretty pathetic to begin with." She sighed sadly.

"Well you made it a fine home. It sure wasn't anythin' to begin with. Looks to me like people live here now. And that always looks good."

"Aw. Thanks." She smiled in turn.

Another long silence settled in. Clay sucked his teeth and sighed.

"Look, this is a little forward, and I ain't any good at this stuff to begin with," His voice was smooth as he spoke, like water flowing lazily through a pebbly creek bed. It was soothing, she liked the sound of it. "I just wanted to know, if I was to ask you out sometime, you know, in the future, if you'd be willin' to go out with me."

Kelli stared at him. He stuck one leg out straight under the table and rested one hand on it as he pushed himself back in his chair a little, waiting for her answer. He held onto his glass with the other hand, looking at her intently. She felt herself blush.

"I'd like to, really." She rolled her eyes a little, "I'd so like to get out and do something some time..." She trailed off as he cracked his broken grin again. "...It's just that I have the kids all the time, and its kinda hard to go on a date with two toddlers in tow."

He stuck out his bottom lip and nodded a few slow nods, thinking. "Nah. I know just what we could do."

"Really?" She looked at him dubiously.

"Yup." He pushed himself up with his palms on the table, brought the glass up with him and swallowed what little was left before stuffing his hat back on his head, "How about tomorrow? Around noon?"

Kelli nodded, a little stunned.

"See you then." He said as he took a few strides to the door and let himself out.

What just happened? Kelli followed him a moment later, looking out the little window on tiptoes. He had resumed his position in Marty's lawn chair on the porch across the driveways. Her stomach felt something other than knots for the first time in nearly three months. Butterflies. She was excited. She also had nothing to wear or dress the kids in. She decided to wash some clothes in the tub and hang them to dry over night. It would work well enough.

The sun woke the kids up at 7:30 the next morning, but she managed to snuggle them in her bed for another hour and a half as she dozed and listened to their little voices play and talk about things. Joshua had celebrated his second birthday quietly the week before and seemed to be marking the occasion with a new slew of words and an inch worth of rapid growth. Ruby would be four in the fall. She sighed and wished she had been smart enough to weasel some guilty-conscious- clothes out of Tim before he left last month. They were all in need. She was going to have to dip into their little savings before too long to satisfy the growing demand.

She had just enough time to bathe them all, feed and dress herself and the kids, and do her hair and makeup before noon. True to his promise Clay knocked on the door just as the minute hand clicked.

"Mornin'." He smiled, holding his hat in one hand as she opened the door.

He stepped in and looked at them all. Ruby's eyes

grew as big as saucers as she stared at him. Her thick hair was pulled up in a fat ponytail, and Kelli had slipped a yellow sun dress on her for the day. Joshua wore a little pair of jeans and a cowboy shirt, and he exclaimed and pointed at Clay's shirt when he noticed they were similar.

Kelli had opted for jeans and a pink tank top with lace on it for herself. She had no idea what he had planned, but the day promised to be warm and she could at least prepare for that.

"Y'all look finer than me." He said, setting his hat on the counter and putting his hands on his hips as he considered the stunned children before him.

It was silliness. He was wearing a new pair of jeans and a crisp red plaid shirt with short sleeves. His big belt buckle gleamed. He looked fine himself. And imposing, the more Kelli looked at him. He carried himself slowly and confidently, something she was not used to. Tim had always zipped along; as though he were some how trying to avoid detection; Clay sauntered. She was unaccustomed to country folk. Especially the world of cowboys. But she began to think she liked it, at least if Clay represented it.

"Clay, this is Ruby and Joshua. Kid's this is Marty's friend. He's taking us out today." She herded them towards him.

"Very pleased to meet you." Clay said, bowing low to take Ruby's hand, and shaking Joshua's like a man.

"Are you a real cowboy?" Ruby asked breathlessly.

"Sure am, how'd you know?"

"Your boots and your hat." She said with finality, "Those are cowboy boots, and that's a cowboy hat."

"You're pretty smart. And pretty pretty. Just like your mom."

"Thank you!" She said, pleased with herself.

Kelli flushed as Clay glanced her way, checking to make sure she'd heard his compliment. He flashed his goofy grin, satisfied that she had.

"Ready?" He asked Kelli. She nodded and grabbed her cell phone and bank card off the counter and stuffed both in her pants pocket.

"We'll have to take my car I guess. For the car seats." She said as she followed them out the door.

"My truck has the latch system, I don't mind movin' them." He answered and she eyed him curiously. "I have a nephew I haul around with me some times. He's only a few months old, but my sister gave me quite the lecture on how to properly install a car seat." He explained.

She smiled, it sounded great; relaxing, "I like that idea. It'd be nice not to drive." She pulled open the back door to her car and started unhooking Joshua's car seat. Clay opened the one opposite and did the same.

"You drive a lot?" He asked, taking the car seat from her and carrying them both to his waiting pickup truck.

"Every day. I work for the hospital system, collecting blood samples and things from other clinics, doctors offices, nursing homes and stuff. Bringing them in for processing."

"We ride too." Ruby said, dancing with excitement.

"Too, too! Me too!" Joshua added one of the few phrases the had mastered.

Clay looked at Kelli. She shrugged, "I can't afford childcare I trust. So they ride with me all day."

"Why not?" He lifted the seats into place and began buckling them.

"I don't want them in a state run daycare, I worry about them being... hurt or abused. Or worse. And I can't afford to pay someone to stay with them all day at home. I don't even know anyone I'd trust to do it."

"Marty might do it." He said jokingly as he pulled the belt tightly, locking Ruby's car seat into place behind the drivers seat.

"I'm sure he'd love to." She answered sarcastically.

He worked on Joshua's seat while she lifted Ruby in and buckled her. Joshua stood eagerly beside him until he was finished, and he lifted him into place and carefully, as though Joshua were made of glass, buckled him in. Kelli grabbed the small bag of diapers and wipes and such from her car and tossed it in at Joshua's feet before climbing up into her own seat. Clay bounded in and shut the door. He looked around at them with a smile.

"Here we go!" And he slapped the truck into gear.

"Where are we going anyway?" Kelli asked as she watched the houses pass by. Soon they were out of the dingy part of town and moving into an area where the houses became larger and nicely kept.

"To the park. My Mom's church is havin' a cookout this afternoon." He turned them down a series of streets. "And he's not so bad as he seems."

"Who?"

"Marty. You guys want air conditionin'? Or windows?" He looked at the kids in the rear view mirror.

"Windows!" They shouted in unison, and giggled as the air from the opening windows messed their hair.

"I didn't think he was. He's a mystery though."

"Nah, its all a bluff. You just have to wait him out."

"Is that what you've been doing?" She chuckled to herself, "You been waiting him out?"

"I have actually." He gave her a side ways glance and curled his lip into a grin.

The truck bounced and they lurched as he pulled into the park driveway. Vehicles were lined up in all the parking spaces so they were forced to join the outcast of cars parked in the grass at the end of the lot. In the shade of a series of poplars and cottonwood trees stood a pavilion where a couple dozen people milled around a line of smoking iron grills on posts.

Clay climbed out of the truck and unhooked Ruby's buckles, while Kelli did the same with Joshua. She carried him around the truck and gathered up Ruby's hand and walked with Clay to the gathering. He put his hand on her back and guided her up to a man at the grill who waved warmly as they approached.

"Clay my boy! Good to see you! Your mother didn't mention that you were coming." The little man waved around a pair of grilling tongs as he spoke, and his smile was invaded by a bushy black mustache that threatened to cover his teeth when he grinned. He was stout, his cheeks were red, and he stood barely taller than the grills. Kelli liked him.

"Glad I could make it, Pastor. This is my good friend Kelli and her babies, Ruby and Joshua." Clay pointed each of them out.

"Hello Pastor." Kelli smiled. Ruby swirled her skirt bashfully and Joshua pointed at the smoking grills and exclaimed that they were hot.

"Come here and give me a hug boy, before you run off to your mom." The aging minister toddled out from behind the grills and wrapped his arms around Clay, who towered comically over him. They swatted each other's backs in a manly fashion before Pastor pushed him away a little and shook his finger in his face, "Your mother's been worried sick. It's been enough years of this nonsense, Clay. Time to call it quits."

"Yessir it has. This is my last season." Clay assured him.

"The Lord hates a liar Clayton. You told us that last summer."

"Yes, he does, and, yes, I did. But this is truly my last season, my body can't take this no more."

"Don't tempt the Lord, Clay. Its a miracle you're even walking around today." Pastor turned after he slapped Clay's arm and returned to his post at the grills, as though he'd suddenly forgotten they were even speaking.

Kelli eyed C l a y suspiciously, and was about to inquire about the exchange when a tall, wiry, woman scuttled up to him. Her rich brown hair was cut short and curled and brushed away from her face, probably in the same way she'd been doing it since she was a young woman in the 80's. It reminded Kelli of her mom's hair when she was a child, and brought back a surge of childhood nostalgia. Her arms were thin and strong and outstretched as she flew in for an embrace. She looked weathered and tanned. Light colored jeans clung to her slim waist and her blue flowered blouse draped neatly across her strong shoulders. She hugged him tight and then held him at arm's length, smiling. Her face was similar to his: thin, straight, lips, wide eyes, the same mousey hair.

"You break a mother's heart, Clay."

"I know Momma. I'm sorry." He looked a little misplaced for a moment before he introduced her to Kelli and the children.

"Aw, pleased to meet you kids. Glad you could come, I'm Patty." She shook Kelli's hand warmly and slid in next to her, running her arm across her shoulders, "Over there is the play ground, Cindy's watching the kids with her two grown daughters." She pointed the short distance to the play area where a mess of children were running around, corralled by a middle aged woman and her teenage daughters, "Over here's the food tables, help yourself to some drinks or chips, the meal will be ready in just a few more minutes. Oh and over there are restrooms. So glad to meet you, Honey." She pointed both areas before patting her on the back and slipping off towards a group of similarly aged woman under the pavilion.

"Thank you!" Kelli called after her as she walked away.

"Can we play Mommy?" Ruby tugged at her shirt bottom.

"Sure, Honey." She set Joshua down and the pair ran off to the slides. "I just want to follow them over, so I can kinda keep an eye on them, too." She said to Clay.

"Okay, I'll get us some drinks." He sauntered off in the direction his mom had gone.

The park was busy with different groups and families. Some filled picnic tables, while others ran around in the open spaces chasing balls or children. Another group had taken up residency at a different pavilion and was also barbequing. The recent rains had left things damp and smelling of leaves and wood from the mulch laid around. The tufts of cut grass that were drying in the heat of the noon day sun smelled sweet and warm. Little white and blue butterflies danced about on the breeze and the leaves of the shady canopy above rasped quietly as the air breathed.

It felt nice to be outside. She hadn't bothered to stop at this park before. It was on the opposite side of town from their trailer park, and the fast food stores with their playgrounds of tubes and foam were closer. She made a mental note to try to get the kids to the park at least a couple times a week, now that she'd seen it. It wasn't as far as it seemed, but then again, maybe the time had just flashed by under the circumstances.

Clay returned and sat down next to her, offering her a can of orange soda. His body was warm near her and she noticed now that he smelled of Old Spice and leather. He scooted around a little so he could face her better. When she failed to take her pop can he snapped the top for her and scooted it a little closer.

It was a simple act, just like going to get the drinks in the first place had been. It spoke volumes to her, a strange foreign language she had never known yet somehow understood. Clay was nice. The more time she spent near him the more she realized about her ex.

Tim had never been a thoughtful person, although early in their relationship he had run the usual gambit of pleasantries. He had bought her flowers and treats; taken her on nice dates. But they were teenagers then, and looking back on it she felt as though he had been reciting a learned equation to her. Even when he asked her to marry him it had been an obvious conclusion to their dating, it was neither special nor uncommon, it just was.

She looked at Clay a minute, her cheek resting on her fist; elbow on the table top. His hands were thinner than Tim's, but bigger, wrapping around the entire can as he held it to the table before him.

"Thanks, Clay." She smiled.

"There weren't many options, there's so many little kids here and pastor's wife can't stand children drinkin' caffeinated pop."

"No, I mean for asking me out." She glanced at the kids merrily playing the short distance away, "I haven't been out in the sun and grass in a long, long, while."

"I know, I had figured. It's not healthy." That he had noticed her at all, let alone the hours of labor she kept struck her.

She exhaled a snuff out of her nose, "My days seem to bleed together right now. I needed a break."

He only nodded in reply. His hat tipping up and down with his head. He seemed to notice it just then and took it off, laying it out of the way on the table.

"Your accent doesn't fit this far north. Even for a cowboy." She said lightly, bumping into his side a little for effect.

"Yeah, I was born in Arkansas. I came up here with my momma in time to start high school. But the southern draw has stuck for the most part." He took a swig of his own orange soda, "How 'bout you? Grow up here in Dakota?"

"Heck, no." She chuckled. "Tim moved me down

here after we got married, he had gotten a job in Bismark. We both grew up together in Michigan."

"Why didn't you go home after you split?"

"There is no home anymore. My parents divorced a few years back and moved south. Neither had the space or time for us. Although they each help us out whenever they can. I haven't seen either of them for a few years now. It's hard."

"That's hard, I'm sorry for it." He said sincerely.

Everything about him was sincere.

"It is." She sighed, "I am sorry for it too." "You still love him?"

She thought about the night she ran after him in her underwear. Remembering that Clay had seen the whole thing: Tim's leaving and her pathetic race to catch him. And also her defeat at his leaving. She flushed a little.

"I've never loved anyone else, I don't remember ever not loving him. We've been together since ninth grade. I am not *in* love with him, though part of me still loves him. He was my world all these years. We have kids together. It's hard to truly hate that. I resent him, for sure, and there's anger..."

"Another woman?"

She breathed a thin chuckle and nodded her head, looking at the drink in her hands. "Yeah. I didn't see it coming. A police officer actually delivered the divorce papers one morning after he'd left for work." She shrugged a little, "I guess I am just now realizing it's really over. Some how I thought... well. Well, you know. He came back and I thought a lot of wrong things. But it's over now."

Clay nodded. "You're gonna be alright, you know."

He grinned so reassuringly at her, and his voice was so smooth when he spoke. She teared up and had to catch herself before she cried.

He put his hand on her back quickly, it was wide and felt as though it spanned the entire distance there, "Sorry. I shouldn't've brought it up."

"No no." She sniffed down her emotions and forced a smile, "Its okay. It's just so good to hear someone say that."

"Say what?"

"That I'm going to be okay. I don't *feel* like I'm *ever* going to be alright again."

He laughed out loud, big and strong. "Girl, You're gonna be alright. Storms only knock you down and wash you out. That's all." He sounded so sure, so confident, she could imagine herself believing him on it. He stood and pulled his legs out from the table's bench seat. "C'mon, lets walk you in some sunshine and grass. Cindy's got the kids; she ain't never lost one yet."

She followed him out from the trees and into the mowed grass that baked contentedly under the summer sun. She kicked off her shoes and carried them in one hand. He stuffed his hands into his pockets and kicked at the mounds of clumpy mowed grass as they came along their path.

Kelli breathed in the summer smells. The noises of Dixson were muted by the sounds of people playing in the park. College was out for the season so most of the students were back home, leaving only the locals. The day was perfect. No ugly billowing storm clouds threatened the horizon, just pretty tufts of white rolled shady spots across the prairie below. It was a calm day for the wind, too, instead of pressing against them and whirling around objects as it hurried along it only breathed; soft, slow puffs of summer warmth. They kicked along slowly, Kelli very much enjoying the slow warmth and Clay's quiet company.

"So now you know my story, a little anyway." She plopped down on the grass, still within ear shot of the playground. "I gotta know why you're sitting on my neighbors porch day and night."

He chuckled again, in the slow deep way that seemed to be his own. He eased himself down on the grass near her, sticking his feet out before him. "Well, that's quite the story. I'm not sure you've got the time."

"I have to be to work Monday, other than that I am free." She smirked.

"I suppose that's almost enough time." He plucked a piece of grass that stood taller than its uniform neighbors and flicked it away. "Marty's my Mom's brother. He owes me for a colt I gave him a few years back, but he don't wanna pay me the money since I use it for entry fees. I like to keep my money separated right; the money from the few foals I sell off goes to entry fees."

"Entry fees for what?" She glanced at the belt buckle, the dots connecting themselves in her mind.

"Bull ridin'. That's what Pastor was hollering at me for. No one likes me doin' it. But some things get stuck in you, like your childhood accent."

"Is your dad here today, too?" She said, glancing over her shoulder at the people in attendance.

"My dad got killed when a bull landed on his head during a ride. I was ten, my sister was eight."

"That's horrific, Clay." She gasped, though Clay recited it almost without feeling, "What on earth possesses you to follow that?"

"I honestly dunno. I got dared to ride as a teen. I was a lot shorter then. I'm too tall for it, but it stuck. We don't pick what comes natural." He shrugged a little, "You can't help being beautiful, and I can't help bein' good at ridin'."

She flushed a little and changed the subject, "Did a bull land on you the day we met?"

"Day before, and I landed on him. Down in

Shelbyville, Missouri. A big brindle bull called Frack'n. I got my eight seconds in, but he threw me over his face at the buzzer. My side caught his horn and he kicked my face with his knee as I landed. Cracked three ribs and fractured my eye socket."

"Lost the tooth?" She said, pointing faintly in his direction.

"Nah, I did that on my first circuit, got in a fight at a meet and greet. He busted out my tooth and I broke his nose. We called it even."

"Sounds... exciting." She smirked a little. It was a whole different world from the one she'd known.

She'd grown up in suburbia, in a little bedroom community of five acre homesteads. Her parents had kept a pet llama, and she had grown up with chickens. Tim had grown up in town and held an office desk job for his whole adult life. She had been a middle class suburban housewife less than a year ago. It was intriguing to her, the thought of ranching and rodeo. She'd never considered any other lifestyle than her own. Her mom and dad had both grown up on farms, but it was Michigan- they raised dairy cattle. But she knew nothing of it.

"I wasn't lying to Pastor. This isn't what I had seen for my life. Not what I intended. It's entertaining. But it's gettin' old. Or I am." He shifted a little under the uncomfortable admission.

"You're not old. You don't seem old to me anyway." She mused.

"Didn't say I was; said I was getting'." He said a little defensively and she giggled at him.

"So you ride bulls for work?" She changed the subject on him.

"Hell no!" He laughed out loud again, it made her smile, "No, hah. I pocket some decent winnin's from time to time. I might ride full time once in a while, a few seasons every couple years when it strikes me. But my real money is in the ranch. All I earn I put back into it. I raise beef and rodeo bulls." He leaned back on his elbows a little, "And a colt here and there. Like to get into feed grains at some point."

"Doesn't seem to eat up much of your time, this ranch." She said, not convinced.

"It's the family ranch. Mom's family. She doesn't work it anymore, her body's shot from it. It's damn hard work on a woman. It's the reason she sent my sister away after school, hoping she'd settle into something easier."

"Did she?"

"Oh, yeah. She works for an insurance company back east. It keeps her busy, she only just recently got down to marryin' and havin' kids."

"That's right, you mentioned your nephew."

"Dillon. He's amazing. He's nearly nine months old. She came out to visit for a few weeks recently, her husband and the baby, too. It was good to see him. Did something to me, see'n my baby sister with a family and me with nothin' but my horses and cattle. Made me jealous, I guess. I've had my head down so busy chasing titles and bottom lines that I lost track of time, I guess."

She pursed her lips a little, considering his honesty. "So you just up and chase the first next thing you see?"

He chuffed, flicking another piece of grass, "I've seen plenty, I just know what I'm lookin' for, is all."

She laughed out loud this time, snorting a little at the end. "Lord have mercy, Clay. That's quite the statement."

He sat up, indignantly; pushed his hat down a little tighter on his head. "It wasn't a line, Kelli. It's the truth. God hates a liar."

"Well, Lord have mercy, that's some plain talkin'."

She poked his leg with her foot, "I didn't mean to offend you." she said apologetically.

"You can't." He said flatly, then, "What're you doing tomorrow?"

"Not much. Laundry. I have a mountain of it. I haven't had a chance to do anything with all this work, and the kids, and being so darn worn out. The trailer's a mess, we're wearing clothes I hand washed in the bathtub last night after you left, for God's sake." She sighed. "Joshua needs a haircut. And clothes, he's outgrown all his pants." She grew quieter as she rattled off the list, "Ruby needs shoes and shirts. My clothes don't even fit..." She looked away and grew silent.

Clay watched her as her mind wandered and she chewed her pouty bottom lip worriedly. She looked over to the playground where the red beacons of her children's heads bobbed around in play.

"You know Cindy lives just a few blocks from you. I've known her nearly two decades now, she and her girls babysit all the time." He said softly, "I might be outta line, but I'd pay for a sitter for you if you wanted to come out with me tomorrow night."

Kelli squinted to see the light haired Cindy standing in the mulch of the swing set and slides. Her blonde haired daughters chased children around as they laughed and screamed with excitement and play. Ruby was running full tilt with a couple of girls, Joshua tagged along behind her happily.

She ached to get away. To be just a person for a moment. Even before the divorce she rarely had time away from the kids or the house, not unless she was grocery shopping or driving around aimlessly. Her girlfriends had all worked during the day and sent their children to school or daycare. They'd grown apart as their lives bore down on them in full force. She sighed, considering the temptation. She didn't know Clay from Adam. But these people seemed sincere, and he seemed honest enough. And she so very much longed, craved, to have some little life of her own. Finally she relented.

"Yeah. Okay." She turned to him and nodded. "I'd really like that.

He smiled wide, his comical missing tooth flashing black. "There's a rodeo in Elgin, I ride at eight. I can pick you up at 5:30?"

"Phew. Elgin? That's a haul."

"It's not so bad. I'll drive, I don't mind it. You can sleep on the way back, and I promise not to stay late. We can leave after my ride."

"Who's gonna drive if you land on the bull again?" She gave him a suspicious look. "I don't drive stick. Not well anyway."

"No? Man. We gotta do somethin' about that. You can't live in cowboy country and not drive stick."

"I've been here almost eight years, it hasn't caused an issue until now. Maybe you should drive an automatic."

"Real trucks are not automatic." He said playfully.

"Real cowboys don't land on the bull." She leaned in and whispered smartly. Kelli stood up and brushed the grass off her saggy, oversized, pants, "We better eat, everyone else has made plates."

Clay smiled softly and agreed, pushing himself up too. He walked closely beside her, though respectful of her personal space. Even as they sat at the table she could feel him near her. It felt good. Better than good, even; she thought.

It was getting dark when Clay finally pulled the truck into the trailer park. Ruby and Joshua's little heads bobbled awkwardly as they slept in their car seats. Their day had been full of hard busy playing, and they had not taken any time to nap. They had fallen asleep even as Kelli carried them to the truck as they left the park. Clay had jogged up to her along the way and scooped up Ruby, the heavier of the two. He repeated the duty back at their trailer, quietly carrying the sleeping girl as Kelli balanced Joshua to fish out her keys at the door.

He was so at ease with the kids, it made butterflies tickle her stomach. Even Tim had been awkward with them, especially as infants, she couldn't imagine him with a stranger's children. Timothy's last visit had been so contrary to their every day lives with him, typically he wasn't interested even in holding them or anything that could be construed as interactive.

Clay strode through the house behind her, pulling his boots off with his toes and leaving them beside the door. He pulled his hat off and laid it on the island as he passed and he followed Kelli down the hall and waited for her to put Joshua down and take Ruby. It was as though it were the most natural thing to him. If doing something so gentle and quiet came so naturally, and riding ferocious hulking bulls also came naturally, she wondered what didn't.

She tucked the kids in after pulling off their shoes, and kissed their sleeping faces. "I love you babies." She whispered as she carefully shut their bedroom door.

Clay was standing just inside the front door, as though he were waiting to step out.

"Are you leaving?" She surprised herself that she sounded so disappointed.

"Well, I was gonna." He smiled a little, "I gotta go wear down Marty. Get my entry fee for tomorrow."

She laughed a little. "Okay. Doesn't sound like a good way to spend the night before participating in a rodeo, though."

"Yeah, it's gettin' old. Or maybe that's me." He joked. "It shouldn't be too hard tonight, he had the day to himself, so he should be in a better mood."

Kelli's phone started jingling and she answered it as she watched Clay pull his boots on.

"Hey, Sweetheart." Tim's raspy voice slithered in her ear.

"I don't want to talk to you, Timothy." She turned away sharply and growled into the phone.

"Aw, Baby, you're not still mad about before are you? I thought I might come out and check on you and the kids. I've been missing them really bad. They must be inches taller by now. Is Joshua talking yet?"

"No, Tim. No, I don't need checking in on. We're fine." "Don't call the police on me okay?" She heard gravel popping under tires outside and the sound of a car door shutting.

She glanced at Clay who stood still, by the door, looking solemnly at her as she grew white. Her mind raced. She dreaded seeing Tim. She knew she had to make good on her threat to call the police, but she feared taking that step. Uncertain of its outcome; uncertain if he'd retaliate in some way. What if he decided to file for custody? To take her to court to see, or worse, share, the kids. Could he do that? She couldn't afford a lawyer and she honestly didn't know the laws. Tim was the one with all the money. Clay bent his head and slowly put his hat on with one hand, his other rested on the door knob.

"Are you outside?" Kelli breathed into the phone.

"I have a real contract this time, Baby, I brought it out with me and everything." He assured her, hanging up his phone as the sound of his steps hit the stairs.

Tim grabbed the door knob just as Clay pulled it open. They stopped short and stared at each other. Tim was startled and he took a minute to gather himself before entering the kitchen. Clay only stared fiercely down at the shorter man. No one spoke for what felt like an eternity. Kelli's head spun and her stomach twisted in a series of nauseating knots.

Finally, Tim walked over towards Kelli; the island standing between them. He laid a stapled packet of papers out for her. "Who's your friend?" He said, jealousy dripping green from his mouth.

"This is Clay. Clay, this is my *ex*-husband Timothy." She gestured between the two, emphasizing his demoted status.

"Nice to meet you, my man!" Tim zipped over, his hand thrust out in greeting.

Clay shook it forcefully, pulling him a little closer with each pump of his arm, "You'll want to step back, friend." He sneered in warning as Tim lurched and wrenched his hand free. Then he added, "That's right, I think I saw you tear outta here the other night in a fine hurry, it seems."

"Easy, buddy. I'm just being polite." Tim said, unsettled. Kelli knew he was embarrassed and becoming angry with each passing breath. She knew him well enough.

"So'em I." Clay said, leveling a stare.

Kelli watched their short exchange, her jaw nearly agape.

"You look like you were headed out, don't let me keep you." Tim said, over his shoulder. He turned away brushing his hand at him.

It was like watching angry dogs circle each other. Clay glanced at Kelli, and back at Tim. Both men bristled. Clay relented.

"I'll see you in a bit, Kelli. I'll just be sitting on the porch over there." He made eye contact with Tim as he thumbed in the direction of Marty's trailer.

"Alrighty, Clay." She barely squeaked, "I had a great time today. Thanks so much."

"Night." He said to her, his voice calm and smooth, but to Tim he spoke through his teeth, "Pleased to meet you, Tim." He touched the rim of his hat as he ducked out the door, pulling it loosely behind him.

Tim smoothed out a little in his absence. He grabbed up the papers and carried them to the table, sitting down in the far chair.

"Where's the kids?" He asked, suddenly looking around him.

"They're asleep."

"It's not even bedtime yet!" He said, dejected.

"We were at the park all day, they didn't nap." She said flatly, regretting that she was alone with him. The sight of him made her want to vomit. As did the thoughts of their intimate encounters last month, which unfortunately came flooding back as she made her way to the table.

"That sounds... fun." Obviously unsettled at the thought of her out gallivanting with his children and a strange man.

"It really was." She liked that the idea seemed to scratch him wrong.

He shook it off.

"Anyway, here's that contract. They're offering less than we're asking, but they can close in two months time." He slid it across the table to her as she sat in the chair opposite him.

"How much less?"

She skimmed through the papers. Twenty thousand less. That was a full ten grand she'd loose. A third less than she had been expecting to get.

"I can't do this Tim. I need the full amount, I can't keep your children in a trailer forever, and I can't get us out of it without that money."

He tisked at her annoyingly. "Calm down, Baby. Lets just counter at one-ninety. That's only a loss of five thousand."

"Five thousand is a down payment on a mortgage, Tim. I need it."

He stood up and walked behind her as if he were truly troubled by her concerns. His thick, hot, hands rubbed the knots across her shoulders and upper back. She tried to shrug him off, but in all honesty it was a welcome relief to her aching muscles. He knew all the places where she carried tension, his hands were experts on her body.

"If it bothers you that much, Honey, I'll give you the five thousand out of my cut at closing."

She sighed and nodded. "Okay. What about your cut?" She asked, hanging her head as his hands worked up her neck and the back of her head.

"What about it?"

"If you'd give me more of your cut I could take better care of your children, Tim. We're barely scraping by- even though I'm working full time. Besides that, you know my car isn't going to run forever, and I am putting thousands of miles on it every month."

"Shhh. Okay okay. I'll take care of it." His clothes rustled as he bent down to kiss her neck, but she swatted him off before he could.

"Don't." She hissed. "I am not a play thing, Tim. I am not your whore. You already have one of those, remember?"

"Tiffany isn't a whore." He said, defensive.

"Well, she surely wasn't and isn't your wife."

"Aw, Baby, let's not fight. Look, I already told you. I love you. I'm not lying. I just get so confused between want I want and what I need. I need you. I need you and the kids. You all are my life, really. I mean that." He stood quietly as she read through the contract again.

Eventually he started paced about, considering different items around the space. Looked out the windows. Opened the fridge. Finally he pulled her out of her chair and to the couch he'd bought her, sitting down beside her, as if trying to change the subject or the situation. He flicked the remote, but the TV only showed snow and static.

"Jeez, you guys need cable. How about if I call up the cable company and have them come install something for us on Monday? Huh? I'll have them mail me the bill every month. The kids would love to have their Disney Channel back, I bet." He pulled her against him and smoothed the hair on the side of her head.

Her heart ached. She hated him. She despised his words. But he was everything familiar. Just as much as he claimed she was his home, he was *her* home. It was awkward to be with him in a place that was hers and not theirs, and it was awkward that she hated his words and dreaded his advances, but his touch, his body, all of it was the same to her as her own. All at once her mind wrecked. She couldn't deal with any of it a second longer.

She rose up finally. "I need to shower."

Tim Shrugged. "Okay. I'm just going to sit here and fill out the changes on the contract for you to sign when you get out."

"There's pens in the left island drawer." She wandered down the narrow hall and shut the bathroom door behind her.

Kelli's head was swimming. She leaned against the closed door and pushed the hair back from her face. When did it end? She wanted to imagine a different life, one where she could explore the ideas that Clay presented of what a good man might be like. Instead Tim seemed to surface at her

every turn.

"Oh God, get me out of here." She shuddered, stifling tears. "Get me out of this life. Whatever I did, whatever was so horrible, I am so sorry." She turned the plastic shower knobs and water cascaded into the dingy shower, stained from all the oil workers who had lived there before her. "I'm so sorry." She finally sobbed, droned out by the sound of the shower.

She stood for a long while in the hot water searching for some kind of resolve. At long length she climbed out and toweled off. She looked in the little mirror above the sink. She wondered what Clay was playing at. She looked old and haggard. She barely recognized herself. When Tim and her had first started dating, and for years after, she'd been slim and firm. Even now, even when her pants barely stayed on and she was in the same clothes size as she had been in her youth, she was softer. Her lower stomach had purple and white scars from pregnancy, and the lip formed by the loosened skin that hung from below her bellybutton disgusted her. Her breasts seemed flappy and also scarred with white and purple lines and dents, all consequences of pregnancy and nursing. She stood on tip toes and glanced at her bottom in the little mirror. Even it seemed to sag, despite all its muscle, and it was wider than it had been years ago.

She might look acceptable, even attractive with her clothes on, especially if she actually owned some that fit, but without them, in just her skin, she knew she looked... used. Tim had never complained, of all the things he had seemed disinterested in with her it was never sex, but he'd always known her. Surely that made a difference. Besides, even if the sex was okay for him he still kept another woman on the side for years. Doubtless one who's body was still well put together and certainly not ravaged by having children.

She sighed loudly. She was twenty six. She shouldn't feel this worn out.

Outside came the clamor of car doors and shuffling feet.

She pulled the privacy-towel out of the tiny window frame and glanced around outside. Clay was unloading the kids' car seats from his truck in Marty's drive and putting them back in her car. He even took the time to install them one by one, pushing down hard with one hand on the seat while the other pulled the latch belt tight. Like someone who cared; someone who knew what they were doing. She watched him do all this, he was slow and methodical. He pulled the little diaper bag out from the floor of the back seat last. He held it for a moment, looking at its little flowery design before he carted it, too, back to her car and placed it carefully on her drivers seat.

Kelli thought for sure he'd climb into his truck and leave, but instead he sauntered back to his seat on Marty's porch and kicked his heels up on the railing. He glanced at her trailer, then pulled the rim of his hat down over his eyes, crossed his arms over his chest and grew still.

Kelli pulled her clothes back on slowly, building up her courage. She brushed her teeth and combed her hair. Finally she unlocked the bathroom door and walked out into the rest of the house. Tim was still sitting on the sofa, reading through a local real estate magazine she'd had laying foolishly by the couch for when she felt like daydreaming.

"There's the most beautiful girl." He flashed his grin at her.

"You should leave." She said, walking to the door and opening it.

"I just got here!" He sat up, a little put out.

"Just go back then." She said, pointing to the door.

"Kelli, Honey, come on. Let me see the kids, I'll leave tomorrow morning, I promise."

She padded over to the table and signed and initialed the contract that sat there. She double checked its accuracy as best she could and then held it out to him.

"No. Get out. Don't come back again, Tim." She pushed him towards the door where he fumbled into his shoes, still protesting as she opened it wide.

"Come on, Baby, lemme see the kids. Lets do some stuff together. No hanky- panky, I'll sleep on the sofa." He promised.

"No. Oh, and you know what? Y*our* children need clothes, Tim, and I can't afford to buy them for them."

He pulled his wallet out of his back pocket and counted out what he had on him, she watched him thumb through a couple hundred dollars. "Here, take this and put it towards what they need, okay? Better yet, lets take it tomorrow to the mall and we'll buy them whatever they want." He held the cash out before her, waving it a little.

She reached out for it, closed her fist around it, and he grabbed her wrist with his free hand. His eyes snapped and he flashed his old dashing grin. He pulled her against him and kissed her hard on the mouth. Kelli struggled to get loose, and he chuckled as he held her in place with a single arm.

"I'm sorry Kelli. Really I am. Come on now, don't fight. I swear I'll let you go. Just promise me you'll let me stay. I just want to visit with you and the kids." He kissed the side of her neck and shoulder, still damp from the shower. She pushed against him, trying to free the arm he had pinned behind her back in his strong grip.

"Let go, Tim!" She nearly shouted, wrenching her arms.

Still he held her fast and chuckled. Tim leaned in again and nuzzled her neck.

"You need to relax a little. Man, you're so uptight." He crooned, pulling the contract from her grip.

A shift of movement outside caught her attention. Her eyes grew big as she peered out the door behind Tim, who was flexing hard to hold her still. Fast as lightning Clay was crossing the distance between the trailers. He leaped up the three steps of her trailer in a single bound. Pulling the flimsy screen door open he reached for Tim's collar. The smaller man jumped instinctively, loosening his grip on Kelli as Clay pulled him backwards down the steps in one expert motion.

Tim writhed on the ground before jumping back up, but Clay was already standing over him. "What the hell asshole?" Tim seethed, steadying himself.

Clay shoved him back on the ground and grabbed the back of his collar again, this time pulling him up and shoving him ahead of himself towards t h e silver SUV in the drive. Clay pulled it's door open and stuffed the T i m through the opening.

"I think that's about enough." Clay growled, pausing between words to wrangle Tim. But he leaped at him from the SUV, making the suspension creak and rock.

Kelli ran out, grabbing the dropped contract and still holding the money in one hand. She landed on the ground just in time to see Tim swing one of his short, powerful, arms at Clay. He caught him square on the jaw. Clay's head nearly spun around, sending his hat flying into the driveway, but his footing and body stayed square.

"Yeah, not so big now, are ya?" Tim jeered, fists raised for another blow.

"I'm pretty sure you're 'sposed to be leavin'." Clay flexed his jaw, practically grinding his teeth together.

Tim took another swing, but this time Clay dodged it. "What are you, huh? Her damn guard dog? She's not your woman. She's mine." Tim almost laughed.

"She ain't yours." Clay leaned in and shoved him back towards the open car door again. Their feet scuffling in the dirty gravel.

Tim swung yet another time, still missing "She's just your booty call then? Eh? Is that it?"

Clay shook his head slightly and pursed his lips, it was obvious Tim had gone one step too far for him to bear. Tim's mouth curled into a menacing sneer as he prepared to say more, but in the time it took him to produce his threatening face Clay slammed him with his fist. The impact from a man so much taller than himself sent Tim reeling straight onto his butt.

Clay squatted down and grabbed him with both fists at his shirt collar and pulled him up; he stuffed him into the SUV a second time. He was so enraged that it seemed to take even less effort.

"You get out of here, and don't let me catch you crawlin' around here no more, or next time you'll be hopin' she make's good on calling the police before I land your sorry ass in the hospital. Understand?"

Kelli had wandered up to them as the exchange happened, horrified and embarrassed. Yet thrilled and piqued by Clay's power spent on her protection, how could she not be? Clay glanced over at her and noticed the papers in her hand just then. His face was angry and dreadful with his thin mouth set hard and his wide eyes narrowed. He paced to her and snatched them from her hands. His arm swiped a bead of sweat on his bow as he walked back and threw them on Tim's lap.

"Get home to your woman, Tim. She's likely wonderin' where you are." He slammed the car door shut as Tim started the engine.

Tim touched his nose and checked his hand, finding blood. He wrenched the rear view mirror down and looked at his face, flicking a seething glance at his opponent. After wiping himself he turned on the headlights angrily and backed out into the road, slowly making his retreat.

Kelli stood silent and wide eyed as the slow motion of their heated exchange returned to real time. Clay paced back and forth before her, breathing heavy, calming himself down. His big boots crunched the gravel. He stooped down and scooped up his hat, dusting it off with the side of his hand. He put it on his head and tamped it down, turning it a little to set it in place. Finally he turned and looked at her, clenching his fists a few times before he blew out a big breath.

"I'm sorry. I just can't handle that kinda thing from no one. Are you okay?" He asked finally.

"Are you?" She was shaking now.

Suddenly Marty's porch door flew open, interrupting them. He stuck his head out as usual and glanced around wildly.

"Damn noisy kids. Darn noisy woman! I can't sleep when you're out here making so much damn noise!" He hollered in their direction in the dark. Unsatisfied he flipped his porch light on, hoping to get a better view of the peace disturbing bandits.

Clay spun around, still riding a wave of rage, "You know what Marty, you sleep all day and work all night, its ten in the p m, who do you think you're foolin old man?! You ain't sleepin' in there! Give me my money!"

"Boy! Don't you pick a fight with me." The older man growled, stepping out on the porch in his jeans and bare beer belly, his fist raised into the night air.

"I just got warmed up, old man, I got enough steam for you." Clay shouted back.

Marty shuffled around, sputtering and muttering to himself. "Oh, take your damn money, bust your brains out under some rage filled bovine. I'm sick of trying to keep you alive, you thankless bastard. It'll be a good change to have my damn lawn chair and *silence*." He turned back into his trailer and slammed the door.

Kelli shrunk down inside herself.

What a horrible way to end such a perfect day. She felt stupid and mortified for letting Tim in. She was always allowing herself to be taken advantage of by him, like some fool. It made her stomach hurt to think about Clay having his jaw smashed by her jealous ex-husband; who she let walk right in and cause this mess. And that he was good enough, or interested enough, to defend her was frightening. Not because she didn't like him. She knew she felt herself wanting to like him, wanting to try for some kind of relationship with him... But surely now that he realized what she was mired in, who she really was... He'd come to his senses, if he had any, and run. Probably grateful he'd avoided more trouble.

Tears clawed at her throat as she thought about it all. Holding her breath she choked and sniffed quietly, trying to get them under control. She felt so emotionally drained, so out of control of herself and her mind and feelings lately; it felt like being insane some times. She hardly knew what she was doing, or why. There was nothing but chaos and worry in her head. And for the first time in months she'd looked up from it all, and found Clay. Someone who seemed genuine and good. He was just so easy to be around. She didn't want to compound the day's events by crying. But it couldn't be helped. She quietly sucked in a breath as tears rolled down her face.

"Are you cryin'?" Clay asked turning towards her. "Don't cry Kelli. Marty and me, we don't mean that stuff. We do this all the time, you just never hear it. Every time I end up here askin' for money this is how it goes. We're always rough with each other..."

She shook her head and covered her mouth, trying in vain to reign herself in. He shuffled over, unsure of what to do. He hovered near her for a few minuets, shifting his weight from side to side. He put his big hand on her back for a moment but removed it. She shuttered quietly, unable to explain herself, unable to move away. He tried putting his arm across her shoulders, but retracted that, too. He huffed a few times out of frustration and sucked on his teeth. Finally he gave up and hugged her.

Kelli covered her face with her hands and sobbed quietly, her head hanging low against his chest. He locked his knees and wrapped his arms around her and just didn't say anything. But inside him, with her ear pressed against his shirt, she could hear his heart racing. He seemed so cool and unaffected by anything on the outside, even when he was angry. Its quick tempo surprised her.

After a few minutes he scooted her in the direction of her trailer steps and sat her down beside him on the second one. His long legs reached the ground from his perch, but beside him she could only reach the bottom step.

"Don't cry, Girl. It undoes me." He said soothingly. "I don't know what to do when you cry."

She hiccuped and swallowed her tears, regaining a little more composure. He shushed her, his arm tight around her, holding her against his side, her head on his chest. He was smaller and some how bigger than Tim all at the same time. His body wasn't as thick, and his arms weren't as round, but he felt even stronger than him some how. She wanted to stay like this the whole night, but inside she had to run away. From life. From him. From her divorce. From the possibility of more failure.

A June bug buzzed through the air and smashed into the naked light bulb behind them. It crashed to the ground and sputtered noisily. She concentrated on it for a few seconds, shutting herself down.

"I am so sorry about all this, Clay." She whispered at length.

He chuckled a little at her. "Sorry for what?"

She looked up at him, his big eyes were almost black in the dim light, and his face was shaded by his wide hat. His eyebrows were set so kindly on his face and his long cheeks were stubbly at the end of the day. She noticed that he had the slightest cleft in his wide chin. She could also see a knot rising on the left side of his jaw. Her insides grew flighty and she felt panicked and constricted.

"You can't do this. You have no idea what you're getting into. I don't know what will happen between Tim and I, I don't even know what tomorrow looks like." She said quietly, reaching up to gently touch the growing bruise on his face.

"Well, tomorrow looks like goin' to a rodeo." He said hopefully, "With me." He added to remind her. As if she'd forgotten.

A cry raised up in her again, but she talked around it, "I don't know how to start over. I just don't. I was just a child the last time I was single. I don't know how to do this. I don't even know what I have to bring to the table anymore." She stopped to sniff and sigh, Clay smoothed her upper arm with his hot hand slowly. "I've got these two small kids that need my every free minute, a job that I'm thankful for- really- but I have no free time at all. And this stupid..." Her voice broke as she thought about it, "This stupid trailer to pay for, and I hate this place. And I'm tired. I don't know what I have to offer anyone. I feel hollowed out and pulled tight, like skin set to tan."

"I don't see it that way at all..." Clay started, but she cut him off.

"And I know everything looks okay right now, like this, all dressed up, but this body's been through two children." She sniffed and started crying again, but she added, "And not well, either."

He hugged her against him again, a little tighter this time.

At length she muttered, "I'm just so darn *tired.*" She sniffled as the tears retreated.

"You know what I think?" He said after some time.

"That you should run fast and far? Because that's what you should be thinking." She sniffed.

He chuckled slowly and shook his head, resting his cheek on the top of her head for just a brief second.

"No, I don't think that." He cleared his throat a little, "I think you're just scared, and I think you think you're alone." He took a big relaxing sigh and let it out slowly through his nose. "You're not though, you know. I'm right here. I've been watchin' all this time, you comin' and goin', workin' and dragin' and workin' more. You gotta slow down some, Girl. And if you're too scared of me, or whatever, well, I guess I'll just wait."

She felt awkward. Pegged, and awkward. She was scared of him. Or rather, scared for him. "You'll find it's not worth it in the end. Tim did." She said with finality.

Clay laughed heartily. Marty's living room lights flipped on, and he laughed even harder, daring the old man to pick a fight. He had to slow down a little though, and pick his words. He gave it a good amount of thought before he finally spoke.

"I've been through almost every buckle bunny that chased me down hard enough, and every girl that I ever took a shine to. I got pretty serious with a few of 'em, too. I've been through this ride, and seen enough stock, to know just what I'm after. I know potential when I see it." He shook her a little, "And I know a lost cause when I see it too. Just 'cause a little filly's got some baggage don't ruin the whole thing."

She wasn't convinced. But she deeply appreciated his words. They felt balmy and cooling in her mind. Even if he did liken her to livestock. Twice.

"Where do you live, anyway?" She asked suddenly.

"What?" He was lost by the lack of thoughtful segue between the topics.

"Marty's going to give you your money, so you'll be headed home, but I don't even know where that is." She sat up and looked at him, then glanced up at her trailer. "You know where I live."

"We'll that's a fair question." "Is it far?"

"A bit. A little over an hour. Close to the South Dakota boarder. In fact we own property on both sides. I'll show you some time if you want." He shifted a little bit, resettling himself.

She sighed. "That is far."

They were quiet for a moment. The *hiss hiss hiss* of katydids surged with the growing chorus of crickets until Kelli thought her head would begin vibrating from the intensity of it. Clay took a deep breath and let it out over tight lips.

"You know, my mom was alone a lot, most of my life she's been alone. I was older than your kids are now and I remember her going through this time. Tryin' to raise us, keep us housed and fed. Stay alive herself. It's not easy. I remember her sitting up at night cryin' when she thought we were asleep.

"She moved back home after two years, Marty and Joe, her brothers, were runnin' the ranch then. She went to work with them so she could be home when we needed her. Tore her body all up workin' that way. Like a man. I hated it for her...Well anyway. You're not alone, okay?"

Kelli nodded, resting her head against his shoulder. "What if he comes back? I'm not afraid of him hurting me, I'm afraid of him taking the kids, or playing me. I get stupid when he's around."

"He's not comin' back." He sighed again, a little harder this time. "You want me to sit on Marty's porch tonight? Get my money from him in the morning?"

"No, I already feel bad that your jaw is bruised because of me."

He stuck his chin out and felt around his jaw line. "It don't hurt. Besides, I like a good, fair, fight. It's why I ride bulls." He made a silly face at her when he said the last.

"Would you..." Kelli paused, glanced at him awkwardly, "if you don't mind I mean... would you sleep on my sofa? I'm not trying to be forward, and I don't mean anything more by it. I mean, I'm not a prude, I don't think, but I'm not trying to be inappropriate either. I just... well. Just tonight? This one time?" She scooted away from him a little, afraid she'd given off the wrong impression. It's not like they really had any sort of relationship. Aside from saying hello to him while he was hopped up on pain killers a month ago they'd only just now met yesterday, really. "It folds out." She added, a little embarrassed.

He laughed loud again as he stood up, and it made her smile. "Girl, I'd sleep in that piddly little lawn chair over there if you wanted me to, a fold out couch sounds like heaven compared to that." He stretched his arms up over his head and worked his shoulders after he dropped them. "Sure, just for tonight, if that's what you want."

Kelli nodded.

-CHAPTER FIVE-

"So how do you know Clay?" A young woman asked Kelli, having noticed them showing up together.

A skinny blond girl and her brown haired friend were leaning on the fence behind the bullpen and catwalks where Clay had left Kelli half an hour earlier. Their bright colored tank tops were laced with sequins and were cut as low as their jean skirts were short. Their faces were only slightly less painted than the rodeo clowns inside the arena. Kelli felt old, and irritated, looking at their tight shimmering cleavage and glistening mid-drifts.

"We're friends." She said. She moved away a few steps, but slid back to them a moment later, "Do you know him?" She had to shout over the din of spectators and the roar of the microphone.

The blonde girl giggled. "Oh, I know him." She looked down her nose at Kelli and smiled suggestively.

"Good for you then." She mused disgustedly, stepping away.

The metal fence they leaned on vibrated as cattle and horses in the pens farther down bumped into the poles as they paced agitatedly. She felt severely inadequate imagining Clay feigning any sort of interest in her after having bedding such a beautiful, fit, young women who couldn't be twenty yet. She wondered if the girl was insinuating that she'd slept with him.

"He's doing really well this season. We both thought for sure he'd miss the rest of the circuit after that bull got him in Missouri." The other girl said to her, shouting over the din.

"You were there?"

"This is my second circuit, Jessica's third." She

pointed at her friend. "I've never seen you at any of the rodeos."

"That's because I've never been." Kelli felt grossly out of place, "This is my first."

"First ever?" Jessica said, wide-eyed; unbelieving. Kelli nodded and the girls looked at each other grimly.

The blonde patted Kelli's arm, "You should sit in the stands where you can see better." They were nearly a decade younger than her, yet they spoke to her as though she were out of her league.

"Thanks. I think I'll wait here. Good luck tonight, though." Kelli said coolly, standing her ground.

In the arena a calf bolted from a box and was chased by two men on horses. They whirled bright colored ropes in loops above their heads. The steer calf was roped quickly around its nubby horns by the first rider, and a moment later the second man deftly ensnared one of its rear hooves. Their horses skidded to a stop and the calf was stretched tight between them before dropping to the ground. It was quickly released and leaped to its feet, trotting away unharmed.

The crowd cheered maniacally, clapping and hollering from the bleachers. The announcers called that there was only one event left until the bull riding began. The crowed cheered again.

Clay wandered back into view from the bull pens. She'd lost sight of him after he left her a while before. When he left he was carrying a pile of equipment, but as he returned he was wearing bright blue and black chaps that were of a ridiculous width and a protective black vest. He sauntered over and climbed the fence; stuck his heels over the second rung and sat down on the top tube of metal and looked down at her. She smiled, laying her arms along the top of the fence as she stood near him.

"Havin' fun yet?" He yelled at her over the noise.

She nodded.

He looked up and flagged down a man carrying a plywood board over his head filled with cones of cotton candy and a lidless cooler filled with cans of beer hanging from his neck. He bought two of the red cans and holding them in one hand helped her up beside him. Clay popped the top on the beer and handed her one.

Kelli tottered a little as she gained her balance on the fence beside him. Just as she'd gotten settled and tipped the can to her lips the fence shook and she nearly fell. Clay's strong hand caught her back and helped steady her. The two girls she'd met earlier had been giggling as they watched the stretching routines of the cowboys on the catwalks behind the chutes. They climbed up expertly to sit on Clay's other side, watching the spectacle. Each cowboy was taking turns bending and stretching and shaking out each leg and arm as they paced back and forth behind the chutes that contained the placid looking bulls.

"Hey, Clay" The blonde girl purred an she sidled up beside him.

"Megan." Clay said coolly, tipping his hat at her. "What're you girls up to tonight?"

"Just the usual, came to see your ride." Jessica the brunette, said sweetly.

"It's gonna be a while yet, I'm second to last tonight."

"The best is worth the wait." Megan slid her hair away from her face, baring her bronze shoulders. "How about a home cooked meal again tonight, cowboy?"

Kelli glanced around her date at them, sneering in disbelief. Did she not exist at all? She fought the urge to jump down and claw their pretty painted eyes out.

"We made beef stew and biscuits." Jenny added.

"Aw, thanks anyway girls, I already ate." Clay patted Megan's knee absentmindedly, but caught himself suddenly and added, "You know, Cody McAllister's been talking about you two over there." He pointed to a group of wide brimmed hats leaning on the corral fence further around the pens, "I think he was lookin' for you."

Kelli sipped her beer and watched as the two girls sashayed away. Clay grew silent, she imagined he was suddenly second guessing having brought her to his conquering ground.

"Almost every buckle bunny, eh?" She quoted him flatly.

"Not them..." He started to say. Clay considered his rapidly emptying can of beer, turning it slowly around in his hand. He winced a little bit, struggling to find some words. He sucked on his teeth and finally settled for, "I don't do that stuff anymore. I've been doing this a long while, you know."

She looked at him severely, "They certainly haven't."

"This is not a fair fight." He said.

"It's not a fight. I'm just questioning your overall motives, that's all." She slipped down off the fence, less gracefully than she had intended and leaned back against it.

"I never imagined regretin' later... Or having a good reason to." He mused, low. "I quit do'n that."

But she ignored him. She knew she couldn't rightly hold his former life against him. At his age he'd surely dated and been with other women. Though she quietly wondered to herself if sleeping around was chronic behavior. It could be, except that those men started right off trying to get in a girl's pants. And that certainly hadn't seemed to be Clay's angle. She couldn't imagine it ever having been.

Women on horseback were turning up great clouds of dirt and dust as their horses grunted and rounded a clover pattern around three barrels at one end of the arena. She took a few large gulps from her can of beer. She never drank and the single beverage was making her legs feel swimmy. The charge in the air from the crowd and the mingling smells of earth and animal dander and leather swarmed around her. She wondered about Clay. She found herself desperately liking him despite not knowing anything about him. Except that he was a good talker and made her feel important, and offered her a welcome escape from the rigors of her strange new life. Her shoulder rested against his long leather covered thigh. The blue fringe of the chaps hung over her shoulder and tangled with her hair. Kelli polished off her drink and handed the can up to Clay.

The last of the ladies rounded the barrels. Her horse threw its head as it spun around and raced back to the gate. The woman, a petite young girl, pulled up out of the saddle and swatted the horses flanks with the long ends of the reigns. Once past the gate she pulled the chestnut animal up and it crow hopped to a stop, waving its head around in protest. She settled it with a few earnest pats on its neck. The red digital clock beside the gate flashed her time at 14.8. The crowd cheered but she hung her head. She'd missed the top time by a fraction of a second.

The announcer called out a three minute break and a big Dodge pick up full of high school kids toting garden rakes slowly circled the arena. The kids hopped out one by one and began raking the dirt divots created by the racing horse's hooves. The bulls that had been wrangled into in the chutes grew antsy, they were veterans and knew the routine. A big gray bull with a huge hump across its shoulders scratched his horns against the gate and side of the enclosure. Another brown bull hopped in protest as a team of men laced a bucking strap around its loins.

"I gotta get goin'." Clay interrupted her wandering thoughts.

"How many are ahead of you?" She asked before he could walk away.

"Nine." He centered his hat and pulled it down a little tighter on his head. He seemed a little preoccupied as he spoke. "It's not a big venue, it shouldn't take long. It's mostly local farmers who ride for fun."

Kelli smiled, "I'm in no rush. I can't remember the last time I've been out. It's been a lot more than a few months, I know that."

Clay looked relieved. "I figured you were gettin' bored."

"Heck no. This is great fun." She smiled, and she meant it. The little tarts may have enlightened her to just how far out of her comfort zone she was, but it was fun nonetheless. There was something simple and slow and enthralling about the strength and pageantry of it all.

"Wanna see the bull I pulled for this ride?" He nodded towards the bull pens.

"Sure, you have time?"

"If we're quick."

He helped her back over the fence so they could walk around the corral perimeter. There were two pens that held half a dozen bulls each. Their long horns had been ground down blunt, and their tails swished across their wide poop stained back sides.

"That one over there, by the chute gate." He helped her climb up on the bottom rungs of the tube fencing and pointed at a blue roan that was intently licking the hind leg of its red neighbor. "He's called Tough 'n Ready."

Kelli watched as the cow blinked slowly, still licking it's friends leg. Its huge head shook up and down with the effort.

"He doesn't look so tough."

"He's tough enough when you're on 'em." Clay mused. "I had him at the beginnin' of the season, before the one that smashed my face. I barely missed the buzzer. He unloaded me into the fence and lit into one of the barrels." He helped her back down from the fence, even though she didn't require it. Obviously using it as an excuse to touch her. "Welp, I better get."

Kelli wished him luck and walked back down to her original position which offered a better view of the events. Her level of trepidation grew with every rider that was turned out of the chute. One cowboy, hardly old enough to be out of high school, got thrown back through the gate not a second after the bull was released. He landed headfirst into the solid metal panel around the bottom perimeter. Instinct and adrenaline spurred him to crawl, chaps flaring and arms flailing, for the fence. Rodeo clowns chased the bull through the exit gate and the boy fell to the ground as the pain of his injury hit him.

Paramedics on site ran to him, and after a few minutes of quick movements and silent words they stood him up and walked him back to the parking lot. The crowd stood and cheered in awe and respect, and he waved his hand and stooped painfully to pick up his hat as it passed by.

Two of the riders that followed managed to keep their seat for the full eight seconds. The rest were dashed to the ground almost immediately. Most of the bulls were fairly tame and only hopped around, but a few leaped to such unbelievable heights, their back legs kicking up so far behind them that Kelli was certain they'd topple over onto the tiny looking men on their backs. At the conclusion of one ride an enraged brown and white bull nearly broke the barrel its targeted clown dove into. Kelli cringed at how narrow his escape was, and winced in anticipation of the bull shucking him from the barrel like a nut from its shell. But men on horses distracted the enraged animal and corralled him into one of the waiting bull pens.

Finally they loaded the big blue bull into the chute and she watched as Clay stretched and squatted and shook out his arms and limbs. He hoisted himself up over the sides of the chute and through much nudging on the part of the men helping him they centered the bull and he wedged himself on top of it in the small space. He seemed to take an eternity setting his grip on the rope around the beast's ribs, undoing and redoing it, slapping his fingers down tight each time. Finally he nodded enthusiastically, his big black hat bobbing.

The announcer had called his name, citing that he was ranked t h i r d in the region this year. The booming voice echoed over the din of the people watching and the metallic clanking of fences and equipment. All at once the gate was thrown open and the bull who was moments earlier placid and calm jumped four feet straight into the air. Clay leaned back until he was almost rigid as the bull's front end dipped low to the ground and his rear half twisted him around high in the air. Almost before all four hooves were on the ground he leaped up and twisted in the other direction. Clay's left arm was waving around wildly in the air, and the rolled up sleeve of his right arm exposed the huge bulging muscles that anchored him to the animal. She'd never imagined how huge his arms were, she realized now that it was no wonder he had felled Tim with a single blow.

Clay seemed tossed around like a rag doll, but each way the bull turned the man seemed to anticipate it and follow. Finally the buzzer sounded after what felt like an eternity. The clowns had been closing in on the bull as the time counted to eight seconds and now they waved their hands and danced defiantly, trying to gain the bull's attention as Clay struggled to release his grip from the rope. The bull charged around the arena, starting for a man perch atop a big painted horse, but Clay finally fell off before the animal reached them, and his fury was turned on Clay.

Clay had landed hard on his upper back, the rest of him curling nearly in a back flip when the animal had bounded and flung him free. Then the bull spun and pressed his huge head into Clay's chest, pushing him along in the dirt before him.

The rodeo clowns slapped the animal, one beat at his head and pulled his horn while the other yanked hard on its tail. Kelli screamed in terror as without an instant's warning it turned on the painted clowns, forgetting Clay as it charged after them.

As one of the cowboys on horseback eased up beside the bull and pulled the bucking strap around its groin loose Clay crawled to the safety of the fence and pulled himself to his feet. He watched as the slightly less enraged blue bull was escorted into a pen as he dusted himself off. It all had taken only a pair of seconds, but to Kelli it seemed like an eternity.

The crowd went wild. People hooted and screamed with all their might and stamped their feet on the metal bleachers where they sat. Clay stuffed his fist in the air and strode over to his hat and placed it on his head.

"Eight-four-two!" The announcer yelled, his voice crackling and booming over the speakers on wooden poles around the arena.

The already stirred crowd rose into a fevered fervor. "Unless Lee Goddard can beat that it looks like Clay Tackett will be taking the purse tonight!" The announcer yelled over the shrieking from the stands. "Seems we all show up just to watch you crash, Tackett."

Clay did a salute in the middle of the arena and strolled to the gate that lead to the pens and hoisted himself up and over. The last rider was getting settled to go as Clay navigated the main passage between the pens to where Kelli waited. She climbed up on the fence as he got nearer, the crowd began to cheer as the gate was pulled and the last pair released from the cute.

"Are you okay?!" She yelled, bending down over the top rail of the fence so he could hear her. Her eyes, concerned, looked over his dusty frame.

He grabbed her face suddenly and planted a kiss on

her mouth, lingering just long enough to disqualify it as an unintentional impulse. "Yup, am now." He said, his comical gaping grin flashing at her.

The last rider fell before the buzzer, but the amped up crowd cheered him enthusiastically anyway. Clay spun around and hooted, waving his hat around in the air. He'd won the prize money for the evening. It'd been a good night for him. A small gaggle of participants and spectators engulfed him, slapping him across the shoulders and congratulating him. They threatened to pull him away, but he fought back through the group to Kelli and after helping her over the fence carted her along behind him. She cheered and laughed with the group, caught up in the excitement around them.

The sun was low on the horizon outside Clay's truck window as he turned onto the road in his big black pickup. Kelli felt awash in a myriad of tangled feelings as she watched him navigate the road and stuff his prize check into the sunglasses compartment on the cab's ceiling. His profile was highlighted by the orange sun, making his tan skin look bronze. The brown stubble on his chin and cheeks looked darker by contrast. He pushed his hat up with one hand and scratched his head, drove with his right knee and found a radio station with the other hand.

She was certain she liked him. Sitting there driving, his ego still inflated from his recent success, he looked like something out of a country music video. Rugged and chiseled, simple and plain talking. And he felt good. He felt good to be around; to be with. Her hand had felt good in his rough grip and she liked it, just as much as she liked his wide hand spread across her back reassuringly. And his lips felt good pressed up against hers in a fast, excited, kiss that had sparked like static.

But she thought of his rigid body crushed helplessly under the powerful head of the angry blue bull he had won riding on. She had never worried about Tim when he left the house. If he went to work it was across town, sitting in a little glass office working at a desk. No risk, no danger. But Clay seemed to flirt with danger, even death, as though it were an addiction. Then she remembered the smooth skin and plump smiles of the buckle bunnies behind the livestock pens. And jealously imagined his smooth tolerant voice and big rough hands touching them. She couldn't keep up with that life. She snapped out of it at the sound of his voice.

"Whachya thinkin'?" He asked, turning the music low.

Kelli shook her head a little, "I dunno. Nothing I guess." She shrugged, "A little bit of everything."

"Like what?"

She looked past him at the glowing summer sun that had swelled enormously large as it neared the ground. She sighed a little.

"You know, me and Tim, we'd known each other since we were about fourteen. We were best friends, we did just everything together. Until we had kids I mean. But even before then, he never talked half so much as you do." She folded down the center console and rested her elbows, propping her head up.

"You don't like talkin'?" He smirked.

"I like talking. I just didn't expect that you would."

"I got it from bein' around my mom so much. I'm just not one of those slow talking, quiet, ranchers I guess."

"You sure you're okay after the bull ground you down like that?"

"Yup."

"Clay, that was terrifying, how are you okay?"

He mused for a moment before answering, "Well, I guess my chest hurts a little. But the vest took the worse beatin'."

She considered what he said. It was a little after nine and she was rapidly running out of steam. Everything around her felt dangerously safe. Clay included. So good; so likable; so restful. It made her fluttery and nervous somewhere deep inside. Especially at the thought of losing him, to some accident or beautiful girl. In her deepest heart she worried about depending on another person again when she could barely depend on herself. Her life with Tim made her feel unqualified to be in a relationship. She'd not even noticed the signs that he'd been cheating. How could she not notice *anything* for all those years?

"What's wrong?" He asked, turning the radio off entirely. Even his insightful awareness of her seemed too good to be true.

"I'm just tired." She smiled softly.

He nodded a little, agreeing. "Did you have a good time?" He ventured.

She sighed. "You already asked that before we left."

"Well, it wasn't a proper date. I don't want you feelin' gypped."

She shook her head and they rode in silence for a few miles. He stole knowing glances at her, begging her to tell him whatever it was she was thinking about. She tried to remain emotionless, but her brows knit anytime her mind wandered off, making her look worried. And he picked up on it each time, generating an awkward quiet between them.

"I got my card this spring with the PBR. I made it to the touring division. I'm plannin' on joinin' the circuit next week."

She looked at him blankly.

"Professional Bull Riders." She blinked.

"I jump in in Montana next Friday, and then they head down south to Texas and then back up to..."

She started to speak but couldn't seem to imagine the right words. It seemed silly to feel so let down, she didn't even know him. This was their first time out alone. Maybe it was all a game for him anyway. Maybe she was just some entertaining occupation for his free time whenever he was in town. She *should* be guarded, it was wise; prudent. Kelli looked out

her window.

Clay looked at the road.

The clumsy silence grew thicker. Clay sucked his teeth and turned the radio back on. They remained quiet and stiff. A few moments later he turned the music back off.

"You know..." He said smoothly, "This evenin' is not turning out at all like I had planned."

"I'm sorry." She looked at him honestly.

She really was sorry. Everything felt too good to be true and the more she distanced herself mentally the more the problems glared in her eyes.

She stood at the brink of having feelings for this man that she knew far too little about. What she had learned about him that night had been exhilarating and yet at the same time terrifying. She didn't want to fall in love with someone who might be on tour all summer, or spend his time being chased by long legged, barely-legal, girls that she'd have to always try hopelessly to outdo. Or worse, a man who might get trampled to death by a bull like his father. How could Clay seem to be so in control, so confident and in charge and still be so helplessly, horribly, reckless. Suddenly he seemed like a mirage. Real and dependable, but nothing but vapor when you got up close to it.

Finally she blurted out, "I can't do this, Clay. I'm so sorry." She felt like crying again, for the umpteenth night in a row. It felt like throwing her dreams away, but she knew it'd be easier now than later.

"Can't do what?" He said hesitantly, slowing the truck down to a crawl as he crept into the berm and parked it. She realized they were only just outside of Dixson now. She had unwittingly wrestled with her feelings for over an hour.

"I can't..." She trailed off, trying to form her thoughts into something coherent. "This lifestyle, Clay, I didn't know anything about it. I can't be the other woman to a bunch of good looking young girls that are a decade younger than me. I can't be the next best thing to a one ton killer animal. I can't risk the possibility of falling in love with a man that's not around half the time. Or wondering if he's leaving me for something better. I did that once before, and I just can't do it again. Let alone live afraid that I'm going to get a call from a hospital telling me you've been gored to death on national television." She bit a quivering lip.

"Love?" He started questioningly, but changed the subject, shaking his head a little, "Kelli, Girl, you ain't gotta worry, its my last..."

"No, Clay." She looked back at him and wiped the silent tears that had slipped from her eyes, "Your own mother can't keep you from this, you already promised your pastor many 'last seasons' before this one. I don't want to hold you back from something you love so much, but I can't attach myself to it either."

"This *is* my last season." He stated pleadingly.

"Your father *died* doing this, Clay. You seem pretty serious about seeing if we work together, but I don't want to end up like your mom." She looked back out her window. "It's not too late, you should still get home at a decent hour. Just drop me off, I'll go pick up the kids at Cindy's."

"Alright. If that's what you want." He said, dejected.

They didn't speak the rest of the way to town. Kelli watched the yellow-orange glow from the street lights illuminate the cab and then fade as they passed. Everything looked tired and sleepy in Dixson as he drove along the railroad tracks before turning to cross them and swing back around to her trailer park road. He hopped out and opened her door for her as she gathered her few belongings and climbed down.

Kelli pulled her keys from her pocket and walked to her steps, Clay close in step behind her.

"At least let me get your number." He said, lightly grabbing her arm as she raised her foot to the first step.

"Do you even have a phone?" She asked, surprised. She'd never seen him carry one.

"Not a cell phone. There's a land line at the house." His face was long and sad looking. He looked thoroughly defeated.

"Come on in, I'll write it down for you."

He followed her inside solemnly. At the door he kicked the dust off his boots before entering, and he pulled his hat off by its crown and laid it on the island while she fished a pen and scrap of paper from the drawer there. He had followed so close though, it was hard for her to concentrate.

Kelli put the pen to the paper. Clay ran the back of his finger gently down her upper arm. She jotted down a few numbers, but realized she wrote them wrong and scribbled them out and started over. Her arm felt on fire where he had touched it, and he stepped close enough for her to feel the heat from his body against her own.

She finally got the numbers right on the paper, and even managed to write her name by them. Because Clay was now so close behind her when she turned she was trapped between him and the edge of the kitchen island. He stared down at her, his big dark eyes soft and intent.

He seemed to tower over her, his broad shoulders shielding her view from the rest of the room so that he was all she could see. It felt oddly good to be hemmed in, between his hard body and the island. He stepped a little closer, until their bodies were only millimeters from touching. She wanted to shy away, to shut him down and stop him. She was so close to having irrevocable feelings for him, she dreaded anything he might do to push her over that edge. But there was nothing she could do to make herself stop it either.

Clay reached a dusty hand to her face. She didn't move, didn't dare to breathe. He ran his fingers through the long strands and gathering them up he pushed them back over her shoulder and pinned them to her head with his palm. Still his eyes were focused, as though he were searching for something and not simply blundering through an intimate moment on a wave of rampant emotion.

Her world grew infinitesimal. All the burden, all the cares, all her worries ignited into weightless ash. All that was left was the soft rhythm of their breathing and the faint rustle of the fabric of their clothes. A world no larger than the space between herself and this man.

He bent down to kiss her, his prickly face brushed across her own, but when she didn't pull away he stood back up and looked at her again. The places where his face touched hers burned after him, leaving an instant aching desire for his lips.

Still he watched her, almost curiously, as he ran his hands, soft as feathers, up the backs of her bare arms and down again. He was looking for something. Something in her face. Her stomach pulled tight and hollow and she inhaled a broken breath. But she matched her eyes with his, silently screaming inside her head, begging him to save the self she was locking away in the name of self preservation. When his hands reached her elbows they deviated and enclosed around her waist. She remained still, her stomach on fire and rolling as if on an angry sea, waiting to see where he might take them.

Finally, with great care, he picked her up and sat her on the edge of the island. His rough hand melted the skin beneath her shirt as he ran it across her back. Carefully he pulled her against his chest, pressing himself against the island between her legs.

Inside herself she was shouting. She was at war with the part of her that wanted to love and be loved. Telling herself to stop, warning that she was at risk of falling, but the lover in her was winning. Her eyes closed as Clay kissed the corner of her mouth. His breath was hot on her lips, and he smelled of sweat and leather and the dust from the stadium where he had landed after being thrown from the big blue bull hours earlier. Her arms instinctively encircled his neck.

Lightning coursed across her skin under his skilled hands. The intensity of the new sensations threatened to steal the oxygen from her lungs. He matched her caught breaths with small gasps of his own that left them both hungry and teetering ever closer to the edge of their self control.

Kelli felt in awe of the pleasant differences between Tim and Clay. Clay's hands were weathered from hard work where Tim's had always been smooth and soft. Tim was stout and thick, but Clay was tall and lean; their bodies in complete contrast. She felt small and delicate inside his arms, where with Tim she'd always felt equal; the same. His hands made new paths across her back and arms, different paths from the one's Tim's hands had mapped out. He held her neck and face and then her waist and hips, with hands that were gentler and bigger than Tim's. Slower, more careful. Methodical.

It was too late. She fell away from herself.

She recognized the affection inside her and the passion that, all at once, ignited. It broke her heart already, even through the flaming desire in their lips and the crashing of lightning in each touch, she was aware of the pain that lurked just beyond. She'd send him away, back to the life he'd had all along. He'd go on to be chased by girls who's looks and bodies held temptations far beyond her own. She'd turn him back to his dreams and dangerous aspirations where he'd undoubtedly succeed and go on to the next place down the road, far away from her.

But for herself, she knew there would be nothing. He'd have distractions and a world of opportunities and she'd fall to pieces alone in this stifling trailer. Her body shuttered as she drew a breath from the skin below his jaw and she pressed her cheek into the soft cool form of his ear as a tear traced its familiar path down her face.

Clay pulled her back and caught up the tear with his thumb, following its trail to where it originated. He looked through her, seemed to see everything she was trying to hide. And though his eyes remained clear the energy that sparked between their bodies betrayed his coolness. When she could take it no longer and looked away.

It had been no more than a pair of minutes. But in them she'd felt as though an entire life had played out in her mind. Wonder and adventure, mystery and love, contentment and happiness. And all of it vanished like an inflated image on the skin of a bubble.

"You'd better get going." She said, hoarsely, forcing herself to end the moment.

Clay's strong hand pushed strands of hair behind her ear again and he looked at her as if she were the only other person that had ever, or would ever, exist in his world. Her heart tore apart in a million different directions. She unlaced her fingers from behind his neck and let them fall down the muscular contours of his chest and into her lap. If she didn't push him out of her life now she'd be unable to. Tomorrow would only hurt worse if she didn't.

Kelli made herself turn away, forcing him to let her go. "I have to go get the kids." The little clock on the wall said it was less than an hour until midnight.

Clay didn't answer, he just watched her solemnly.

He pulled her down from the counter and handed her her car keys from the island where he'd also picked up his hat. She opened the door to let him out but he took her hand in his and walked her down the steps before closing and locking the door for her. Her hand felt dainty and small inside his and her throat was constricted by the emotion of how much she longed to just leave it there. He opened her car door for her, placed his hands on her shoulders and kissed her cheek softly. The stubble on his face drew goosebumps down her neck and arms like electricity, all over again.

"Good luck with the tour, Clay." She whispered as he straightened up to leave, "I mean it." She sat down in her drivers seat and looked up at him. "And Clay," She moved her head to catch his eye, "promise you'll be safe."

He nodded and croaked, "Yup."

He turned and walked to his truck with no further drama, though he did pause mid step once as though he might double back, but didn't. He climbed in the cab and the diesel engine roared as it turned over. She shut the door and started her own car and waited as he pulled out from the space behind her and out the trailer park drive. He went left at the stop sign, and she went right. Sooner than she could hear his tail lights disappeared around a corner and he was gone.

-CHAPTER SIX-

That first night had been hell for her. She barely slept, imagining she was hearing Clay's truck pull back into the drive, or his boots on the steps outside. Every pop and creak of the settling house jerked her awake with the hope that he had returned.

Daylight did little to alleviate the pain. As she drove around in a sleepless, broken, haze that following Monday she had checked her phone diligently every few minutes. She rechecked the ringer settings multiple times just to make sure it was really on.

He never called.

The days dripped away, and soon the weeks faded into the passing of a yet another month. She began to resign to the truth that Clay was really gone. Whatever they had was simply only what might have been. The spark, the surge of desire that resonated with all the tones of destiny, faded quietly into the bland nothingness of necessary routine.

August began with a horrible heat wave. The typically cool prairie mornings started instead with the shimmering heat of a noonday sun and the rising smell of baking grasses and pavement that lasted through the night. The heat made the stink of the railroad outside almost unbearable. Her tiny trailer had no air conditioning so they were forced to open the windows and rely on fans to move the air, which served only to suffocate them in the smell of coal and oil.

Kelli had also been forced to beg for childcare from Cindy during her work day. She was glad for Clay every time she dropped them off there; without him she never would have found any sort of sitter she could trust. Thankfully it was still summer and between her and her

two teenage school girls they were willing to keep the kids. She hated leaving them all day long, and her car felt horrible and empty without them, but Cindy's little ranch home had central air.

Cindy's church had even been willing to help cover the cost of the childcare, but in her pride Kelli had refused and instead set the money aside each week to pay for it herself. Some how it felt like taking more from Clay to accept their help. Cindy had graciously only charged her twenty dollars a day, less than half what most day cares would have charged for a pair of toddlers. It may have only been a hundred dollars, but it was the money that would have otherwise gone into her savings account in the hopes of getting them into a better home.

August cicadas were screaming high in the trees in front of Cindy's house. It was a little after five on Friday. She had the air conditioning blowing full blast in the car, which she left running in the driveway as she walked up to get the kids. It would be baking hot before they could return to it, no matter how fast she was.

"Mommy!" Her children bounded up to her and leaped into her arms as Cindy pulled the door open for her.

"Hi babies!" She struggled to lift them both from where they clamored at her legs. They were growing and her body was constantly hurting from stress and work. As simple as driving was it did take a toll on her posture and legs.

"They were fantastic today." Cindy said, closing the door behind her, "We made you some pictures." She said cheerfully, reminding Ruby and Joshua.

They sprang loose from her arms and ran to the kitchen. When they came back they produced colored pictures from behind their backs. Joshua had scribbled Noah's Ark in red. The entire picture. The crayon was layered so thick it made the paper stiff and crusty. Ruby, who was naturally artistic had used the proper colors for every person and animal and stayed nearly entirely within the lines. She was very proud of herself and beamed at Kelli.

"Wow! These are my favorite pictures! I can't wait to put them on the fridge!" She set them to pulling their flip flops on and turned to Cindy. "I have to stop back tomorrow and drop your money off to you, I'm sorry. The line at the bank was incredibly long when I passed by."

"Don't worry about it, Honey." Cindy said reassuringly.

"We're going right back out to the laundromat when we get home, so I'll hit the bank then if I can. I could even drop it off to you on our way home." Kelli hated owing people money, it made her uncomfortable, especially since she had had to pay Cindy so much less than the going rate. She felt as though she were looking a gift horse in the mouth expecting her to wait even longer for her meager earnings.

Cindy patted her arm, "It's okay, you can just leave it in the mail box when ever you get a chance. No rush."

The older woman hugged the kids good-bye and shuttled them out the door. She did the same to Kelli. She thanked her again for the week and loaded her kids into the running vehicle.

At home she left the kids waiting in the car while she loaded four big baskets of laundry into the trunk and front seat. She ran back in and made the kids quick meals of peanut butter and jelly and carrot sticks. She grabbed an ancient apple from the empty fruit bowl on the counter and ran out to the car.

She hated going to the laundromat. It wouldn't be so hard if she went more often, but it was all she could do to make herself go on Friday nights. The baskets were always overfull and heavy. Her neck and shoulders always burned and pinched from hauling them out of the house and into the car, and out of the car and into the laundry, and then doing the whole thing in reverse again. Plus children must be carried and minded and entertained during that time. Then all the folding. Not to mention this time of year the building was always suffocatingly hot and humid. And all of it at the end of an already exhausting day and week.

A few moments later they pulled up outside of the brick- front building. It was in the dead section of down town, where the hollow fronts of vacant stores were broken up by only a cut-rate insurance office and an auto garage that looked as though the last painting it had received was half a century ago.

Kelli sighed as she slid the car into park. Her air conditioner was not working properly in the car lately, it only blew slightly cooled air. The kids were sweaty already, and so was she. The windows of the store were dripping with water vapor from the driers inside, giving no promise of relief. It was like facing the very gates of hell.

"Come on babies, let get this over with." She unbuckled their car seats from where she sat and opened the rear passenger door outside to let them out. "Stay right with me while we carry these in." She reminded them.

After the sequential trips back and forth she directed them to sticky plastic chairs near the windows. They sat, their little faces exhausted from the heat and munched halfheartedly on their soggy sandwiches. Kelli filled the washers and fed the notoriously temperamental change machine a twenty. After half a dozen tries it finally accept the tender and spat out a fistful of coins. They clanged against the metal catcher as they were counted, echoing loudly. Two driers were running, but that was the only noise except for the quite hum of a muted tube television perched on a metal arm high in one corner. It was showing golf, which was marginally less exciting than watching the spinning driers below. The dingy yellow walls were streaked with orange where they sweated near the ceiling.

There were several floor tiles missing here and there. Kelli purposefully stepped in the gaping hole left where one should have been. She smiled. It reminded her of Clay's missing tooth.

She sat down with the kids and pulled out her check book and a pile of receipts from her back pocket. She needed to reconcile the account, she had a sickening suspicion that she'd taken too much out the days before being paid. She was forced to check her math three separate times, interrupted by a slew of questions from Ruby and also to break up a fight over who had eaten who's crust. She blew out a deep breath. She'd come down to within two dollars and change. She munched on her dry, grainy, apple while the kids raced quietly down the empty rows of washing machines. Finally she opted for staring, hypnotized, at the spinning dryers instead of watching the golf on the muted television while waiting for the washers to spin out.

After an eternity she was at last able to switch the laundry. She felt elated. It was down hill from that point. It always felt so progressive to stuff the wads of damp clothing into the perforated barrels on the walls. She had filled five washers, but only required two dryers. She'd be forced to run them for almost an hour and a half though, to get the clothes completely dry. But in the long run it saved her five dollars. It always required a handful of drier sheets, too. The driers ran on propane gas which made the clothes smell tinged with eggs and burnt things.

With that herculean task completed she turned to retreat to her chair. The television caught her eye. In the fifteen minutes it'd taken her to change machines and dole out quarters the program had changed entirely. She stopped where she was and stood, hands limp at her side, staring.

The camera panned around a massive stadium full of cheering onlookers. At its center was a dirty floor ringed by red livestock panels and plexiboard ads. The banner across the bottom of the screen boasted "Oklahoma Professional Bull Riding Invitational". A wave of sickening excitement washed over her, settling in her gut. She scanned the scrolling names of the bull riders jealously, searching for Clay's name. She'd missed the first half of names and had to wait for them to be shown again. Finally it switched back. He was listed at number four. She wasn't sure if that was his rank or the order in which they rode. She felt giddy and looked around, but there was no one to share her excitement. Again she was reminded that she was alone.

Kelli watched impatiently as some man was thrown from his bull only a few seconds into his ride. He scrambled to his feet and waved his helmet as the crowd cheered before he exited, a hop in his step. The camera scanned the bull pens as it replayed the event, she searched the view as it panned looking hard for Clay.

His back was turned as he stretched to reach something, but she saw him. His black and blue chaps and black hat were bent over the top rail of one panel, his arm was extended out to someone below. They recapped the scene again as her insides tore apart. This time she watched for where he was reaching, but the screen cut the image. She wondered jealously if it was another woman. It'd been many weeks, naturally he should have moved on. She had no right to feel jealous, or let down. But she did.

Back in real time the camera showed bulls being loaded into chutes and riders finding their seats on the backs of the angry animals. She spotted Clay perched over a huge white bull with a massive hump across its shoulders. It bucked in protest at the man who's legs spanned the gates on either side of its body. The screen flicked to a short bio. It showed Clay grinning with his arms crossed on his chest. He was turned slightly so you couldn't see the gap between teeth. In the reel he tipped his hat as the screen scrolled his information.

"Clay Tackett" it read, "Age 36, Hometown: Texarkana, AR, Height: 6' 0", Weight: 182" It listed his winnings and standings and rank. Finally the screen cut back to the chute. This time Clay was actually sitting on the animal's shoulders. His black hat was missing and he instead wore a hard helmet with steel bars across the face. He wound the rope around one hand and beat his fingers down with the other. A team of men jostled and worked around him. Finally his head bobbled back and forth and the door was swung open.

The terrible looking bull lunged out, nearly spinning back into the wall of panels. Strings of foamy spit flew like streamers from its nostrils as it leaped into the air. Clay grimaced as his face nearly made impact with the massive rising head. The seconds ticked away in slow motion, it seemed, even though the numbers counted by too fast to read. The bull lurched and bucked, spinning one way and then the next. The numbers stuck at eight seconds and she watched nauseated as he loosed himself from the bull and allowed the animal to toss him head first into the ground. A pair of rodeo clowns sped in and diverted the animal as Clay stood and dusted himself off. He pulled his helmet off and made eye contact with the camera. For a moment it was as though they were together again. He stared emotionless at her through the screen and her mind slipped back to their parting. She could almost feel his hands in her hair. The whisper of his touch on her arm.

Kelli sucked in a tight breath. The camera angel changed and she saw he was only looking at a big red screen showing his ride time and score. The crowed was jumping and throwing things into the air as he walked slowly, ignoring them it seemed, back to the gate and disappeared. He had surely won the evening, the score was unbeatable. But he did nothing to celebrate it. He only noted the screen and disappeared quietly.

Everything in her felt singular and foreign. She sat back down in her chair and listened to the puffing driers. Sweat trickled down her neck and cleavage. The children had grown too hot and tired for their running game and had collapsed in impossible positions on the cracked plastic furniture beside her. She felt bittersweet and jealous. Jealous of the teaming throngs of spectators that got to spend their time with Clay while she sat, parched as a drought, in a small town laundromat. It wasn't fair, and it burned her up.

She desperately wanted to know what might have been. Her heart needed the reassuring strength of his soothing words. Her shoulders ached for his comforting embrace. And her body hungered to race down the path they'd left unexplored the night he left. She threw the clothes into their baskets without folding them when they were finally dry. She didn't care, she told herself. What was, was for the best. It would never have worked out. He deserved someone who understood his world, and she had no time for it.

It was nearly nine when she finally got home. Her car had sputtered and chugged on the way there. She barely made it into the driveway before it died. The air conditioning refused to blow anything but tepid air. She laid her forehead on the steering wheel, defeated. She had just paid rent with her last paycheck. Their savings account only had six hundred dollars in it. And her bills for this month would barely be covered by today's paycheck, it left nothing for food. She was already going to rob Peter to pay Paul just to buy groceries for the week. If the car didn't run she'd be stranded without an income.

Her head hurt. Her back and shoulders hurt. Her neck hurt. Her stomach hurt. Everything hurt. Her heart hurt. She sighed. It had taken her nearly four hours to do the laundry and go to the bank. She hadn't even taken the time yet to drop the little envelope of money to Cindy. She pulled herself out of the car and forced her body to go through the motions.

With Ruby in tow and Joshua on her hip she climbed the little steps to her door. A pink slip of paper hung from a piece of tape at the window. It was from CPS. She opened the door and dropped everything inside as she read the paper. Child Protective Services had been notified of a possible case of abuse or neglect. It was not a notice of pending action, and it was not a notice to appear in court, it stated. It was simply a home visit from a case worker who was investigating the claims. Kelli folded it neatly and laid it on the counter with her keys. She couldn't even think, her head spun so wildly out of control. And there was no one to save her from it. Her throat hurt as she swallowed those emotions down and forced herself to finish the tasks at hand. But there was no stopping the few hot tears of desperation that escaped as she went.

She carried in the laundry. She had to go back out to get her phone and wallet, which she swore under her breath for forgetting on one of the trips with the baskets. Even though it was twenty minutes too early she pushed Ruby and Joshua through their nighttime routines and got them into bed. After the mad dash of diapers, potty, tooth brushes, stories and a million questions she crashed on the couch at nine fifteen. And feeling exceptionally sorry for herself cried herself to sleep.

Dreams of big slobbering bulls and dust and Clay's tender hot kisses fluttered through her mind. And burning things and Tim on fire. Then she dreamed nothing at all for a while.

An engine outside stirred her from her sleep. She heard a car door open and shut. It was close enough to rattle the window in the kitchen. Her heart leaped as she flew to the door imagining her love had raced to find her, reuniting them, searching her out in the miserable bleak black of another lonely night. But she realized as her hand fell on the knob that it was too long of a drive for the vehicle outside to belong to Clay. Fear tickled her spine as she considered who it might be. It was too late to be CPS returning, ad that left only a single last option.

She peered timidly out the diamond shaped window in the door, propped up on tiptoes. But ducked instantly. It was Tim. His face was scowled and his hair was shaggy and unkempt. He tore open the screen door and pummeled the steel between them with his fist furiously. She leaned against it and waited for him to stop. She only had the one lock on the knob, she prayed it would hold.

"Open up Kelli!" He roared like an animal.

She didn't answer; didn't move. Fear trickled down her back and arms like molten lava.

"Open this damn door or I'll kick it in." He roared as he resumed hitting the door.

Kelli felt the massive thuds of his fists pass through her body like the rhythm of heavy music from a speaker turned too loud. She was horrified. Nothing about the man beyond the door was familiar, and that terrified her.

Suddenly her cell phone sprang to life on the island. She crawled over to it and grabbed it and scrambled back. It was Tim's number. He was calling her from outside.

"I can hear the fricking phone Kelli. Open up. What's the matter, Baby? Your guard dog not here to protect you? Huh?" He kicked the door a few more times.

The windows were open because of the heat. Fans whirred noisily in the bedrooms and living room. She heard him jump from the steps and stomp around the outside of the trailer. The openings were too high for him to look straight into, but she heard him puffing around below them. Quietly she crept to the kids' room and peered in. Kelli thanked God they were sleeping soundly, exhausted from the heat and the day. She couldn't imagine the impact it might have on them knowing their father was trying to break into the house forcibly, like a crazed madman.

From outside the kitchen walls she could hear Marty shouting about damn loud kids. Tim swore at him and she heard his shoes shuffling through the gravel of the driveway.

"You take a step closer, Son, and you'll be meeting your maker." Marty growled.

"Who the *hell* are you old man? Huh? You want a piece of this?" Tim hollered at him

Kelli didn't dare look out side.

She heard the chucking sound of a shot gun being cocked and the distant blare of sirens growing louder. There was a tender pause.

"Please, God, just let him leave." She whispered.

Her pulse raced in her throat and she crawled back towards the bedroom, leaning against the open door jam of Ruby and Joshua's room, afraid to do anything else. She covered her ears, anticipating the sound of a gun.

An engine fired up outside and tires sprayed gravel against the trailer before peeling on the torn up asphalt of the drive. A few short seconds later the alternating blue and red lights of a police cruiser sprayed color through the white rooms. She hurried to the door and opened it just as Marty was about to knock.

"You're alright, Girl." He said, his voice uncommonly soft, sounding just like Clay.

It made Kelli hungry to hear his voice, and in the moment she consciously pretended Clay had said it and not his old hairy uncle.

A voice boomed over a loud speaker, "PUT THE WEAPON ON THE GROUND AND PUT YOUR

HANDS ON YOUR HEAD!"

Kelli noticed only then that Marty was carrying his shotgun. Relief spread over her as she realized the gun had been Marty's and not her Ex's. Marty growled and obeyed the orders, laying the firearm at his feet and putting his hands on the back of his head. Two police officers charged him even though Kelli was yelling that it was her ex-husband and not this man who caused the disturbance.

After a few minutes in handcuffs the police turned Marty loose.

"I'm the one that called." He said, his voice angry. "Damn kid's were keep'n me up. Some hot headed man nearly beat the door down over here, and when he turned on me, well, I just grabbed my damn gun and told him where to go."

Outside, beside the cruiser, the police officer took notes. Another spoke with Kelli.

"Does he have a history of violence?" The man in the black uniform asked.

"No." Kelli was shaking, she turned her head back to the trailer, listening to hear if the children had stirred from all from the commotion. They were so exhausted from the heat and the week that the whirring of the fans had kept them asleep through the entire event.

The radios on the officer's shoulders buzzed and muffled voices chattered as they pulled the event from Marty and Kelli. Kelli answered a few more questions as Marty tromped back home, his untied boot laces dragging through the gravel and dirt.

The officer before her pulled the radio from his shoulder and responded to one of the muffled spurts of information. He turned to Kelli, "Describe your husband to me again?"

"Ex. *Ex-husband*" She said forcefully, wanting to make the point clear.

"Yes Ma'am." He scribbled something on his notepad.

"I don't know exactly what he was wearing tonight, but his hair is blond, he's about five eight and one hundred and eighty pounds. He has green eyes. And a noticeable freckle on his upper lip."

The officer relayed the information. He took more notes quickly as he clipped the radio back to his shoulder, "Yeah, they got him over on twenty-two. Pulled him over for drunk driving. Mrs. Christi, is your husband..."

"Ex. Ex husband."

"Right, ex husband. Is your ex husband a violent man when he's been drinking?"

"I've never known him to be drunk?"

Kelli tried thinking over the course of their long relationship. In the eleven years she'd known him he'd only been drunk a handful of times. Most of those times were when they were reckless teenagers.

"Once when we were kids he got in a fight while drunk. It took four of our friends to pull him off the other guy. They were fighting over a football game." She smirked at the memory. That had been a very long time ago, in a whole different world.

She suddenly remembered their years as children as though seeing it all for the first time. As if she were alone. As if there were no flashing lights or men in uniforms shining flashlights and talking loudly at her.

The fury of dating, the drama of high school. Kelli walked herself through their whole relationship. Suddenly it took on a different hue. She always had imagined him as a dependable, reliable, partner. Someone who was in love with her, a trustworthy man. But the more she thought the less she could remember anything that proved that. He'd always been busy with his plans and aspirations and she'd always just been in tow. In fact when they had graduated and he got the job in

Bismark he never even asked her to move. He just told her they were, expecting her to be excited for his fortune. And she had been. She'd gone along with it happily, not questioning his loyalty and motives. She trusted he had her best interests in mind.

She realized, too, he'd even bought the house that he liked best, not that she had disliked the house. He had asked her what she liked about each one that they had looked at, and although she had favorited a large ranch in an older neighborhood he had chosen the big french chalet style in the subdivision. Everything that she had done had been by his urging, or his idea.

And he'd never really been around. She'd been content to follow him on his many activities, to his friends or his sports games or his business dinners, but that was the extent of their time spent together. Kelli also suddenly saw that, even as teenagers, their mutual friends had been comprised mostly of his friends who had accepted her into their circle.

He'd even been the one that picked out the car she was still driving. She'd been happy and placated to live her life in his company, never realizing until now that she was always just an accessory to him. She'd never been in charge of anything in her own world, she'd always shared or given that responsibility to Tim.

"Ma`am?"

Kelli snapped to attention, "What?"

"I asked if you wanted to file a harassment charge or an order of protection."

Kelli thought it over for a minute. "I don't know. How long do I have to make up my mind?"

"Well, he's been picked up on a DUI, with added aggravated assault he'll probably be in over night until he sees the county judge tomorrow afternoon. Unless he posts bail. You have the time to make up your mind. But I suggest, just from what you've told me about tonight and the scuffle last time he was here, that you take his actions seriously and assume he intends to do harm." He pointed at the trailer, "You got little ones to take care of, they don't need to be seeing you getting beat up by their father."

Kelli nodded dumbly. She watched as the officer clicked his pen and slid it into his pocket. He asked her again if she was okay and she insisted she was. But when they drove away, their sirens silent and lights on top of their cars extinguished, she still stood in the empty driveway. And it was long after Marty switched off his porch light that she crept back into the trailer.

She dragged her tired and aching body into the bedroom. It was early morning, soon the sun would set the sky ablaze with a tiny flickering of blue flame along the horizon. But she was so wound up she couldn't sleep.

Kelli peeled her sweaty clothes off and stood in the running shower until her muscles relaxed a little. The small room was sweltering, even with just the cold water turned on she felt warm. She left the door open while she bathed, partly because the room was too stuffy, but mostly because she wanted to hear the house and the kids. Even though she knew Tim was surely gone for the night she still worried that some how, some way, he'd make his way back in the dark.

She still didn't exactly fear him, but she did loath the thought of any kind of interaction with him. She couldn't really imagine what their next meeting would be like. What he'd be like. Was he really a threat? She didn't believe so, but his behavior lately was certainly unsettling. But surely if he were sober he'd be in his right mind. Belligerent, obnoxious, but certainly not a physical threat.

Suddenly her thoughts drifted to the pink slip that had been taped to her door. She sat on the the floor of the tub after turning the water off and choked on her tears. She feared nothing more than losing her children. The thought of some stranger, part of a government bigger than her entire world, swooping in and stealing them away and placing them in a strange home tipped her mind in a dark direction. Visions of racing to the Mexican boarder filled her mind. She tried to consider the logistics of hiding in Canada. Even in the heat of the bathroom she began to shiver. She couldn't stand the thought of it anymore, she'd deal with it later, when she could at least pretend to be stronger.

Only after moving the sleeping children into her own bed with her was she able to even consider calming down. But not before remembering that the car was not working. She moaned dreadfully. She'd probably have to pay to have it towed as well as fixed. She hoped inside her that it would not come to more than the $600 she had in savings. But she had enough knowledge about vehicles, although limited, to know the symptoms of a dying water pump. Those were never cheap, and they took a long while to fix. The going rate for a mechanic was nearly eighty dollars an hour.

She couldn't imagine a way around missing work Monday. She'd be lucky to even find a garage tomorrow, let alone one that could tow her car on a Sunday. Or a tow company she could afford, for that matter.

Thoughts of the car and drying bank account slipped into thoughts of Tim and what exactly he intended to accomplish by showing up, apparently drunk, and trying to beat her door down. The rapidly growing understanding of their previous relationship opened her mind to the concept that he had always been and always would be an ass. She felt intensely embarrassed, even though there was no one to notice. How could she have wasted half of her life believing something so entirely wrong about the man she'd been with?

Kelli wondered about Clay. If she had been so intensely deceived by Timothy, could she have been mistaken about him as well? Maybe his comfortable, protective, actions weren't as safe and pure as they seemed. She resolved herself that she had dodged a bullet.

She was better off alone. She was strong, she assured herself. Besides, women live alone their whole lives, on purpose, and enjoy it. She could do that.

But still she missed Clay horribly, and the mile long list of what they might have missed out on and what could have been rolled out before her almost constantly. She needed a friend and he had been there readily. She needed a shoulder to cry on and arms to hold her and someone to calm her fears with a heartfelt, "You're gonna be alright.". She needed a better job and a house that wouldn't blow away like a pile of sand in a tornado. She needed a new car. She wanted to love and be loved, but apparently she wasn't worth it, and was unable to judge people properly. It all seemed horribly out of her reach, and she was so exhausted. Her only option was to keep her head down and keep plodding forward.

Kelli snuggled in the hot bed with her babies and cried herself to sleep.

Ruby woke her up what seemed felt only a moment later.

"I'm hungry mommy." She said, sitting astride Kelli's middle.

Kelli stretched and yawned and nodded. "In a minute Honey. Let mommy wake up."

"I want pancakes." Ruby sounded groggy and grumpy, but a second later she added, "Please" sweetly, barely remembering her manners.

"Oh Ruby, not this morning. We'll make pancakes tomorrow morning. Mommy will make you some cereal and toast."

"Oooohkay." She sighed, disappointed.

Joshua woke up from the commotion of talking and moving about. He popped up in the bed, smiling. Kelli always loved how babies started the day. Their beaming little smiles and enthusiastic energy. She longed for that sort of amplitude when she opened her eyes. Lately though every day felt like the same day. She merely picked up where she left off every morning.

Her cell phone was ringing as she exited her bedroom. It was vibrating and jingling on the island counter where she'd left it the previous night after unloading the laundry. She didn't answer it in time, but when she opened it the screen informed her that she'd missed nearly a dozen calls. One number she didn't recognize had called her every thirty minutes since six am. Another had called her last night; she must have been in the shower. The last call was from Tim's cell phone. There were no voice messages. It was too early to care about who was calling, she laid it back on the counter and pulled out bowls and cereal for the kids.

"I want lucky charms." Ruby said, climbing up and sitting demurely like a lady in her chair at the table.

"Yeah!" Joshua stated in agreement, also climbing to his seat.

Kelli filled their orders and placed the bowls before them. Her cell phone started buzzing again. It was Tim. She weighed her options. She didn't want to talk to him, especially first thing in the morning, but she was also curious about what he might have to say for himself. She accepted the call and squeaked out a feeble greeting.

"Kelli?" Tim voice was rougher than usual.

"What, Tim?"

He cleared his throat a little; hesitated. "I'm so sorry, Babe."

"That's all you ever say to me these days, Tim. I really don't care." She felt herself rise up. He was the reason her world had fallen apart. She hadn't done anything except faithfully stand by his side and bear him children for the past decade.

"Baby, really, I don't know what I was thinking. I

hardly remember driving out here."

"Well you certainly did." She snapped.

"Tiffany left me." He confessed.

She let the silence creep in. She didn't give a crap. In fact, she felt a little tinge of bitter excitement that his world was crumbling. Tim seemed a little nervous that she hadn't responded.

"I guess I just didn't take it well. I went out drinking with some buddies from work." He paused again at her silence. His voice stammered a little. Finally he sighed, "Is Clay there?"

"No." She answered flatly, "He wasn't here last night either. I assume that's what you were here for. To finish your little fight."

"I suppose so. I didn't mean it though, Kelli."

"I think you did, Tim. Drinking just makes a person more honest. It's okay for you to have your little whore on the side, but I can't have anyone. Why the hell are you so bent on ruining my life? What did I ever do to you? You already won, Tim. You got everything. You have a house, a job that affords you everything you want. You don't pay for your children, I do. You left me with nothing, what more do you want from me?"

He stuttered a little, "I don't know. I guess I just want you."

"Well there's a piece of truth for a change. That ship has long since sailed, Tim." She paused to rub her brow, which had already started to ache. "I have a broken car to get fixed, and no money to fix it with. I have a job that I can't get to, and children who have a constant need for all the money I can make. I really don't have time for your issues. You made this bed, you lay in it."

"What's wrong with your car?"

"I think it's the water pump. It's not blowing cold air anymore, and its chugging and sputtering. I can't drive it. It barely made it home last night from the laundromat." She answered him without thinking. It was none of his business what her issues were. She had immediate regret.

He paused for a moment and then cautiously asked, "I have to be back for court this afternoon, you want me to stop over and give you some money?" He sounded genuinely guilty.

It was tempting. She almost said yes on an impulse. But she remembered their last encounters. Every time he felt guilty, or alone, he had whisked in and shelled out money all while acting as though everything was normal and she was his and they were the regular family they had always been. She cringed. She'd rather be alone and struggle than have Tim thinking he somehow owned her or held her indebted.

"No. I'll find a way on my own Tim." She felt hopeless, but she was glad to be separate from him. Any delusions she held before had dissipated, and there was at least a small sense of accomplishment in that. "I don't want your money, or your help." She added.

"Kelli, please. Don't shut me out."

"You shut yourself out."

"It's someone else isn't it. You and Clay?"

She sighed irritatedly, "No, Timothy. There is no one else, it's not even your business if there were. Whatever it is it does *not* involve you."

"Kelli! Please!"

"I am still deciding whether or not to file harassment charges after last night. Oh, and I know you called CPS on me you bastard. I have a lot to deal with right now, Tim. We'll talk later." She almost hung up but just before she did she added firmly, "I'll call you."

She slammed the phone on the counter and hid her face in her hands while she regained her composure. She felt empowered. She could do anything. She didn't need

Tim anyway, or anyone for that matter. She'd find a way to get the car fixed. She just needed a phone book.

"Sit still babies, Mommy's just going to run to Marty's and grab a phone book." She called to the kids at the table.

"I want to come!" Ruby said, trying to hop down before Kelli answered.

"Yeah! Too! Too! Me too!" Joshua added his piece.

"No, no. You two sit right here, I'll just be a second."

She threw open the door and kicked the screen before she turned her head from the kids.

She nearly tripped over a pile of man sitting on the second step outside her door. He jumped up and grabbed her before she could tumble. She was face to face with Clay. He'd been sitting on her porch for God knew how long.

"Hey, Girl." He said, pulling her into a warm embrace before she had the chance to accept it. He pushed her back and set her straight before turning loose.

"Clay? What are you doing here? Wait, how long have you been here?" Kelli wanted him to grab her back up. Any resolve she had built up to go it alone in life blew away like driven snow at the sight and touch of him.

"I dunno, I guess since about six this morning. I called a bunch." He told her and she remembered all the strange calls on her phone.

For a moment they stood in the newness of the day. Everything was crisp and hot around them, and illuminated by the bright white light of morning. It had drizzled some where during the night and made everything smell like railroad.

His face had an old bruise fading on it. But she was so happy, so elated, just to see him she hardly noticed. In the blink of an eye she relived the smokey passion in his hands and the tenderness in his kiss at their last encounter. She wanted to throw her arms around him and kiss his stubbly square jaw and red weathered neck. But instead a tormented cry scratched viciously at her throat. Kelli swallowed it down forcefully.

"But why?" Her voice wavered. Clay's hand ran up and down her arm to comfort her.

"This is all my fault Kelli. I never should've left that night like that. I didn't want to go, it ate me up. But I told myself I'd just give you some time and space. I'd finish the season out, chase you down when I got home..."

"It's okay, Clay. It's not your fault. Tim was looking for you anyway. He was drunk, looking for a fight. I'm alright." She paused when he took her hand in his. It felt softened against his scratchy calloused palm. "You didn't have to come back." Her voice cracked, broken by his tenderness and sincerity.

"I wanted to. I guess I did have to." He whispered.

"I saw you on TV last night." She chuckled a little, "At the laundromat. I got to see you ride. You did pretty good."

"I took first." He pulled her arm a little, "Kelli, Girl, listen."

"No, Clay, really. It's alright." The softness in his voice was too venerable, too intimate. It ached her heart. She had no resolve at all if he talked to her like that. "Why don't you come in and sit a while? I gotta find a garage to come get the car and fix it." She sighed a little, trying to change the subject, dodging his piercing eyes and the strong warmth of his hand around hers. "It died in the driveway last night and I have to work Monday..."

"What's it doing?"

She described the waning air conditioning and the other symptoms. He listened to her, enthralled, as though she were telling him his favorite story. Still she evaded his eyes and tried to ignore where their skin touched in his grasp; his long fingers working gently over her knuckles.

"Lemme fix it. I took a few days off, I wont have nothin' to do if you don't keep me busy."

Kelli laughed out loud a little. "You must think I am a fool. All that stock on the ranch, and all the work of running it, all your escapades in the PBR..." He tried to interject but she pressed on, "And the limp in your step and the bruise on your face, and you expect me to believe you've got nothing to do?"

"I ain't a liar, woman." His eyes narrowed a little in jest, "I have nothin' I want to do more than be at your beck'n call."

Kelli tried to keep from looking at his face, but in the end her eyes drifted to his jaw and lips and eventually his eyes. She could have read a thousand words into his look, but she dared not.

"I'll get you the keys." She managed to say under the weight of his stare. It was useless to refuse, she knew that. And most of all, she knew he knew that.

He didn't readily let go of her hand, but instead followed her inside from where they'd been talking in the doorway. He lagged behind a moment as he kicked the dust from his boots at the door. He stood grinning just inside the kitchen, his hands on his hips.

"Cowboy guy!" Ruby said enthusiastically, having forgotten his name in the weeks he'd been gone.

She leaped from the table, as Joshua carefully slid off his chair. Both their fronts were covered in milk and bits of cereal. Her hair was a mess from the night and frizzed out in all directions around her face. They both ran to Clay and jumped at him. Clay gleefully snatched up Ruby and tossed her in the air a little as Joshua wrapped himself around his leg.

Ruby pushed herself away from Clay's chest as he

settled her on his arm and looked at him ruefully. "Where's your cowboy hat?"

Clay patted his head and laughed. "I left in such a hurry last night I forgot it." He raised his eyebrows at her, pretending to be astonished and regretful.

Kelli handed him the keyring. "How did you get here so fast, anyway? Kansas is quite a few hours away."

He shook his head. "That wasn't live. We did that rodeo two nights ago. I was only in Gillette, Wyoming."

"You really left your hat?" She asked, unbelieving.

"I keep tellin' you I ain't a liar." He set the kids down and pocketed the keys she gave him. "I left it in the hotel and didn't even notice until I got to sittin' on your stoop."

"How does someone such as yourself forget their hat?"

He smirked a little in response, and traced the back of her arm with the tips of his fingers. "It slipped my mind." And he turned, heading purposefully for the door.

"Did you have breakfast yet?" She said through the swimming feeling stirred up by his touch.

"Nope." He pulled the door shut behind himself and the growing warm of the summer weekend.

She sighed with relief. Just having Clay nearby seemed to ease the weight of the whole world from her shoulders. She could breathe again. Where she'd been weak and hopeless for weeks suddenly she felt as though she were able to conquer any obstacle. Even the biggest ones.

Armed with that determination she set herself against the scariest task she had at hand. Kelli grabbed up the letter left by CPS. She felt sick reading it again, but instead of fear the sickness made her angry. It requested that she call the investigator as soon as possible. She decided to get it over with while Clay was busy and she still had some emotional control and confidence from the wave of hope he gave her. She turned on the TV for the kids and sat down at the table with the paper and her phone. She took a deep breath; her hands shaking as she dialed the number.

"Tina Jackson." A woman answered, stating her name.

"Hello Miss Jackson, I received a letter from you taped to my door last night."

"Kelli Christi?" She asked. "Yes, ma'am."

Kelli heard some papers being shuffled and Tina muttered to herself as she read through notes. "Missus Christi.."

"Miss." Kelli corrected her.

"Okay, Miss Christi," She repeated, bemused, "We received allegations that your children are not being cared for properly and being neglected by yourself while you are at work."

"My ex husband filed that shortly before showing up drunk at my house in the night hell bent on attacking people. Timothy. Timothy Nevins."

"Mmhmm..." The woman said absently as she flipped through papers, no doubt checking to see who filed the complaint. "Miss Christi can you provide me with proof that your children are being cared for during the day while you are at work and not, in fact, being left unattended in your vehicle?"

Kelli chuckled under her breath, impressed that the same circumstances that riled Tim's anger and accusations had also lead her to Cindy's house for childcare. Otherwise the kids would surely be riding in the car still.

"Sure I can. I can give you the phone number of the woman who watches them for me, as well as the police officer's name that was here last night. In fact, I think I am in the process of filing a harassment case against Tim and I can supply you with those papers also if you'd need them." Clay pushed his way through the door and towered over the table beside her.

The woman on the phone sighed irritatedly, "Half of my work load is this crap. Give me your contact numbers and fax me over the police report."

"I don't have a fax. You'll either have to wait for it to come in the mail from me or have the sheriff's office fax it to you." She felt powerful, in control. It was delightful that it worked.

"I can call the sheriff. Unless things are not as you say they are we should not have to do a home interview. I deal with these inflamed ex's cases all the time. The less time spent on them the better."

"I have to admit I was sickened when I found the note. I couldn't believe he'd stoop to such low levels."

"You never really know someone until you divorce them. I suggest you take your law suit seriously. A lot of the times these actions are just saber rattling, but some times they can erupt into cases of terrible violence. It's good to have official records on your side."

"I really don't think Tim's capable of hurting me or the children." Kelli was disgusted that she was defending him. She glanced up at Clay to see if he noticed. He only looked at the keys in his hands as he turned them over in turn and inspected each one, pretending not to listen.

"I'll be in touch Miss Christi." Tina ended the call. Kelli smoothed her face with her hands and sighed.

"It's the water pump and the alternator pulley." Clay laid the keys down on the table before her.

Kelli sighed again. Her stress levels were suddenly and without warning at maximum. She wanted to crawl back into bed and cry herself to sleep. She ran her fingers through her hair.

"You up for a road trip?" He flashed her his silly looking grin with its missing tooth.

"Very funny."

"No seriously, I'm going to go rent a dolly and drag your car back to the ranch so I can fix it. All my tools and things are there." He said, dead pan.

She considered him for a moment. A mischievous grin slowly growing in the corner of his mouth. He looked so handsome, just his presence in the room altered the feeling of the entire world around her for the better. If she was honest the thought of getting out of the house and away from town sounded splendid. It tore her heart open being around Clay, knowing that she'd have to turn him away and let him go again. But pretending they were okay; that someone else had control of things, was worth the pain she'd pay.

"Okay." She said, letting go; her smile matching his.

-CHAPTER SEVEN-

A sea of rolling hills and bluffs arced out around them in all directions. Boundless fields of cut hay dried in the sun under fluffy cotton ball clouds. Clay's truck roared down the endless empty road towards the family ranch nearly two hours south of town, her broken car in tow behind. Kelli laid her head back on the seat and closed her eyes. She drifted into a series of relaxing daydreams, drinking in the sun on her skin. Clay rolled her window down and the wind blew her hair across her face. She breathed in the warm air sweet with the scent of hay.

She rolled her head to face Clay and opened her eyes. She found him glancing between her and the road. He smiled so sweetly at her that she found herself grinning at him sleepily before she could even think about it. He reached his hand off the wheel; she expected him to hold her hand or push the hair from her face but he unbuckled her seat belt instead. She looked at him questioningly as he took her by the hand and pulled her across the seat without saying a word, tucking her head into the crook of his arm as he swung the middle belt around her waist so she could re-buckle.

The kids had nodded off in their car seats miles ago. Except for the rush of air from the cracked window and the hum of the engine it was quiet. Clay smoothed the hair on the side of her head and she snuggled closer against him, her feet tucked up beside her on the seat. She could hear his heartbeat, racing, betraying the slow coolness of his face and actions. And she could feel the whoosh of every breath he took. Kelli closed her eyes again, letting the rhythm of her breathing match his.

God, how much she wanted this. She wanted to feel

small and delicate and loved. She realized she'd never really felt loved with Tim. He loved her, he had said so. He took care of her, she always had a roof over her head and money in the bank. But he was never there, never in tune with her personal needs or issues. Never concerned with whatever little thing she might be going through, however trivial it might have been. A slow tear crept from her eye as she thought about the end of her time together with Clay. When his days off ran out and he'd have to rush back to finish the rodeo circuit and get on with his life. And she'd have to get on with her own life, treading water in an endless eddy.

As if he could sense its existence his hand brushed the tear away. He bent his head down and kissed the top of hers. She let exhaustion take over and she drifted off to sleep, letting the miles pass by under his care, blissfully absent from everything. Her vision was bright behind her eyelids, she wandered aimlessly through waist high seas of prairie grass, her palms skimming over their scratchy, nodding tops. In her dream the warm air smelled of leather and old spice and dirt. And she was weightless.

She had slept for the rest of the trip, waking only as the truck lurched over a cattle grate at the end of a long driveway.

"Is this it?" She asked, rubbing her eyes.

"Yup. Scruggs' Ranch."

"Where?" She stared in all directions, but there was not a fence or a building in sight.

"Everything you see. There's close to three thousand acres."

"Wow...Where's the house?"

"Down this way. At the end of the drive here." The truck lumbered on down the gravely lane, the tires straddling a strip of overgrown grasses.

The driveway was nearly a mile long. Eventually they crested a small roll in the earth and she was able to see an arrangement of gleaming red tin roofs not far away. There was a long horse barn closest to the drive, and a series of small sheds and equipment barns. A square two story home with a wide porch clear around it stood in the middle of it all. A few big cottonwood trees towered around, shading its small yard. Clay pulled the truck and its car-in-tow alongside what appeared to be a small workshop.

"Who lives here?" She said breathlessly.

Kelli was taken by the place. The barns and the house were all gleaming white. The grasses near the home and buildings were trimmed low and grew greener and thicker than the tall field grasses that surrounded. All of it was capped with gleaming red metal roofs.

"Momma stays here with her brother, Joe. Joe runs the place with his sons and me when I am around. Grandma died a few years back and left the place to her three children, Joe, Momma and Marty. Marty doesn't care for ranch work. He retired from it to work the oil rigs."

"It's beautiful out here." She turned and stirred the sleeping children in the back seat.

Clay pulled open Ruby's door and pulled her out of her seat carefully.

"Where is this place?" She asked, still half asleep.

"This is my ranch, far away from your place." He said, sweeping his arm across her view.

"It smells good here." She said, wiping the sleep from her eyes.

"You wanna ride some horses?"

"Yes." Ruby's eyes grew big and she grew so excited that she could do nothing except shiver with anticipation.

"Too! Too! Me, too!" Joshua screeched from Kelli's arms. He'd heard the conversation as they came closer.

"Come on, Little Cowboy, lets go find you kids

someone to get that old cow pony out of the field." He set Ruby down and held his hands out to Joshua who readily reached for him. Clay sat him on his arm and strode across the wide driveway and up the porch steps to the house. Kelli had to jog behind to keep up.

"Who's in this house?" He called, letting the screen door slap after he let Kelli in.

"Clayton?" His mom stuck her head out of the kitchen doorway. "Boy, you're like the wind. I will *never* know where your coming from or where you been."

His boots echoed through the big rooms as he made his way down the hall, meeting her halfway.

"Hey, momma." He said, leaning in to kiss her cheek before passing into the kitchen.

"And here's Kelli. And little Ruby and Joshua, too." She said with an enormous smile, taking little Joshua's face in her hands and smooshing his baby cheeks together a little.

"I can't believe you remembered us! And our names even!" Kelli exclaimed.

Patty chuckled a little and blew out a quick breath, "As if I don't hear about you all enough. Every time I manage to get this boy on the phone he's gotta know if I've seen or heard of you or the kids."

Kelli shot a look at Clay who desperately pretended to be busy pouring himself some iced tea from the fridge across the room. He carried his glass with him, stopping to kiss his mother's cheek before leaning his backside against a nearby counter.

"Momma, these kids are ate up from sittin' in the truck all morning. Can't someone pull Strawberry pony out of the pasture and lead them around a bit." He smacked his lips after a long swig.

"I don't understand why you haul out of here to chase those damn belt buckles. What's it all for Clay?" She replied, looking away from the children and leveling her eyes at him.

"Dang, Momma! Now?" He eyed her sternly. But she met his gaze, narrowing her eyes at him. She may have been smaller, but she was fiercer.

"Joe's down the ravines with the boys rounding up a bunch of new young stock he bought off Tyler's for vaccines tomorrow." She said implying that he should be doing something about it, her eyes still crinkled and her lips pursed tight.

Clay only stared at her, sipping from his glass nonchalantly as he kept his eyes on her.

Finally she smiled a little smirk that looked just like Clay's and clapped her hands together, "I gotta toss some hay at the horses anyway, and that old Strawberry's been all but rotting in that field. You kids come help me with the hay and we'll see about some pony rides. Does that sound like a deal?"

Ruby stamped her feet with excitement and agreed emphatically. Joshua copied her like all younger siblings do so well. Patty gathered up their little hands in her expert ones and lead them back out the door.

"Don't you worry, Momma," She called to Kelli over her shoulder, "We'll be right here in the barnyard the whole time."

"Thanks so much!" She called after her, then she turned to Clay, "Every time she gets you on the phone, huh?"

"Seems she likes that I have a cell phone now and she can call night and day." He said dryly. He took her by the hand and hauled her out of the back door. "C'mon, I'll show you where the cowboys bunk up."

In a flash he pulled them off the porch and back out into the sunny yard. He lead her to one of the low cement buildings beside the equipment shed. It was separated in half with two matching windows and a single door on either side. Clay proudly opened the one on the left side for her and let her walk in.

The space was small and the cement blocks were painted with the same thick white paint on the inside as they were on the outside. There were old wood floors that looked as if they had come from a barn a hundred years ago. Just inside the door was a small nondescript sofa and a little pine table with two chairs. The back wall was ordered with a wooden staircase that rose to a loft area overhead and a small kitchenette and a door to a room built into the corner which was obviously a small bathroom.

There was no real art on the walls, just framed prints of horses and bulls surrounded by ribbons and trophies that hung or sat around the place here and there. Clay left the door wide open and paced across the floor to the stairs.

"C'mon up, I gotta grab a hat." He bounded up the steps effortlessly, his boots making a racket as he went.

Kelli followed more slowly, looking at the pictures as she went. There were painted ponies and squat bays and roans with big thick rumps and powerful legs. In a few pictures there was a child looking very much like a young Clay perched confidently atop horses far larger than it seemed a child could manage. There were pictures of a teenage him holding a lead rope high above his head, encouraging a massive bull to hold its head up. It was all marvelous to her.

The roof at the top of the stairs was low, Clay could barely stand under the ridge. There was a single mattress on the floor with a bunch of bedding wadded up on it. As if someone had slept there and left it in a hurry never to return. There was also a small wooden dresser and a naked metal pole stretched between some two by fours that provided space for hanging a mess of shirts. A few different pairs of plain brown leather chaps hung on nails in the rafters. The space was lit only by a square window above the stairs.

"So this is where a professional bull rider hangs his

hat?" She said, looking around.

"This is where he lays his head when he happens to be home and wonders what the woman he cares about is up to." He grabbed her hand and pulled her down with him as he flopped on the bare mattress.

Kelli landed beside him and looked into his big brown eyes. He grinned devilishly.

"Don't say that." She said, propping her head up on her arm.

"Why not? It's the truth."

"Because, Clay, this is never going to work out."

"I can't think of a reason why it shouldn't."

"Because you have to leave and finish with the PBR." She stated, barely managing to get the words out before he drew her in for a long kiss.

The little apartment was hot and stuffy from being closed up and empty in the heat of summer. But Clay's lips were hotter. The contrast sent shivers up her spine and pulled sweat from her pores. "And I don't want to sit around wondering if you're getting killed a thousand miles away." She whispered as he kissed her again, running his calloused hand though the long hair behind her head.

"You already do that anyway." He whispered in her ear, as if he were reminding her of it. As if she'd have forgotten.

It was true. Not a day had gone by when she hadn't dreaded the fact that she had no way of contacting him, or being contacted concerning him. She'd never been able to imagine Marty's knocking on her door to inform her of anything that might have happened. If he should be seriously injured or died it'd be a thing of the past before she'd even hear about it- if she ever did at all. It ate her up.

"I don't want to worry. I don't want to be left

behind while you go try to kill yourself." She tried to focus on all her reasons and rationale as Clay carefully slipped his hand under the edge of her shirt, smoothing his wide palm across her back and chasing her thoughts away.

He pressed her against him with his arm. All the softness of her female form met up against the harsh muscles of his stomach and chest. Energy coursed through her entire being and her breath caught every time his hand moved. She wanted him to rip her clothes off; to run his hands expertly over her entire body. But instead he pulled his hand out from her back and ran it through her hair. He kissed the corner of her mouth carefully and grinned against her lips.

"I wanna tear you apart right now. But I promised myself I wasn't gonna." He hopped up and helped her to her feet. She was a little woozy from her blood rushing, and she grabbed his strong arm for support, "I gotta fix that car of yours, and I have an awful hankerin' to see you ride a horse before the day is out." She followed him dumbly; blindsided with passion that was cut painfully short.

In the bumpy driveway, under the heavy heat of the summer sun, she lay on her belly with her chin resting on her folded arms. She was watching Clay on his back working under the car. He was further under the vehicle than she was, she was only beside his knees. He wore a dirty t-shirt and the muscles of his arms bulged and flexed as he worked bolts loose from the undercarriage. His forearms were red from the sun and shaded with fine hairs that were thinned just above his wrists from where the ends of his leather work gloves had rubbed. All of it was laced together with ribbons of vein. She could study just the movement of those muscles for a lifetime and not tire of it.

"When do you have to be back?" She asked, her head bobbing over her chin that was planted on the tops of her fingers.

"Oh I dunno. In a couple days. It'll take me a while to drive out to Georgia and catch up." He grappled with a wrench on a stubborn nut as he spoke. Grunting a little between words.

"I wish you didn't have to leave."

"I got to. I'm already pissin' off my sponsors."

"Oh." She chewed her lip a little. "When is the season over?"

"November." He grunted again, wrestling a big part free and setting it aside.

She rolled over on her back as he crawled out and switched to working while standing. His boots crunched the gravel beside her as he leaned over the grill and pulled and prodded the mechanics within. He was amazing. She honestly wondered what there was that he couldn't do.

"You didn't call." She stated factually.

"Nope." He matched her tone.

Kelli tossed a pebble at him. It bounced off his thigh and landed back with its brethren in the driveway. He looked down at her. She raised an eyebrow at him. He went back to work.

"Arc Mcgan and Jenny keeping you company?" She asked, imagining the tarts from the rodeo she'd met.

He stopped moving for a moment. "You think that's why I didn't call?" His voice was muffled by the car's front end.

Kelli shrugged even though he couldn't see her. "It crossed my mind."

"I'm not a cheater, Kelli."

"It's not cheating. We're not anything." She picked up another pebble and flicked it across the driveway.

"That's just what you think. What other notions you got floatin' around in that pretty little head of yours?"

"Plenty."

He stood back up and wiped his greasy hands on his jeans. "There's no way I can get this done today. You and the kids'll have to stay over."

"Oh Clay, I hate to impose on you and your family... I already feel bad that you're doing all this work."

"Work?" He laughed a little, "This is all play. Besides, I can't finish this car with you layin' there on the ground like that. You're killin' me. C'mon, lemme introduce you to the finest pair of old quarter horses in this country." She smiled as he helped her up. His southern accent was doubly bad after the month he'd spent roaming the states down there. She liked it.

"I feel bad leaving your mom with the kids all day. And where will we sleep?" She followed behind as he lead her to the long metal horse barn.

"You and the kids can have my bed, I'll sleep on my couch."

"That seems inappropriate." Not that she really minded, but there were other people's considerations of the matter to keep in mind.

He mulled it over as they entered the near end of the barn. "You and the kids can have my bed, I'll sleep on the couch in the house." He said, satisfied with his solution.

The barn was long and lined with horse stalls and washing bays and tack and feed rooms. The stalls were all empty except for a pair of ancient looking paints who stood butt to nose against the stall divider between them. The center isle was clear and covered with rubber mats, and the whole place felt peaceful and serene. The old horses acknowledged their entrance with placid whooshes of breath, but didn't take the time to look up from where their heads hung. Both ends of the isle ended in large open barn doors; flooding the barn with light and allowing the hot summer breeze to flow through.

The warm smell of sweet feed mingled with the scents of horse dander and pine shavings. The thick warmth of the building felt like a narcotic, instantly calming and numbing. Kelli felt so relaxed she wondered in passing if she might die from it.

Clay left her on a stack of hay bales, and walked outside with a pair of red halters and lead ropes tossed over his shoulder. A few short minutes later he returned with two, small, squat horses in tow. A gray mare and a black gelding. He walked them past her and situated them nose to nose in the isle, cross ties clipped under their chins to keep them still.

Kelli ran her hand over the smooth rump of the horse nearest her. Its black flanks gleamed even in the dim barn light. The gelding expanded its ribs taking in a deep breath, and it shook its head as it whooshed out. She patted along under its mane and he dropped his head obligingly as she scratched her way along its crest to the pole. The horse seemed very grateful and nudged her chest in appreciation, requesting more affection.

Clay returned with two saddles stacked in his arms, and a pair of bridles over his shoulder. He heaved the mound onto the hay bales and set about tacking up the horses.

"Have you ever ridden?" He asked, easing the last bridle into the black horse's mouth and flipping the reigns over its head.

"I took lessons as a girl. English, though."

"Tank wont care. He just likes women and chasing cows. Although he doesn't do much cow chasing these days. He's got a bad knee."

She watched as he smoothed the hairs on their backs with his hand before sliding thick saddle pads onto them. Next came saddles. The horses sighed and swayed a little with the effort of them being cinched tightly in place. Finished he offered her his hand at the black horse's side. She stepped lightly into his palm and he hoisted her up effortlessly.

It felt good to sit on a horse. It'd been years. Her seat felt off, and she wasn't used to balancing in the deepness of the western saddle. But the familiar sound of creaking leather and the life that coursed through the animal to her was tangible and sparked her memory.

Clay unclipped Tank from the cross-ties and then his own horse. He turned Kelli around in one of the washing bays and walked her out of the barn and into the bright sun of summer, the gray mare in tow.

"Crap." He said, turning the mare around and swinging the reigns over her head, handing them to Kelli. "I forgot my hat."

He trotted across the barn lot to his little low apartment and darted inside. The horses touched noses and as though they were communicating telepathically. They remained that way until he returned, their tails swishing and teeth crunching as they played with the bits in their mouths. The mare's ears perked at the sound of Clay running up to them. She crow hopped excitedly as he rushed up to her. Clay ignored her antics and shoved her out of the way of Tank's side. He reached up and tucked a ball cap on Kelli's head. Then he centered an old brown cowboy hat on his own before he expertly climbed into the saddle.

"Let's go!" Clay smiled at her as he slapped the mare. The poor beast jumped unexpectedly and tore out of the barnyard, pebbles flying.

Tank followed excitedly. Kelli hadn't ridden in ages and she struggled to keep her balance as the elated horse chased after its pasture buddy.

Clay glanced back at her as they bounded over the hills and dales beyond the barns. He urged the gray mare faster, pushing her into a gallop. The gelding followed, finally breaking into a smoother stride. Kelli felt her muscles remembering the motions of a running animal beneath her and she relaxed. She felt her knees relent from their pressing against the horse's sides and let her weight fall easy into the stirrups. Tank was so pleased with the freedom it provided him that he gathered himself up and surged ahead of the little gray mare. Kelli pointed and laughed as she passed Clay. When he realized he was far ahead Tank slowed down.

"I haven't seen that fat old man run so fast in ages. He'll be lame tomorrow from it if he ain't already." He said as he reached them.

"Don't blame me. I only let him go to chase you." She huffed a little with the exertion of riding.

"You're about as blameless as they get, Girl." He crooned. It was silly flattery, but she drank it up.

The horses walked side by side. After nearly half an hour the gentle hills began to change. Big black mounds of dirt and rock broke through the ground around them. In the distance, a little ways off, there were tree tops visible like bushes. Their height was masked by the ravine that hid them and the creek that fed them. When they neared it the horses shivered and spooked at a group of antelope that fled in their wake from the coolness of the trees.

Single file the horses dropped into the little canyon. It was rocky and less grassy, but protected from the wind there. Nourished by a small stream there was a long winding line of trees and shrubs. Clay slid off his horse as they neared the water, he held Tank while Kelli dismounted.

"These fool horses love the water. Unless you wanted to swim we'd better get off and let them get it out of their system." He said turning them loose.

"Wont they run off?"

"Nah, they're tired now and there's no place for 'em to go anyway."

Sure enough as they sensed the freedom they began

pawing at the waters edge, creeping further and further into the water with each splash. Tank nodded his head and sipped the water before finally laying down and rolling in it. His friend did the same, but not quite with the same level of abandon. They stood back up, water dripping from their sides and from under the saddles they still wore.

Clay took Kelli's hand and lead her away, leaving the placated animals to swim and fall to grazing the short green grasses along the waters edge. Little birds sang in the tree tops and small blue flowers bloomed in patches under the willowy looking trees. He sat down in a large expanse of velvety green and flowers under one of the shady trees. Kelli sat down with him.

"It is beautiful here." She watched the slow babbling water twinkling in the sun before them.

"It is now." Clay said, wrapping an arm around her shoulders, "Usually its just lonely feeling."

She laid her head on his shoulder. "You always have such lovely things to say."

"I have a lot of time alone to think them up." He said mockingly.

She laid back in the grass and plucked a stem from the tangled masses and picked it into pieces. Clay watched her, the corner of his mouth turned up ever so slightly. His eyes were clouded and soft, as though he were watching the most amazing creature he'd ever encountered.

"You never called." She stated again.

He blinked a couple times, clearing the clouds; sharpening his gaze. He sighed long and low.

"Well, in the beginning I didn't have a cell phone. And I was on the road a lot and not sure you'd answer. I wanted to give you space." He laid down beside her, his head propped on his hand. "I checked up on you though. Called Marty and Momma. I made up my mind to call after the first two weeks went by, I even bought myself the darn cell phone for it." He pulled it from his pocket as proof.

"So why didn't you?"

"I dunno. Everyone said you were doing so fine, and the days kept slipping away. I figured I'd wait and visit next time I was in town." He looked down into her face and smiled.

"You didn't stop by either."

"I wasn't home, Woman!" He laughed. "I felt terrible when I heard about Marty's story. I feared the worst. I got a ticket speeding just over the state line, gotta pay the fine since I'm not planin' to go to court for it." He tried to sound lighthearted and casual.

"You feared the worst, huh?"

His face grew serious and his voice deepened a little, "Kelli, Girl, I left when I hung up the phone. It was two in the mornin', Momma had called and woke me up to tell me. I was so scared he'd get to you, or that you'd pack up and leave to God knows where. Or that you'd be alone and scared."

"I wasn't scared of him, or about that. Not after it was over anyway. I was scared for the kids though. You know he called CPS and tried to report me for neglect. If you hadn't introduced me to Cindy they'd have been riding around in the car and I'd be in the middle of an investigation and at risk of losing the kids." Her stomach felt sick just mentioning it.

Clay smoothed the hair that tangled along the side of her face. "I'm sorry, Girl. I never should have left."

"Well you seem in a fine hurry to leave again." She huffed.

"Go'n is not the same as leave'n." He pulled his hat off and laid it above her head. "What would you do if you weren't workin' your brains out, anyway? Huh? I never got to ask you." He changed the subject.

"You could have called and asked." She teased.

"Woman! I should have called. I'll call next time." He poked the tip of her nose with his finger. "It's a serious question though"

Kelli bit her lip in thought. "Keep house I guess. I never really had any aspirations beyond having babies and being a wife. I feel pretty adrift right now with the way things are. I can't keep a house, I can barely run one. I have no time to be mom, and my kids take a second role to the darn bills and work. I hate it. I don't even know what I like to do anymore." She sighed and glanced at the blue and white circular sky above them and the green trees that reached for it, "I like this, though."

"You 'spose you'll have more kids?" He asked nonchalantly, fiddling with something in his fingers, but she saw him eye her out of the corner of his eye.

She shrugged. "I like being pregnant. I like babies. I was lucky to get the babies I got out of Tim. He never really wanted kids, I think he just went a long with it to shut me up. I'd probably have a couple more. If the situation was right." She plucked another stem of grass from the ground and fingered it. "How about yourself? You have any kids?"

"No." He said, laughing with relief, "No kids. Not yet. I always figured I'd have some. Figured I'd have some by now, that's for sure. I just have been so busy with the ranch and the bull riding and the rodeo... all these years passed and now I'm nearin' forty and have nothing to show for it but half a dozen broken bones and the few screws that hold them together."

"You never took the time to get a house or anything either." She pointed out. "You've been here on the ranch all this time?"

"Yup. Never saw fit to leave. Me and my baby

cousins built the two apartments in the equipment shed a few years back. That's about as far away from home as I've gotten I'm afraid."

"That's sad."

"Well, when I'm home I'm workin' outside. Most of the time though I'm gone chasin' the rodeo and things, it seems. Doesn't really make sense to have a place of my own if its just sitin' empty and lonely all the time."

"No I guess not."

"I have plans to build a place here on the ranch though. Up on the rise just beyond the creek bed here. I figured I'd put up a little ranch house. Nothin' fancy. Maybe with a walkout basement and a big deck. Dig a pond out back."

"I like ranch houses. My parents had one when I was a teenager, before they split."

"Do ya now?" He said, raising his eyebrows, acting surprised. "When I get my place built you'll have to come see it."

She shook her head, "I already saw your place. I don't need to see a bigger mess you'd live in."

"You could come help me decorate."

"Maybe."

Clay smiled again, following the silhouette of her side with his hand. Sparks flew under his palm and she secretly wished their skin wasn't separated by her clothes.

"Oh c'mon, Girl. Just come keep my house and have my babies." He said jokingly.

"Just? That's hardly an enticing offer." She said sarcastically. "Or romantic." She added as an after thought.

He thought on it a few brief moments, "You keep my house and have my babies and I'll give you whatever you want. Whatever's fair."

She smirked. "See, we're trading lives here. Mine for yours. My life is babies and houses and all the things that lay between. I'll consider giving you that when you stop riding bulls. Everything else is yours to keep, but the bulls are mine. Maybe we could go from there."

"Consider? That seems pretty steep for just considerin'."

"Well it was your very unromantic proposition."

"Fair enough." He leaned down and kissed her forehead.

Kelli wrapped her arms around his neck and ran her fingers through his hair, chasing his mouth with hers. He tasted like coffee, and his breath quickened as he hugged her tightly in response. Her body pressed instinctively against his, drawn in by the strength of his presence and the heat of the day around them.

Clay slid a strong hand down her back and followed the curve of her bottom and thigh, pulling her knee up over his side and followed the curves back up to where he started. He rolled her over, pressing her into the grass and earth with his weight. She felt small and singular, her pulse rushing through her ears as he lightly sank his teeth into her jaw before smoothing it with kisses.

Suddenly he stopped, pushing himself off her so he could look down at her face. Her hands rested above her head, on the wide tangle of hair that surrounded her. His face showed the struggle between his body and mind. Finally he rolled back onto his side, propping his head back on his hand.

"You're like a little tornado." He bit his lip, looking her over, "Dangerous little thing. If I get too close you'll suck me right in." He hopped up to his feet and drew her along with him, "C'mon, lets get back. It'll be dinner soon and they ought to be drivin' that stock in for the night. Better get some space between us before I end up doing somethin' I don't intend to."

Kelli felt slightly disappointed. "You mean you don't intend to... at all?" She was instantly embarrassed that she had wondered that out loud.

Clay stopped in his tracks and looked at her. He all but licked his lips like some hungry wild thing. "Girl. Don't tempt me."

"I was just asking." She wrapped her arm through his and leaned against him as they walked back to the grazing horses.

"You're askin' for trouble."

"Seem's like trouble finds me these days, whether I ask for it or not." She felt serious and overwhelmed just acknowledging the world she'd left behind for the day.

His smooth voice rang out with laughter. "You're gonna be alright, Girl. You'll see."

They had reached the horses and she threw her leg up over Tank's fat back. "You said that last time and then you left. I don't think I should trust you."

Clay swung up on his mare, looking hurt. But he didn't argue the point.

They didn't race the horses back to the barns, although the animals picked up the pace a little on their own as they smelled home nearing. The barnyard was alive with activity now. There were a pair of huge chrome-lined pickup trucks rumbling in the huge circular driveway. Long stock trailers were hitched to them and they rattled as animals shifted inside impatiently. A couple of men on horseback leaned down from their saddles to carry on a conversation with the drivers. They held onto an extra cow pony each that was tethered to the saddle horns of their own saddles. The metal trailers shook harder from time to time with the sound of anxious cattle. Manure was kicked through the side and rear panels, making a mess in the white driveway rocks.

Ruby and Joshua were fussing over a small palomino horse on the house lawn as Patty looked on at the gaggle in the drive from the shade. Ruby picked Joshua up and he kicked and wiggled, yanking fist fulls of skin and mane as he climbed onto the little horses back. The old mare did little more than swish her tail and pause from munching the grass in the yard until he was settled and continued on unbothered by their childish play.

Ruby had obviously spent no small amount of time braiding the pony's mane and tail. Patty had given her some sort of sparkling paint that looked like a bottle of shoe polish which the child was using carefully to make purple marks on the animals yellow coat.

Clay dismounted and his horse followed him over to the far side of one of the trucks where he leaned in one of the open windows. Kelli followed, slipping off Tank and leading him along behind her to the truck, too.

"'Bout time you show up for some work." The old man behind the wheel looked a lot like Marty, only older and even more wind-worn. Kelli figured he was Joe.

"You seem to be gettin' on without me." Clay answered.

"Where's the money this time? I watched you take the purse in Tulsa." A young man on horseback on the other side of the truck called. "You owe me a thousand."

"That is a grossly exaggerated number, Shawn." Clay replied through his goofy grin.

"We were double or nothing on that damn bull busting you up, five-hundred doubled is a grand. I *can* do math."

"We were at two-fifty, and that was before you owed me for that dang girl's number I got you."

"You boys can figure out your finances later. We have stock to bed down and feed." Joe popped the truck into first and the riders moved their horses out of the way as the two vehicles swung wide and backed along the long side of the equipment shed where a series of pens awaited the cattle.

"I better take care of the kids." Kelli said to Clay

before he swung up on his horse.

"Alright, D a r l i n ' ." She handed Tank over to him as he settled in the saddle. He leaned down impossibly low from the horse's back and stole a lingering kiss from her.

Kelli flushed a little as she realized his family was all watching and listening. She spun around, stuffing her hands into her pockets as she shuffled over to the yard. Ruby came bounding over, her little blue sun dress floating around her.

"This is my best friend now, Mommy." She said, dragging her by the hand to the little horse's head. "Her name is Strawberry. See look, I drew hearts on her. *You can draw on the horses here.*" She whispered the last in awe.

"Oh wow, B aby, that's so amazing." She reached out to Joshua on the horses back, but he shook his head at her. "How about you, Buster? You having fun?"

"Yes!" He beamed, poking a fat finger into the horses shoulder between his legs.

"We've had lots of fun." Patty crooned. "There haven't been kids on the place since Shawn and Luke grew up. You look like you've been having some fun yourself, Momma."

Kelli blushed at the knowing tone in Clay's mother's voice. "I feel bad that you've had to babysit unexpectedly this afternoon. Clay insisted it'd be okay."

Patty grinned like Clay, except all her teeth were in place. "I'm getting pretty old these days. I have to admit I'd lost all hope in Clay ever settling down. Anything I can do to help that along makes my heart swell." She patted the pony's rump as she spoke, brushing the rising dust from its hair. "It's not easy falling in love with children in tow, no matter how old they are."

"You never remarried?"

"Heavens no. Between the kids and working the

ranch... I barely had time to bathe, let alone go to town and find a man."

"I'm sorry. Clay mentioned what it was like growing up. Losing his dad must have broke your heart."

"It did. But I knew how close to the fire we were dancing. It's not like it is now. They had no helmets or vests. The pay certainly wasn't as good. But he loved it. More than he loved us, I'm afraid. And I was never strong enough to take him from it."

Kelli kicked at the grass a little thinking about the life and heartache that must have chased Clay, his sister and mother. "I wish Clay would give it up." She sighed, finally.

Patty mused a thought over in her head for a few moments before she spoke. "He's not like his father. He takes a lot from my side of the family. He rides because nothing more interesting has ever come along. If it came down to it he'd choose life over riding."

"You seem to think we're pretty serious."

"Well, I know he's serious. I know my boy. I've never seen him so in love. He never calls to ask about the farm or family, just to ask after you and the kids. Until Cindy took them in I never had much to tell him except that Marty noted you were still alive and living across the way. Personally I'm glad he's getting a life."

Kelli laughed out loud. "Getting one? He seems to live pretty well, in the lime light. On television, even."

"Honey I've lived that, it is no life. I've been telling him that for years now, but the darn fool wont listen. A mother can only be so right in the eyes of her son."

Kelli and the kids helped return the old pony to its little paddock on the side of the barn. She even blundered through the evening chores in the horse barn, with Patty calling out directions as she powered through the familiar tasks at a much quicker rate. Her mind felt numb though, trying to process the information about Clay that his mother had shared with her. He didn't even know her, yet according to those around him he was lost on her. It was elating and terrifying at the same time. She felt like she had a lot to live up to and wondered at what point he'd be disappointed in her and lose interest.

But the barn work felt good. Her body felt wonderful in motion, her muscles working to pick up hay bales and feed buckets loosened and ached with built up lactic acid. She was weaker than she realized, but she still felt strong working at something so purposeful. Sitting static behind the wheel had truly taken a toll. The work now made her remember her childhood years with her parents few pet animals in their little shed out back. All the work of cleaning manure and feeding and watering them every day that had fallen to her in the summer months when school was out.

The kids scampered about trying to help. A few of the horses from outside came in for the night, including those that had been working all day. They were given rations of sweet feed and lush green hay. One by one they munched on their dinners before laying down and rolling in their airy stalls.

An hour later the big dining room table in the farmhouse had been pulled apart and leaves added to it's length. Long benches and chairs were pushed around to make room for the nine of them. They all sat around chatting about the day and life together; steaming plates of home cooked food all around.

Clay's cousins, Shawn and Luke were much younger than him and seemed to almost worship him in the way that adolescent boys look up to the men in their lives. Luke was youngest and finishing his last year of high school. Shawn was about twenty and worked full time on the ranch with his dad Joe. Pete, who had been on horseback in the driveway when they returned earlier, was an obscure cousin from someone's in-laws that lived on a small farm down the road from them. But he leased his land to the ranch and worked on it part time. Aside from Kelli, Patty was the only woman on the place apparently. Pete's wife worked in town and Joe's woman had run off recently with a man from Colorado, which might have accounted for some of his gruffness.

Kelli took little bites as she looked around the place from her seat. The old farmhouse had been updated some. The kitchen was still traditionally hidden behind doors that opened into the dining room and center hallway, but the rest of the living area had been opened up as much as was structurally possible. The pecan colored floors were satiny and covered with large, soft, areas rugs in places. The whole place had the faint smell of the corn stove that ran in winter for heat, and slow roasted meats that made up the meals each day.

The tall walls were covered in flowered wall paper and wainscoting. Knotty pine deviated from the uniformity to cover the living room walls. And everywhere there were pictures. Portraits of the family through the ages. Old black and white images from the 1800's and series of photographs of Luke and Shawn through their childhood. Whimsical country decorations were peppered through out. In all it felt perfect and whole. And like most things surrounding Clay it drew tears to her eyes. She longed for something like this. It was restful and nurturing. Just like the food that seemed to melt, bite after bite, in her mouth. And the way they included them in their conversations. She so longed to belong; to be accepted.

"Are you a cowboy mister Joe?" Ruby asked around a mouthful of food, interrupting the constant conversation that had been taking place between the men.

"Yup." Joe said coarsely, in a voice much like Marty's.

"Are you a cowboy, Shawn?" She asked the next man.

"Well, I guess so." He said slowly. Ruby nodded, accepting his answer as truth.

"Are you a cowboy, Mister Pete?"

"I pretend to be one so the girls like me. But I'm really just a farmer." He lamented, pretending to confess a secret.

"Oh." She stuffed another bite of food in her little mouth and chewed it as she thought about Pete's answer. She bounced up and down slightly as her feet swung back and forth off the edge of the chair. "Yeah, I like you." She said innocently. The table erupted in laughter around her and she beamed proudly, though uncertain as to why.

She ate a few more bites as the table settled down.

Luke spoke up indignantly, "Well if anyone cares I'm a cowboy, too."

"You don't have cowboy boots." Ruby injected flatly.

"Well. But..." He stamped his feet. "Well, they are boots."

Ruby shook her head. "They're not cowboy boots."

Clay chuckled, almost choking on his mouthful of food.

Kelli laughed, too.

"At least *I* impress the girls." Pete injected and the table roared with laughter again.

Kelli wanted to curl up on her chair and spend the rest of her life listening to them talk. She missed family and wanted it desperately. She thought of all the effort she'd wasted trying to foster it with Timothy. All the pleading and arguing for meals together or quiet time as a family unit. Clay's family held such promise and hope, and she ached to attach herself to them. She smiled so hard her face ached before she finished her meal. Watching her children laugh and interact with the people around them filled her heart to the brim.

After dinner Pete and Shawn disappeared and Luke slipped off to focus on whatever it is teenagers do in the summer in the country. Joe sat down to work the books in his little office off the kitchen and Kelli helped Patty with the clean up. Clay eventually ended up on the living room rug under a pile of small children.

"It's nice to have a woman around at meal time. I know Joe has different feelings but I miss Cheryl. Besides, he ran her off the place as far as I'm concerned." Patty talked aimlessly as she washed dishes at the big country sink under the kitchen window. "I just get so sick of being left alone all the time. I can't handle working out with the stock anymore. I spend most of my time keeping the buildings and horses in order. Plus running this house now that Cheryl's gone."

"Momma I gotta work on that car tomorrow so Kelli and the kids are stayin' over. Do you mind if I crash on the couch in here?" Clay called, poking his head in through the kitchen door, a pair of toddlers clinging to his arms and legs.

"I doubt it makes a difference either way." She said absently, waving a hand. Clay ducked back out at her reply, dragging Joshua on one leg.

"Thanks for the meal. And for keeping the kids all day." Kelli said as she dried the last dish that came out of the sudsy sink. She breathed in the warm scent of citrus cleaner. "Well, and for putting us up for the night, too"

"Well, Honey. Thanks for bringing my baby home for a visit." Patty chuckled warmly.

Kelli hugged her. She didn't really know why, other than she just had to. It felt healing some how to be hugged back. Like being mothered. For the brief moment of the embrace her heart felt like a child. It was a taste of something foreign. Just a taste of being okay.

A little later Clay lead them out the side door and across the driveway to his little apartment. It had gotten late while they had all lingered at the table laughing and talking. And the day wound down further while dishes were done and people relaxed. The men had talked extensively about the branding work to be done the next day and Joe had been slightly irritated that Clay had other obligations. It was compounded by being completed at an odd time of year. He insisted Shawn produced imperfect brands and went into a long story about the week previous when the heifer calves had been vaccinated and branded and Shawn had been kicked in the rear end by a large calf and nearly landed face first on a pile of hot irons. Naturally they'd all laughed riotously at the table, except Shawn. And Joe.

"Do you have a bathtub in here?" Kelli asked as Clay let them in and turned on the lights.

"Yeah. Its not very fancy, though. Just an old antique thing."

Kelli washed the kids up as quick as she could with the paltry supplies in the bathroom. They could barely keep their eyes open as she dried them off quickly and put their under clothes back on them. In the heat of the upstairs she turned a fan towards the bed and dug through the wad of bedding. She spread a thin blanket on the mattress and another small blanket on top. The kids crawled in and she laid down with them, smoothing their hair and talking soothingly to them about the days events, working through their sleepy-time routine. The warm, thick, scent of a man's living area swirled around them and the old barn boards on the floor smelled rich and faintly of outside things like hay and grain. It seemed to sooth all three of them.

"Joshua wants to be a cowboy when he grows up." Ruby said sleepily as Kelli smoothed her damp hair. "And I am going to be a cowboy, too."

"You'd be a cowgirl, Honey." Kelli corrected her.

"I like it here. I like Strawberry." She said through a yawn.

"Me too! Yah!" Joshua suddenly jumped into the

conversation, although he was mostly asleep.

Kelli liked it there, too. She liked the smell of the animals and riding horses in the sun. She liked the steady purposefulness of the work that went on around the ranch and the comfort of sitting around a table with friendly people and laughing. She had no memory of such an event with Tim. And her own parents had worked late when she was a teenager, so the routine of a quiet home cooked meal had died with her elementary school years. The simple reliability that the place and people seemed to emit soaked deep into her bones.

"It is nice here." She kissed their heads as they drifted to sleep in the hot loft. She got up and repositioned the fan so it would hit them more directly before sneaking down the stairs.

Clay was stretched out on the old couch in the open room downstairs. He had turned the lights off, except for the one in the bathroom. The little place was cozy and radiated with him.

It smelled of manly things and leather. Everything was arranged in the way he had placed it, to suit his needs and how he lived his daily life when home. Somehow though it felt familiar and homey to her.

"I thought you'd have gone to the house already." She whispered, sitting on the arm of the couch.

"Did you want me to?" His voice was thick and deep with the night.

"No."

Everything felt so good, even the air around her was comfortable on her skin. She crawled across the sofa and lay against him, wanting his arms around her and the comfort of the press of his body against hers.

She rested her head on him, listening to the slow rhythm of his breathing and the racing of his heart. The muscles across his chest flexed and her head raised and lowered as he moved his arms around her tighter. Her senses were full of him. The smell of horses and sun-baked cotton in his clothes. His breath in her hair and the warmth of his arms and body surrounding her. The sound of his heart and lungs. He ran his hand across her face and through her hair, smoothing the worry that hid there.

Kelli wanted to scream and beg. She wanted to reason with him and rationalize his thoughts. And still she wanted to run away from him and the risky promise of security he seemed to offer. She wanted things to be as simple and easy as they had been when she and Tim had dated. She wished she was not so needy and that her situation was not so threatening and complex. She just wished she could enjoy the unfolding moment without her mind flying to pieces with conflicting worry and desire. All her thoughts roared and swirled together until they were no more than the troubling din of a summer storm. She fought it, but a single tear escaped. His hand ran across it before she could catch it.

"What's the matter, Kelli?" He whispered.

His tone was so soft and soothing that she was barely able to keep from breaking completely into tears. She didn't know what was the matter. It was hard to pick just one reason. Mostly she felt tired and frustrated.

She shook her head against his chest in reply.

"Babe, don't cry. What is it, Girl, what?" His thumb found another tear and wiped it away also, "Why do you always cry when I hold you?"

"I don't know."

She did though. She cried knowing she wanted him, afraid the rest and protection he offered wasn't real. Just like it hadn't been with Tim. She was overwhelmed with the hopeless need to be loved and cherished. To finally be important to someone.

Clay sat up with her and pulled her close against him, helping her fold her legs as she straddled his thighs. He held her face in his hands and looked at her in the dim

P. C. Rogers

light. His big dark eyes and soft brow searched her face for some kind of answer. Her lip quivered and he looked worried by it for a moment.

"Don't cry, Girl. It breaks my heart." He kissed her lip and watched to see if it had some magical effect. He frowned a little when it only produced another tear.

She tried to smile and wipe it away; to shake it off. It was embarrassing. She felt out of control and needy. Demanding even; always crying. It seemed their every encounter eventually ended in some form of tears.

He kissed her cheek and smoothed her hair again. His thumb ran softly along the side of her throat until it reached her chin and he turned her face so he could plant kisses down the side of her neck and collar bone.

He paused to hold her face in his hands again and look into her eyes. It was so probing, so intimate, even fully clothed she felt naked under his gaze. It was as if he were trying to fix her, and pausing every few kisses to see if it had worked yet.

"You don't even know me." She whispered hesitantly. "You act like you love me. Don't do this, Clay. Tim never once looked at me like this. It's scary."

Clay looked slightly shocked. "Well, then, he obviously never loved you, Kelli."

"He said he did and I believed him, and look what happened." She confessed in a little exhale, cramming a sob down her throat before she whispered with a croak, "I wasn't good enough."

His eyes narrowed under knit brows and he shook his head ever so slightly, disapprovingly.

"Do you still love him?" He asked, intense. She shook her head no and he sighed a little with relief. "It wasn't you, Girl. Believe me. It wasn't your fault."

"You don't know that, Clay. Anymore than I know anything about you." Again he wiped a tear away with the rough pad of his thumb and kissed her face as though

178

he were trying to erase its existence completely.

"Whachya wanna know? Tell me and I'll show you who I am. It's not a mystery, Kelli. What you see is what you get. Just a man. Uncomplicated and simple."

He was so strong in her eyes, yet his voice pleaded with her; as though he were begging her to believe him. As though her concern troubled him.

Kelli was too afraid to say what she thought: that it was too good to be true; that *he* was too good to be true. Like a knight in shining armor. On bull-back, instead of astride a gleaming white horse.

"It'd take me a lifetime to explain myself. All my problems. All the broken things inside. You can't even imagine..." She took a deep breath from against his neck where her face was hidden and exhaled slowly, "I don't think I even know myself anymore."

"Well, let's see." He said seriously, "I know you're strong, you've carried the enormous weight of bein' a single mother with no support. I know you're hurt from bein' ignored and let down and bein' treated common and plain. I know you're beautiful and you smell like heaven and the way you move is enough to keep me speechless for days" He kissed her mouth, carefully; convincingly. "I know you're an excellent mom, and you make beautiful, smart, children who should never have to survive the shame of a father who so rashly threw away the most precious gift ever..."

"Please don't go..." She blurted out.

"Darlin', I am not leavin'. I just have to finish the circuit. People pay me money to."

"Just give it back. I'll work; I'll get it back for you." Kelli pleaded.

He pulled her shirt down on one shoulder and kissed the bare skin there, desperate to sooth her despair. The room spun around her and she clutched at his arm to steady herself. "It doesn't work that way." He breathed against her.

She broke down and cried finally. "I don't want to lose you. I don't want you broken or ruined or killed. Or a thousand miles away. I don't want to be alone anymore. This is too perfect, something will ruin it. If you go I might not get you back. I just want you, Clay. I want this to work." She rattled through her confession, still clinging to him as his breath on her skin sent shivers through her.

"Come with me, Kelli." He said finally. He wasn't asking; he was not waiting for a reply. "Just bring the kids and come with me. I can't keep you from having to wonder if I'm killin' myself, but I can take away the other worries." He promised.

Her breath caught as he laid her on the sofa and slid on top of her. His every movement was careful and purposeful. Every brush of his palm; every glance; every motion, it all added up to one loving, possessive, sum. He ran his fingers through her hair, down her neck and shoulder and along her side. The hard muscles of his stomach pressed her into the cushions where it felt that nothing terrible could reach her.

Kelli slid her hands across his back and shoulders, slowly considering the rise of each blade and the knots of thick muscles around them and the valley that ran between. His skin was just as hot and smooth as his breath on her neck, even through the fabric of his clothes.

"I have work... and rent..." She wanted to let go. She wanted to close her eyes and never see that horrible, lonely, life again. And as much as it terrified her, she wanted to trust that if she jumped he'd catch her.

"I'll take care of it. We'll work it out." His hands slid under her shoulders and carefully untangled the worried muscles there, pressing her tight against him with each movement.

The tiny apartment was warm, though the windows

were open. The sounds of cattle and crickets sifted through the screens and billowed the thin curtains like the ghosts that haunted her mind. The ever present scent of baking prairie grass filled every corner of the space. And although it was foreign, there was something singularly familiar about all of it. Like lingering dé·jà vu.

"I don't want to live a rodeo life." She said. Kelli wanted to give in, but the thought of being so transient was not appealing. She wanted to be planted, the two of them, and build a life together.

"This is the last season. When it's up I'll bring you home and build you a house and spend all my time findin' new ways to make you smile. And anythin' else you get in your mind that you need." He was practically begging. "I need this, I need you and even the kids, too, Kelli. A man can't be alone chasin' the world forever. It gets lonesome."

"But what if you change your mind? Clay, think about it." She looked at him, pleading, "You are so good, Clay. I'm afraid you'll wake up and realize I'm not worth it, and all that good will leave with you."

She imagined him growing weary of the stress of raising a family and keeping a wife. There was no time for anything else besides that most of the time. Even in a well-aged relationship where the children belonged to both partners. But he listened intently to everything she had to say. Every worry seemed to instantly plague him as much as it did her. And yet he seemed to always have a ready solution to relieve her of it.

"Never. I've had months to think about it. And besides, I already made my mind up long ago. I planned to chase you down when I got home next, same as I planned to call you but chickened out. I bought the cell phone and all, but I so wanted to see you with my own eyes... I kept tellin' myself I'd wait until I got home. In another week, next month..." He paused to watch his hand trace a line down her arm before it found its way into her hair again. He lifted her head slightly and kissed her mouth. "You loved me and I knew it; I never should have left like that. Not without bein' sure you knew how much I loved you back. It was a stupid mistake."

Kelli blinked at him. How on earth did he know she loved him? She had been so certain that she'd never given anything away in her countenance. She looked at him questioningly, remembering his searching eyes and explorative hands that sexually charged night over a month ago. It was surely obvious at the time that she'd been aroused. Who wouldn't have been? She'd understood she loved him that night, so much so that apparently even he knew it. He knew it and didn't run from it. Didn't balk at it.

"Come with me, Girl." He breathed into her ear, sending a rush of goosebumps down her arms. "Let me take care of you." She finally nodded; a tear of hopeful relief slipping from her closed lids.

"I love you, Kelli. As big as this life, I love you." His voice was desperate; hopeful. Reassuring.

"I love you, too." She whispered in confession, overwhelmed. She was finally leaping away from who she'd been. And she was letting him save her.

"Yeah?" He smiled against her mouth. "You'll come with me, then? You and the kids? Be mine?"

"I just don't know if it's a good idea, making you drag us all over the country…" She sighed a little, "I'm just some girl you met, with kids. That's a lot to take on."

"Marry me then." He looked at her sincerely, "I'm serious. I am *that* serious, Girl. If that's what makes it a good idea for you, I'll put an engagement ring on your pretty little finger first chance I get to buy one. I'll get down on one knee, right now." He shifted to get up.

"Clay…" Her voice was reluctant. "I don't know anything about your world…"

"Three months and I'll hang up my rope and never

touch it again, I swear." He sat up, holding her against him. "I'll put a ring on your finger; the biggest rock I can find. Monday morning." He sounded excited; his hushed voice grew raspy as he planned it all out. "Marry me, come with me. You belong with me, we belong together, Kelli. I know it, you know it. There's no sense in you wasting all this time and upset over being alone. Not when I'm right here."

She nodded slowly, clinging to him, letting his words wash over her.

"I promise you, you will never have to feel common again. Or taken for granted. I'll do this life with you like it should have been done the first time." He kissed her harder, smiling wide between each one, "Startin' with the biggest darn ring I can find..."

"I don't need a big diamond..." She chuckled, straddling him again as he leaned back against the arm of the couch, his knees against her back.

"And then we can have a wedding the weekend before Thanksgivin', as soon as the season's over. Pastor'd love to see me hitched." His hands ran up and down her sides, following the curve of her form idly as he imagined it all.

"I can't go traveling around with you unmarried, though, Clay. I just can't. I'm not that kind of woman... I wasn't raised that way." She said quietly, whispering and embarrassed, "I'm sorry."

He was quiet, too, for a moment. His hands froze where they had begun smoothing her arms. She closed her eyes as insecure dread crept in. Just as she considered despairing he exhaled noisily.

"Well, no. I guess not. It don't seem right for you I suppose." He sucked on his teeth thoughtfully. "We gotta get married before thanksgivin', then, obviously..." He sighed loud again, "I really wanted to have a big frilly wedding. You know, like you girls are always plannin'...

But there ain't time. How 'bout day after tomorrow?"

"What?" She laughed, believing he was being facetious.

"Why are you laughin', Woman? I'm serious."

Clay looked at her intently. She stopped before chuckling again and thought about it at length.

"I'd hate to take your wedding away from you, but I also know I gotta have you and the kids with me, too. Pastor'd do it; he's never busy on a Monday. There's no waiting period, we'll just run to town, get a license and be mister and missus before noon. We'll keep it secret if you want, momma'd watch the kids for the night, and this fall we could have a weddin', a real one. We wont tell no one here that you're comin' with me. You don't know anyone but Cindy and Pastor anyway. And they'd keep it secret. It'd be easy as that."

"Really?"

"Hell, yeah." He stroked her cheek and smiled, "The luckiest thing that ever happened to me was having you all but fall in my lap. I knew you were priceless the first moment I saw you. You were like a little glowing phoenix rising from the dull black horizon."

Kelli snorted and laughed out loud, "That's because you were high on painkillers, Clay."

"No. That's because you're the one, Kelli. I knew it the second I first laid eyes on you. No one's ever struck me that way, not in all this lifetime. And I was certain when I saw you chasin' after that worthless piece of garbage ex of yours in your underwear that night." He paused to smile and kiss her again, "God, you were so heartbreakin' in the dark; those long legs of yours and your hair all a mess. You crumpled me right up, I haven't gotten straightened out since."

"That night was so embarrassing. I was such a fool." She moaned, hiding behind her hands.

"No, you weren't. You were innocent and trustin',

even though you'd been treated bad by him. I knew I wanted you to trust me like that; to love me like that. That's why you gotta marry me."

She giggled a little again, "I can't believe you're serious about this. You'd really take me on? Me and the mess I'm in with Tim and two kids that need me and all my issues..."

He reached into his pocket and pulled out his cell phone as she rattled on. After punching a few numbers he cleared his throat and spoke. "Sorry Momma. I didn't mean to wake you. I wanna get married day after tomorrow, can you watch the kids?"

Kelli stared at him wide eyed; speechless. It was all so silly and awesome. She could hear the shrill excited voice on the other line, but Clay didn't seem to be listening to it. He was watching only her and grinning. Finally he snapped back to the phone conversation.

"Yes, of course I'm serious. I wasted enough time, no sense in wasting more... No. Yes. Well, we'll keep it secret and have a big o'l weddin' in the fall. Around thanksgivin'... of course Pastor'd do both... Well okay if you want to call the man in the middle of the night. Okay. Yup, love you. See you tomorrow." He shut the phone off and laid it down on the floor, looking at her expectantly.

"Monday?"

"Monday. Crazy woman's callin' Pastor right this minute." He said. "And in the fall I'll make it up to you. You can have whatever weddin' you want. We could honeymoon in Tahiti! Whatever. We'll go tomorrow and get you a ring... get us rings." He corrected himself, emphasizing "us", smiling dreamily at her.

"Nothing big, Clay..." She drifted off in thought, "Just image little Joshua in a tux!" She gasped, her mind wandering back to wedding thoughts.

"Yup. And you in a pretty white dress with flowers

in your hair..." He pulled her back down to him and kissed her hard. "I can't wait." He ran his fingers through her long hair and let it fall across his chest.

"Can't wait to get married?"

"Yeah." He nuzzled her neck and raised a shiver from her, "You know what comes with that?"

"Shameful. Shameful man." She poked his side with her finger and he squirmed away from her a little. "Your momma's gonna know what you're up to in here." She chided.

"Shh. It's bedtime and she's sleepin'." Clay sighed loudly, "You 'spose the kids will be okay with me being... you know..."

"Their dad?"

"It feels presumptuous to say..."

"I think they adore you. You don't even know how uninvolved and cold Tim could be towards them. And you're so..." She searched his face, "You're just so in tune. And caring. If they don't love you already they'll learn to. I'm not at all worried about it."

"Wow. I woke up this mornin' all by myself. But here I am goin' to bed all attached." He kissed her again and paused to smell her hair.

"Where do you stay when you're on the road? And when do you leave again? I need to pack for me and the kids when you get the car done." She was already thinking of what it would take to live like gypsies for a few months. Kelli tried to imagine what that life would be like for the kids, but she couldn't really.

He chuckled wickedly, snapping her out of her thoughts. "The car is done."

"What?"

He broke out into a muffled laugh as she punched him in the stomach playfully, "It's finished already! I finished it while you were makin' dinner with Momma! Ow! Quit!"

"You had this whole thing planned! You liar!" She punched him again, devilishly.

"Ow... OW!" He grabbed her wrists and held them tight, "Maybe most of it. I just wanted you out of that damn trailer and where I knew you were safe. I swear I haven't slept a full night since I left."

She stretched back out on him and hid her face against his neck. "Why?" She whispered.

"'Cause I worry somethin' awful about you. There's about eight seconds every few days when you're not the first thing on my mind..."

"No, I mean *why*? Why me?"

"Dang, woman. Why not?" He glanced down at her and saw she wasn't satisfied with his answer. "Because I said so, that's why." He stated matter-of-factually, wrapping her tight in another embrace.

"That's not really an explanation, though. I don't know how you can just make your mind up like that. You don't even know me, we don't even know each other. "

Clay's eyes unfocused a little and his hand cautiously skirted under the hem of her shirt as he thought about it.

"You gonna marry me on Monday?" He asked deadly serious, suddenly seeing her again.

Kelli nodded; courses of energy surging out from her stomach where his hand was slowly exploring.

"Come're, Girl. Come're and let's get to know each other a little. Let's just be us a minute."

-CHAPTER EIGHT-

The air was hazy with dust and the smell of livestock. The closed-roof stadium was almost full with spectators who watched the unfolding events below with beers in their hands and trays of nachos on their knees. Sticky faced children with cotton candy fingers hopped around charged with sugar and excitement. The din of hundreds of people talking at once hummed behind the reverberating voice of the announcer over the loud speakers. Ruby and Joshua stood with their mother against the short concrete wall at the bottom of the seating, staring at the bull pens and cowboys on horseback shortly beyond. Their eyes were as big as saucers. Every event was just as exciting as the last for them.

"Oh Mommy! Look at all the cowboys!" Ruby cried breathlessly staring at a group of hat-and-chaps wearing men on horseback on the other side of the barriers. One older man smiled sweetly at them and waved and Ruby returned it with triple the enthusiasm. He laughed.

"That! That! Horsie!" Joshua cried. Clay had bought both the kids cowboy hats and Joshua wore his proudly, even though it nearly sat on his nose.

They had been on the road for over four weeks and had just that afternoon made it into South Carolina. Clay only did the one event, so he didn't need to haul a horse. He'd been used to flying to the longer distanced events, but with the sudden addition of a family they'd settled for driving to all of them. In the end it was incredibly less expensive, though he wrestled with getting a motor home every time they struck out on the highway. The other participants that brought family along for the ride drove enormous rigs the size of Manhattan apartments.

Kelli very much did not want to be at the rodeo. Not because she didn't like the sport; she wasn't any more immune to the energy that sparked through the air than anyone else in the stadium. She simply felt nauseous with dread having to be there where Clay could be breathing his last dusty breath. It had been fun the first few times, but the sick sinking dread crept in after the first couple nights. It got worse with every rodeo they showed up to. She usually waited at the motel, but they had gotten in so late that there was no time for him to drop them off before getting ready for his ride. They were only halfway through the night's events and there was a good amount of time left to waste.

She spotted Clay walking past one of the tunneled entrances to the lower level under the cement rise of seats; where the participants staged events and prepared for their sports. He was swaggering along with a group of fellow riders. He stood nearly a head above them all. She'd overheard people talking about how he was too tall for a bull rider at her first rodeo. The men had been amazed that he was able to be small and quick enough when there was so much more to him for the bull to catch. It seemed to be a common theme concerning him at every event. Many wondered openly about his next fall or injury. And it only compounded her dread.

He doubled back with a couple of his buddies and waved at her from across the arena. She waved and blew him a kiss and his friends on either side slapped his back as they sauntered out of sight below the seats. She felt a new sense of pride knowing that he had likely told them of their marriage and he had the reward of his buddies approval. If he approved, and they approved, she must be quite the catch. It was an interesting thought to ponder.

She twisted the big diamond band on her finger thoughtfully. Every night, at least once, he had someone he was excited to introduce her to. And every night she received a rash of lavish compliments and stunned reviews of awe from the people that knew Clay. He was like a child with treasure, and everyone else seemed excited and jealous for him. It made her feel ten feet tall, though she felt she was the one who had won the prize. Clay's flaws existed, just like any man, but compared to what she had known previously they shrank to unnoticeable sizes when stacked against his merits.

Kelli left the kids against the railing and sat back down in their bottom row seats. Her cell phone said it was already nearly nine at night. The kids were exhausted from the long drive from the last venue four long states away. They'd been forced to drive it almost clear through. Clay had mercifully gotten a cheap hotel room for a measly six hours to break up the nearly 24 hour drive; that had been last night. In all honesty she was exhausted from the long drive herself, but the pulling rush of adrenaline from the unfinished event gave her the jitters.

Her phone began vibrating and jingling in her pocket. She pulled it back out and checked the number. It was Tim. She ignored the call and stuffed it back in her back pocket. The cowboy on horseback beyond the divider moved his horse to the end of the taller panels and let it stick its head over the metal bars of the fence there. He beckoned the kids over and waved nicely to Kelli after catching her eye, asking silently if this horse-petting arrangement was okay. She smiled and watched as the stocky brown cow pony eagerly reached its velvet muzzle down for the kids to pat.

Again her phone sprang to life and she pulled it out to look at the number. It was Tim again. He'd left her a voice message before, her phone told her, but he called again anyway. She crammed it into her pocket and jumped a little as Clay unexpectedly pressed his lips into the side of her neck. He swung over the seats and flopped into the chair next to her.

"Hey, Girl." He said smoothly, wrapping his arm around her shoulders and pulling her against him.

She kissed his cheek. "How much longer until you ride?"

"Oh, 'bout twenty minutes."

"Which bull did you pull?" She glanced over at the deceptively quiet bulls chewing their cud and licking each other in the bull pens.

"Another Menace." He pointed his finger from where his hand was draped over her shoulder, "The big black one over there. He ain't so bad. I haven't had him yet. He scores low most of the time and just 'bout everyone gets their eight seconds on him."

"Are you going to the after party tonight?" Her phone buzzed annoyingly in her pocket and she pulled it out again. It was Tim, for the third time.

"And miss a minute with you?" Clay glanced over her shoulder at the phone. "Who's callin'?"

"Tim, this is the third time he's called in the last two minutes. He left me some messages but I haven't listened to them." She considered the phone in her grip.

"You should answer it." He said passively, the arena echoing with cheers and talking.

Kelli pressed the talk button and put the phone to her ear.

"Hello?" She said loudly over the volume of screaming rodeo goers.

"Where the hell are you? Where are my kids?!" Tim spat out at her.

"We're out."

"Why is it so damn loud?" He growled, swearing at her, "Where are you?"

"We're at the rodeo." She said, trying to be loud

enough for him to hear, "And stop swearing at me, Tim, you sound drunk. Are you drinking again?"

"With that damn dog of yours? What's his name... Dirt?" He snarled more foul insults at her.

"Clay. Yes with Clay."

Clay pulled the phone away from her and stuck it to his own ear, listening to the reply before she had a chance to hear it. She couldn't tell what was being said, but she could hear the tiny muffled sounds of his shouting through the earpiece, even against Clay's head.

"Hey, Tim. This is Clay. How you been buddy?" Clay paused while the growling hiss resumed on the other line. "Actually I am glad you called.

Kelli watched him as he rolled his eyes listening to her ex's drunken tirade. He bent down and kissed her forehead while he continued to listen to Tim. With his wide black hat, dusty blue and black chaps and dirt covered hands he was her shimmering hero.

"Mmhmm. Alright buddy." He paused to scratch the scruff on his jaw before he went on casually, "Listen, I want you to know, you call this number again and make *my* woman listen to *your* filthy mouth, *I* promise you I'll hunt you down and pull your asshole through your throat quicker than you can decide which direction I'm come'n from. That's a promise, you got that?" Tim had quieted down and she could no longer hear him when Clay waited for him to speak. "Okay bud, remember that promise, now. Here's Kelli." He handed her the phone and she spoke into it.

"Tim?" There was a quiet pause on the other line, then a long breath.

"How are the kids?" Tim's rough voice asked, somewhat sobered and deflated. Tim had always been a coward when it came down to it. He'd puff himself up, maybe take a swing or two, but in the long run he was scared of just about everything and everyone.

"They're great. Having a blast. Clay bought them cowboy hats and he's promised them cowboy boots next chance he gets to find some that small."

"Can I talk to them?"

"Well, they're kinda busy, Tim. And they have such a hard time understanding the situation. How about if I send you a picture with my phone?"

Tim sighed deeply, sounding defeated and somehow more like himself. "That'd be great." He cleared his throat a little, and she heard him take a swig from a bottle, "So I guess things are heating up for you two. I thought there was nothing between you and this guy."

"I didn't realize there was so much something between me and Clay. We're going to have a wedding later this year. I am happy about it. So are the kids. "

"Huh." He said, a little haughty. He was harder to hear since the event had ended and country music blared as trucks hauled out people with rakes to prepare the dirt for the next participants.

"Well I have to go, Clay's about to ride."

She heard the unmistakable draw and squeak of smoke being pulled from a cigarette on the other line. "Ride huh?"

"Yeah, he's riding in the PBR this year. It's his last season."

"Sounds like a big venue, sure is loud." He exhaled through his mouth. A few seconds earlier he had briefly sounded like himself, now the vision of him doing something as foreign as smoking and drinking gave a weird eerie feeling behind his voice. "Is it televised?"

"I dunno. Probably, most of them are. I think the posters said it was live tonight."

She heard him surfing channels on the television. "You're starting to talk like him, you know. I suppose that's considered endearing." There was the sound of him drag another puff of smoke. "So, drinking *and* smoking. You're in quite the tail spin, Tim. Are you okay?"

"You don't know the half of it." He paused a second, "Oh look, here it is. Greenville, South Carolina."

"Yup. Well, look hard, maybe you can see us. I gotta go."

"I'm watching. You know Kelli, you should sleep with one eye open. You're a long way from home, Baby."

Kelli's skin crawled. "What's that supposed to mean?"

He took another loud puff off his cigarette, "Nothing. Good night, Sweetheart."

She ended the call feeling slimy and gross. Clay, ever intuitive, picked up on it.

"Did he give you trouble?"

"No. He just sounds weird." She wiped her palms down her lap as if they were dirty just from talking to Tim.

She glanced at the kids. They were still petting the horse, who had been joined by one of the other event participants and a few more children. They were here, together. It didn't matter what devils Tim was facing, she told herself. But it still added to the overall unsettled feeling in her gut.

"It's nothing." She assured herself just as much as him.

Clay's hand turned her face to his and he kissed her, slowly. "Don't let him talk to you like that again. If he acts up you lemme know. I'll take care of it."

She smiled and nodded. "He's no trouble, Clay. Really. He's all growl and bark."

"A coward can be dangerous enough if he's cornered. Or thinks he is, I suppose." He pulled her up with him as he jumped to his feet and wrapped her in his arms.

"Gotta go dance with a bull."

"Promise you'll be careful." She begged him. He

kissed her another time and nodded.

"Yup." He flashed his silly smile over his shoulder at her as he marched off.

Ruby jumped down from the tubular fencing she had climbed to pat the horses and ran after him as he passed.

"Cowboy!"

He spun on his heel and knelt down as she ran up to him.

Kelli couldn't hear their little conversation over the rising din of elated onlookers. Clay smiled as he listened, nodding sincerely, and then laughed a little. Ruby talked animatedly, obviously trying to be fast. Finally she was finished and ran back to the horse heads resting over the panels. Clay smiled at Ruby and Joshua and then after tipping his hat at Kelli walked off towards one of the lower level passages.

Already the first rider was spilling out of the chute on a big brown bull. Their seats were so close to the action that she could hear the grunts of the animal as its feet ricocheted off the ground. Streams of mucus trailed from its nose and mouth and its hind feet flung dirt out in all directions. Ruby and Joshua had run back to their seats next to Kelli to take in the awesome sight. Joshua stood up on his chair and bobbed with the hinged seat, screaming along with the crowd around him. Ruby sat quietly with wide eyes throwing her hands onto her head and cringing as the rider flew from the animal's back and scrambled in the dirt to climb out of its reach on a nearby fence section.

Kelli realized she had grown tense with anticipation and uncertainty. She relaxed a little and blew out a long breath she'd been subconsciously holding. She was getting a grasp on the scoring used for the game. 100 was perfect, but no one had ever really scored that before. The points were split between the bull's performance and the riders ability. This particular pair had scored an 82.72, which was a pretty decent score. She clapped with the kids who stood and cheered with those around them.

She'd forgotten to ask Clay what order the rides were in, so she wasn't sure who was left before him. Her eyes kept scanning the catwalk behind the chutes for signs of his vest and chaps. He wasn't there yet. She was torn between hiding in the bathroom and supporting the man she loved. She'd only stayed for one of his other events, the first one on the road, back in Atlanta. He'd landed so hard on the ground dismounting she had cringed in wonder as to how his spine hadn't been broken in half from the impact. He had hopped up entirely unharmed though, but it had still made her physically ill for the rest of that evening. She'd guiltily hid in the bathroom with the kids at the other events until his ride was over hovering near a trash can, her stomach lurching with sick anticipation.

Two more riders took their turns before she noticed Clay standing with his feet on either side of the chute eyeballing the huge black bull hidden by an advertisement on the red metal gate below him. A team of men were on both sides shoving and prodding the animal, feeding Clay's rope under the bull's armpits. The animal was leaning against the gate so tight he couldn't squeeze his leg down alongside it. One of the men helping grabbed a fist full of the bull's loose hide and twisted it clear around. The animal kicked and lurched forward, turning its awful head into the gate in retaliation of the irritating pinch. It all made an enormous clanging. Finally Clay was able to find a seat across the wide shoulders of his mount.

Another few moments of settling in, wiggling and resettling found him repeating his familiar gripping ritual with the rope. He pounded his fingers shut when he was satisfied with the grasp. He slid back and forth a little before nodding his helmeted head frantically.

Kelli squinted and bit her lip hard. The bull flew out of the chute, overwhelmingly ticked off; as if a hornet had stung under its tail. She could see the red in its eyes and hear its low huffing grunts as it leaped and spun to the right repeatedly. Clay held on, his face twisted into a horrible gaze within the confines of the protective wire mesh of his helmet. The bull landed forward and jumped back up with barely enough time to touch the ground. Clay threw his raised left arm impossibly far behind him as his face and chest came precariously close to the neck and head of the animal. He managed to keep from touching it somehow and at the sound of the buzzer prepared to slide off the animal's backside.

Something went wrong in the fraction of a second between turning the rope loose and rolling backward. The bull flung its hind legs into the air unexpectedly, throwing Clay forward. He bounced shoulder first into the bull's head and rolled onto the ground. Rodeo clowns swarmed the bull even as its terrible head fell onto Clay's legs. Clumps of dirt flew in all directions, flung up by both the bulls feet and Clay's hands. The nearly one ton cow scraped its head along the man's body and trampled over him as it lunged for one of the brightly painted bull fighters.

Kelli screamed, pulling her children to her and covering their faces. Everything she had dreaded seemed to be unfolding before her.

"Please, God, no!" She screamed again.

Men on horses surrounded the bull and encouraged him through the open gate at the end of the arena. A team of paramedics and men in big cowboy hats collected around Clay's motionless body. The announcer narrated the fall, recounting it for the audience, as thought they had all not just witnessed it themselves. The paramedic's arms flew about as they checked him over. They rolled him onto his back and then were suddenly unmoving for a few moments. Kelli ran to the fence and leaned out, struggling to hear anything, or see something, but she was unable. Her heart was surely about to burst from beating so uncontrollably. The smell of dust and people swirled around her along with the huge crowded space, making her dizzy and sick. Her head grew thick and her thoughts clouded before she realized she was hyperventilating.

A hush fell on the stadium. All eyes watched the pile of men encircling the fallen rider. *Her* fallen rider. Suddenly there was movement. The men backed away from Clay, and one of the paramedics reached his hand down and pulled him to his feet.

Clay stood and eased his helmet off. He leaned over a little and took a few hard breaths; an arm wrapped around his ribs, and shook his head at one of the questions the EMT asked. After a short moment he carefully undid the Velcro on his vest and pulled it off, wincing. He nodded at the paramedic and stood straighter. He rose his hand to the crowd and waved.

Like a bomb exploding, the place erupted with cheers. The announcer yelled into the microphone, causing the speakers above them all to sputter and hum wildly.

"It looks like Clay Tackett has faced the bull and dodged major injury! This is truly amazing folks! We feared the worst. Mr. Tackett you take care of yourself, now."

Clay looked at the man on the stand along the side of the arena and waved, nodding. The paramedics held him by the upper arms and helped him limp off the field.

"Let's get that score up before he leaves the area here boys. Come on judges and judge that ride." The announcer called as the scoreboard lit up. "Ninety-ONE! Whoo! Tackett is on a ROLL this season! That's the best score I've ever called" He chuckled the last to himself and the people in the stands cheered.

With some small relief she looked on as Clay climbed into the back of an awaiting ambulance at the far end of the arena. She could barely see him through the forest of pens and men on horses. A pair of EMT's and a few of the people in charge of the event crowded around him again. Kelli fought the urge to run to him through the dirty brown corral between them. Instead she bit her lip ever harder and watched from the wide distance. He leaned over from the gurney and pointed in her direction, calling the attention of one of the men there talking to him. She waved slightly, looking with trepidation as they eased the gurney into the back of the flashing vehicle.

A middle aged man jogged to the fence and climbed over, landing with a heavy footfall on the cement walkway at the far end of the arena from her. She grabbed up the kids and walked towards him, hoping he was coming for her and not something else. At length he reached them and took her by the arm, bending down to her ear so she could hear him. Until that moment she had completely blocked out the roar of the crowd over the new rider that was dancing atop another huge brown bull for their entertainment.

"They're taking him up to Saint Francis to take some x- rays." The man said through a thick, graying, mustache.

"Oh my God, is he okay?" She panted with fear and exertion, trying to keep up with his long strides.

"Nothing major." He produced a set of keys from his pocket and handed them to her. "He said for you to follow me over there, so you can wait on him at the ER. He also said he's sorry he wasn't more careful." He handed them to her.

"Nothing major." She repeated to herself. She glanced down and noticed Ruby had fat tears running down her cheeks as she ran awkwardly beside her.

Kelli grabbed the man's sleeve and handed Joshua over to him, scooping Ruby up into her arms as she charged along beside the stranger.

"It's okay, Baby, Clay's alright."

"But I love Cowboy, Mommy. I don't want him to be hurt." She sobbed and choked on her words.

"Well, me either Honey. But grown up men make their own choices." She felt relieved and infuriated at the same time.

What was she doing? Subjecting her children to this spectacle, working them up into a frenzy of elation and fearful dread and tears. What was she doing to herself? As relaxed as she was being with Clay all the time, and as much as it simplified her life, she felt as though she was spiraling out of control into some overwhelming thing she couldn't describe. This lifestyle was foreign not only to her, but also to the kids. They'd never even seen a bull until Clay came along.

Her stomach hurt almost constantly. She still felt sick, and her head hurt terribly by dinnertime most days. And with the passing of each event she found herself more often at the base of a toilet throwing up with dread over it all. She wanted to touch Clay, to see that he was okay; to feel the heat from his body and feel the breath from his lungs and know that all was right with the little world they were creating around themselves.

And she also wanted to slap him and yell at him. And cry. And maybe even throw up again. She wanted to not be uprooted. She felt the need to be nested and still, to shelter the kids and be in a home. To have Clay near her and for all of them to be safe and unmoving in daily routines that suited them. Had she uprooted their lives again for the selfish sake of her own happiness? She glanced at the kids. How was this time on tour going to affect them in the long run? She shouldered through an exit, trying to quiet her mind and focus on the issue at hand.

The man who had introduced himself only as "Walker" left her at Clay's big black truck in the overfilled parking lot. She set to work packing the kids into their seats as he retrieved his own vehicle. Kelli climbed into the driver's seat. She felt like she was swimming in the machine. It was huge. A million times bigger feeling than her little sedan. For a moment she wondered if she could even drive it without scraping it against things or plowing over other cars or people. Let alone manage the big standard transmission.

Kelli turned the key in the ignition and felt the huge engine roar to life as Walker pulled up in his gleaming white Ford. She adjusted her seat, wondering how Clay could ever have such long legs in the first place to even reach the pedals from where she began. She stared at the long shifter on the floor. It'd been more than decade since she'd driven a standard. And that had been her dad's small sports car that he had bought in the throws of a mid-life crisis.

She pushed her seat forward more and stuffed in the clutch, popping the truck into first gear. It sprang into motion. Carefully, she navigated the parking lot and eased the beast out onto the road, saying a silent thankful prayer that she hadn't needed to back out of the tight sparking space. Kelli plugged along behind her navigator and after nearly half an hour veered off the freeway and into the vast hospital parking lot. She slipped into a space way in back. It was clear on both sides and afforded her some grace for pulling the unfamiliar wide truck in.

Walker parked nearby before helping her get the kids into the towering brick hospital. Inside the waiting room she stood impatiently at the reception window waiting for the woman there to acknowledge her. Walker sat quietly with her exhausted children in some chairs beside a big window. There was a table of toys beneath it, but the kids were spent from the traveling and excitement, and Ruby's little eyes were red from crying. They shared a seat next to Walker and held each other sleepily.

"Name." The old woman behind the glass finally looked up at her.

"I'm here to see my husband- he just came in on an ambulance." She whispered, thinking a few seconds later that saying 'husband' felt like the most natural thing she'd ever done.

"Name." The woman repeated, her fingers poised over the keyboard of her computer.

"Clayton Tackett. T-A-C-K-E-double-T." Kelli recited.

The woman considered her screen and clicked the mouse. She slid her chair across the small space and called around the corner to a colleague, "Where'd they unload that rodeo bus?"

"Thirteen, but I think he's in radiology." A man's voice replied.

The woman wheeled herself back to her desk and pulled a yellow band from a roll of bracelets sticking out of a row of similar cardboard boxes. There were various colored bands, some fed into a printer and others were brightly colored and blank. The place smelled like rubbing alcohol and echoed with coughs and moans. The beige walls of the waiting room were stained and the paint was chipping in places. And there were marks on the floor like polka-dots from where people's shoes had scuffed here and there.

"I'll just need to see your ID." The woman said, as though bemused with everything.

Kelli offered her her license and the woman made a copy of it at a nearby printer and after jotting "VISITOR" in capital letters on the yellow band and affixed it to Kelli's wrist. Kelli hadn't been to such a large hospital before, but it did seem like a lot of fuss just to get into the emergency room.

"He's in thirteen, or will be again shortly if he's not now. I'll buzz you in."

Kelli turned to her children, but found they had drifted off to sleep in the chair. She looked at Walker, and then at Ruby and Joshua. She wasn't sure what to do. She'd never met him before, although his face was familiar. She'd seen Clay talking to him many times. She wasn't sure but she thought maybe it was him that had congratulated them before one of the rodeos that first week. But that week had been a blur and she hardly remembered anyone she'd been introduced to.

"It's okay, Ma'am, I'll sit here with them. You go on in, if they wake up I'll bring them to you." Walker whispered loudly through his big mustache. Kelli felt torn, but she decided it was safe enough.

She wound her way through the maze of curtain enclosed spaces beyond the waiting room door. Triage was slow. It was already after ten at night, and apparently it was a quiet night. There were a few people laying silently in the tall beds under white hospital-smelling sheets. A mother and son were in one room, the young boy held a bloody patch of gauze to his head; little stains of blood spatters peppered the legs of his baseball uniform. Things beeped without any rhythm and nurses looked at charts and spok unnervingly quiet to each other.

Finally she found thirteen. The curtain was pulled. Kelli called Clay's name softly as she pushed it open and slipped in. She found him there. His left arm was puffed up to nearly twice its size and he had a huge busted lip and a gash above his eyebrow. He lay with his eyes closed in the bed. There were no tubes or hoses attached to him, aside from a vitals monitor clipped to his right forefinger. She assured herself he was fine, but she still felt dizzy with emotion seeing him unresponsive in the bed.

After a few moments of deep breaths she sat down on the edge of the mattress and watched as his dark eyes opened slowly.

"They give me lots of meds." He slurred sleepily, grinning slightly when he realized she was there.

"Are you okay?" She asked, holding his good hand in hers. She patted his thigh and noticed that his left leg was swollen below the knee.

"Yup. Dislocated and sprained a shoulder, and got a little sprain in the knee." He rolled his head drunkenly and nodded at the hurt appendages.

The walls seemed to boil at the thought of what could have been and she lunged for a nearby garbage can, emptying her already empty stomach. Kelli coughed and gagged as she dry heaved. She stood back up and looked down at herself, feeling as though her body was foreign and under some other control besides her own. She was positive there was nothing more unsettling than throwing up. Clay sat up and swung his legs over the side of the bed lethargically; awkwardly. She pushed him back before he could try to stand.

"You okay? Girl? Throwin' up and stuff..." He slurred his question at her, speaking slow.

"Yeah. No. I don't know what happened."

"It's been exciting." He laid back down on the bed. And hugged his arm to his side.

She felt terrible for how she felt, on top of just feeling plain terrible. She had wanted to be with him, had even cried about it. She'd willingly agreed to come along and be part of this aspect of his life. But now she dreaded it. She felt like she was being cheap and fickle. Like she had become everything a man hates to be bound to in a woman. It was as though she'd failed to meet that high mark Clay and his family had of her. But she just couldn't stand to keep her word either.

"I can't do this Clay. I just can't. I've been sick for weeks. All this worry eats me up, and now you're laying here in this hospital bed..." She started crying.

He pulled the clip from his finger and reached his

only good hand up to her face. The monitor buzzed and beeped furiously beside him. "Baby, don't cry, don't be sad." He said, his eyes half closed.

"I'm not sad, Clay. I'm... angry. With myself. With everything." She whispered, "With you."

His eyes snapped open and cocked his head at her. "With me?! Wud I do? I do what I do." He humphed a little to himself. "This is what I do."

"I'm not watching you do this anymore, Clay. I'll go home and wait for November to get here. There's only a few more weeks left."

"Aww Girl, don't go. I'll be okay. Really I'm fine. It just looks bad, plus the drugs." His eyes closed again slowly, as though he didn't have enough energy to accomplish both looking and speaking at the same time.

Kelli could tell he was forcing himself to talk clearly. It slowed him down comically. His eyes opened a little and he ran his fingers through his hair, scratching his head lazily as he went.

She was still so confused and sick. Mostly sick. She felt she could trust that she was the most important person in his life, but she failed to see why that paled in comparison to trying to get himself killed by an infuriated one ton animal multiple times every week. Why couldn't he just leave this thing behind and settle down with the family he had now? And why couldn't she just support him and see it through like she promised?

A nurse flew in through the curtain and frowned at the discovery of the abandoned monitor clip. She tried to put it back on but Clay waved his hand away from her and shook his head. The short black haired woman searched through the nearby cabinets and pulled a blue fabric sling from a drawer instead.

"I'm glad you're fine Clay, but sitting around waiting and watching for this to happen..." She trailed off. "Ruby and Joshua saw the whole thing. Ruby's exhausted herself crying. She thought for sure you were dead, and then she was ate up with worry that you were hurt bad."

"The swelling's gone down enough now, Sir, let me just slip your arm in this sling." The nurse interrupted.

Clay nodded at her, but watched Kelli as she continued to speak. "I don't have any money, at least not enough to get back on. You'll have to buy us some plane tickets, Clay." She scooted a little closer to him, "I promise I'll count the hours until you come home. Call me this time though, okay? And I'll call you?"

He stared at her dumb-struck. As though he'd just been whacked upside the head with an invisible bat. "But... I thought this was workin' great." He had sobered up a little bit out of unspoken despair.

"Honey, it's working great for you. The kids are exhausted from being so uprooted. I'm sick with worry all the time..."

"You said you'd finish the whole circuit, that's what you said." His eyes narrowed a little under his knit brow, which suddenly looked not so soft.

"I did. But I didn't know what I was getting into, Clay. This is your life, not mine. Not ours. I don't know it. You know I hate this rodeo stuff. I hate wondering if you're walking away from it or being carried out in a hearse. And I didn't realize how hard it'd be on the kids- they're just babies really, and traveling all the time like this is so hard on them..." She looked at him pleadingly, "Don't make me feel guilty for it all on top of it." She wished they were alone and her eyes flicked occasionally to the nurse who was the third wheel to the conversation.

They hadn't had any time alone since setting out on the road. They were always either in the truck with the kids or at the event. Even at night he often had to creep in after the children were asleep and eased himself into one of the empty hotel beds while Kelli curled up with the kids in her own. If he did happen to be with her the kids were always present. There had been no rekindling of the fire they had lit that night on the ranch. Although the sparks flew any time they happened to brush against one another or make eye contact.

He looked at her now like a man wandering into the desert and leaving behind an oasis.

"Maybe if we bought a camper..."

"Clay..." Kelli's voice pulled tight.

"If you want to go home, Girl, I'll get you there." His words were kind but his face looked angry with her. She wanted to fall on him crying and beg him to have some sort of mercy on her. To understand that she was pulled in a dozen different directions and the last thing she wanted was to upset or disappoint him. He was her savior through it all. She shivered a little.

"Please Clay, don't be angry with me."

"Darnit, Kelli, I'm not angry with you." He pulled himself up in the bed a little bit, pressing the button on the buzzer that laid on the bed beside him. "I just can't be in two places at once. I don't like leavin' you alone."

"Well you did a fine job doing just that before!" Kelli spat out. She covered her mouth in surprise and looked at him with big eyes. She started to apologize but he interrupted her.

"I ain't fightin' with you, Sweetheart." He said, brushing her shoulder with the palm of his hand. The nurse slipped back in to answer the call, "Get this knee patched up or I'm walking out of here like it is."

"Sir the doctor will be with you in just a moment." The woman tried to assure him.

"In a moment he'll have an empty bed with another person who can wait to see 'em. Now or never, woman." He sent here away, her white nurse shoes squeaking.

"Clay don't..." Kelli tried soothing him. He wasn't exactly angry, just intense and powerful, even if he was laying busted up in a hospital bed.

"I gotta be in Tennessee by tomorrow night or I'll not make it to the next venue. We better get a move on if we're gonna to get you to the airport and on your way in time."

"You can't ride again Clay! How on earth will you manage that?"

"I've done it before, little ice and some pain pills and I'll be good as new for the rodeo night after next." He stumbled from the bed and it jiggled under her as he left it.

A little bald headed man with an Indian accent slipped through the curtain, catching him in the act.

"Mr. Tackett. If we can just get you to have a seat I'll look over your chart here and have you on your way." The d o c t o r pressed his hand against Clay's broad chest, easing him back into the bed.

Clay sat, defiant, unwilling to lay back down completely, as if obeying was worse than the pain of sitting. The doctor mumbled to himself as he read through the chart he had pulled from the end of the bed. He clicked through a few windows on the computer that rested on a wheeled tray nearby. Finally he searched through the drawers and pulled out three blue colored foam braces of varying sizes. He laid them each against Clay's leg until he found the one he was satisfied with.

"There's no torn ligaments or muscles. The tendons look good. No broken bones or hairline fractures. Not even a dislocation. You're a lucky man, most people would have a lasting injury from this sort of accident." He took the brace from its crinkly plastic packaging and undid the Velcro that fastened it. "How did you say this happened?"

"Fell off an angry bull." Clay winced as the doctor applied the brace and set it in place, locking it there with the straps.

"Mmhmm." The doctor said. He turned to the computer, "I'm going to print you off a couple prescriptions for some pain killers and muscle relaxers in case the knee or shoulder start knotting up on you. Avoid any strenuous activities for at least a week." He pulled open a tall cupboard and produced a pair of crutches. "Visit your primary care physician to follow up with your progress in four days."

"No thanks, I'll walk." He said, turning them down.

Clay lumbered out of the emergency room, dragging is left leg behind him. Kelli felt s h a m e f u l l y ignored and unwanted, as though he had turned a cold shoulder to her. The patient slow man she loved was overtaken by purposeful movements and silent resolve. At any moment he'd leave her, just like she feared. Just like Tim. She could almost hear him placing the puzzle pieces of her together, almost feel his disappointment with the overall picture.

Had they rushed in too fast, that was the problem. No one really spends forever together, especially in such small quarters after only a handful of days spent together, do they? Yet even now, as she carried sleeping Joshua, Ruby clung to Clay's fingers and he let her try to help him along, even though it was obviously more of a painful hindrance than a help. It pained her heart to watch them because it seemed so natural. Time had never possessed patience for the kids, especially not when he was sick or injured. Clay seemed so careful and genuinely interested in the kids. Fatherly even. Her children appeared to genuinely matter to him.

"I don't want to go home, Cowboy." Ruby cried as Clay buckled her into her car seat behind his own. He leaned against the open door frame and laid his head on his hand as he listened to her. "You didn't even buy me my boots yet." She pouted furiously, on the very verge of an exhausted tantrum.

Clay chucked her under the chin, "Don't worry, Ruby. Cowboy'll get you your boots. Pretty pink ones with rhinestones in them."

"I want black ones like yours. Only, with pretties in them, too." She still pouted, but was placated temporarily.

He patted her little leg. "It's gonna be alright, Little Girl." He crooned, "Hey, you get to fly in a big airplane! Think about that."

Kelli had climbed into the passenger seat and stared at her hands in her lap; all the while her stomach coiled tighter on itself. She was obsessively concerned about it, on top of everything else. Her middle had been bothering her ever since the stress of the divorce, it had not gotten much better, but it hadn't been much worse either. Until now. She tried to convince herself it was only stress, that being home, even if it was a sad little trailer in the cloudy stench of the oily railroad, would make her feel better. And it would be best for her exhausted children.

Clay had finally calmed Ruby's fears and slid into his own seat.

"Are you okay to drive? With the meds and all?" She asked quietly.

"Yup." He turned the engine over, "They don't last long, it was mostly just so's they could get the x-rays without me screamin' like a little girl." He still hadn't looked at her, though his voice had softened measurably.

It took him a minute to get the hang of driving the stick shift with one arm while steering with his good knee. And he winced horribly shifting gears as his bad leg was forced to press the clutch down. Kelli looked away before they even made it from the parking lot. It pained her too much to watch him.

They drove around a little while. Clay got lost at one point after Kelli pointed out that they were headed out of town instead of into it on the freeway. The street lights over the highway illuminated the truck cab and then slipped into darkness again on an endless cycle. The little cracks in the roadway pounded out a rhythm through the tires. Clay smelled like leather and dust and animal dander. And hospital. Kelli thought about her churning stomach again. Her neck pulled and her throat tightened, threatening to cough up whatever it could produce from her empty stomach. It took all her concentration to calm it.

The thought occurred to her suddenly that she had felt this way before. Twice. She counted days in her head, but forgot what the date was today and what it had been last time. She pulled her phone from her pocket and opened its calendar program and counted back to her last period. Suddenly everything began to swim around her with a vengeance. She was a full week late, that very day. She'd been so caught up in the bliss of her and Clay's new life and plans that she had never considered that their one night of excited, unprotected, sex would produce a pregnancy. She'd fought so hard to get pregnant with Tim, she hadn't realized it could be so easy. She slid her phone shut and stuck it back in her pocket and stared out the window. She felt doubly tired at the possibility and longed for home; for stillness.

The marriage had been little more than an exchanging of generic vows. They didn't even use rings, other than her engagement band, since they were keeping it secret. And a secret was easy to forget. The state would easily nullify a union so short-lived. She hadn't even filed to change her last name. All Clay had to do was disappear.

In the silence; in the dark; it felt like they were falling apart. Her new found confidence in this man was so shallow, a painful consequence of having been betrayed by another. She thought of Tim's weird advice before he had ended their call that night. The safe security that had built up around her started to crumble back in on her all over again. She closed her eyes and tried to ignore her sick stomach and her reeling head. She had no way to survive pregnancy and delivery alone. If Clay left her she'd be unable to afford anything; she'd quit her job without notice and was certain they'd not take her back. She *had* to work, but babies had a very distinct way of making that nearly impossible. And a third child. She counted months on her fingers. She'd have three children all under five years old. If Clay left her like Tim, like it felt he would, she'd be utterly destitute.

No.

She stopped her head from thinking. She was tired. Sick and tired and stressed. That was enough to make her skip a menstrual cycle.

But the knowledge tickled her mind mercilessly. Surely Clay would come to his senses and tell her what they did was a mistake. He's ask her to sign annulment papers. He'd wish her well in his nice, kind, voice and leave. The possibility of a baby might only send him over that edge. Or worse, make him prove what a good man he was by staying though he dreaded to. He'd likey go find the right woman for him; someone born into this country lifestyle. She dreaded its coming. Any moment between now and boarding the plane would be their last together. Forever. She dared not even catch her breath in her despair, if she did she'd surely vomit.

Eventually they found the signs for the airport and manged to make their way into the tangled parking lot. Ruby had fallen asleep in her car seat, joining her brother in succumbing to sleepiness. Clay reached out and pulled a ticket from the gate at the entrance of the short term parking lot in the garage by the terminals. The engine echoed thunderously off the concrete in the low ceilinged space. Near the elevator to the terminal walkway he found a parking spot and gingerly backed the big truck into it. He set the brake and turned in his seat to face her, wincing with pain as he moved. He sucked on his teeth as he thought for a few seconds.

She had a million things she wanted to say, to ask,

but instead she just looked at him in the same sorrowful way that had seemed to become her default setting with him. She hated it; hated all her troubles that bled out into his world. He rubbed his face with his free hand and sighed.

"Let me call Marty and see if he can pick you guys up from the airport." He said finally.

"If we fly out tonight he'll be at work when we land. And its a three hour round trip from Dixson from Bismark and back. We can wait at the airport..."

He thought for a minute. "I'll get you an early morning flight and a hotel here by the airport, so you can take the shuttle in the morning. And I'll reserve you a car in Bismark so you can just drive home when you get in."

"Can't you stay for a little while with us? Before we leave?" Suddenly she was crying again. She covered her face with her hands and turned to the window. "I'm sorry. God, I'm sorry. I am always crying." She stammered quickly.

"What's go'n on with you, Girl?" His voice was genuinely concerned and he reached out to pull her hands from her face.

"I don't know. It's just there's so much. And I feel so sick. I can't stand watching you do this thing Clay, it kills me. I die every time I know that you're going to ride. I know I should just keep my mouth shut and support you in this, and I want to, I really do. I just..." She took a moment to let her sobs subside a little, she was too scared to admit her biggest, newest, concern. "I just am so afraid of losing you. And I worry about the kids and how stressful it is on them... Seeing them watch that beast tear into you... You're so important to them, Clay. And their little crying faces... they were so afraid. I was afraid..."

"It's only a little while. We're down to weeks,

Honey. That's all." He injected.

She looked at him. His swollen lip and cut face. His arm in a sling and his jeans leg squished under the brace around his knee. Her eyes fell to her hands in her lap and she fumbled with her fingers absently.

"What is it?" He pleaded with her.

"Just stay with us until we leave? Please? I'm afraid you wont come home for me."

He reached his arm out for her and pulled her to him. Up close he smelled like peace to her. It was such a warm safe smell. "Girl, I am comin' home for you and not a thing on this planet can stop me."

"Tonight could have stopped you, Clay. That big black bull could have stopped you."

He kissed her head, and paused to smell her hair for a few long minutes before kissing it again. "Lemme go get things taken care of here for you, and we'll get settled into a hotel for the night." He pulled himself out of the truck with his left arm, pausing to push his hat onto his head, "Sit here with the kids, I'll be right back."

Kelli whispered "okay" and watched as he limped heavily to the elevator and disappeared.

Alone with her thoughts the nagging wondering of whether she was pregnant swooped in like a storm. She desperately loved having babies. She loved watching her belly grow and delighted in the tiny interactions between mother and unborn as it pressed against her skin and shoved its fists and feet into different places inside her. And she loved their wonderful newborn smell that only the animal part of a mother's senses can detect, and their tiny little cries and tiny clenched fists.

Part of her prayed and hoped she was pregnant. To hell with the cost and impossibility and risk of Clay leaving. Part of her prayed and hoped it was only stress and that she'd spare another tiny life the uncertainty of a fatherless childhood and abject poverty.

She wondered about Tim's last words of the day. 'Better sleep with one eye open.' All at once she couldn't stand him or his games. Most of all she dreaded leaving Clay and losing him forever. Or having him send her away, cast aside as she had been once before. But, no matter her fears, her body refused to go another day on the road.

Kelli drifted away in her thoughts about all Tim's gross, blatant flaws and the years she had lost to him. She hated his voice. The thought of it in her memory made the corner of her lip curl in disgust. She remembered the polished smell of his cologne and aftershave. He'd smelled like he had as a teenager for their whole adult lives. She considered all his brutish ways and his thick, stocky, body. He was everything Clay wasn't. Suddenly she had a new rule to measure the entire male world against, and anyone she could think of fell terribly short compared to this new husband. She loved him, and life had taught her to lose everything she cared for.

The clock on the dash clicked down the remaining minutes of the day. She closed her eyes and dozed lightly, listening to the quiet breathing of Ruby and Joshua in the back seat and the ticking whine of the idling diesel engine.

Finally the door popped open and Clay eased himself back into the truck. He sat gripping the steering wheel for a few long seconds. His face was twisted with pain and he took a series of long slow breaths; in through his nose and whooshing them out through tight lips. After collecting himself he scowled though first and second gear as he drove them out of the parking garage. He paused at the toll booths to pay for the parking; handing Kelli his wallet he had her fish out a few dollars while he pulled the parking ticket from his visor. She gave it back to him as they drove on, but he threw it on the dash, too sore to get it back into his pocket.

Finally he passed her some papers from the airline

before pulling onto the surface road around the airport. "I got you guys three seats to Bismark tomorrow morning at seven fifteen."

"Oh Clay, I forgot we'd need three seats. I am so sorry."

"It's no problem, Girl, really." He wound around some little access roads until he ended up at a small motel with a huge blue number sign perched on a metal post outside. "You'll have to take the car seats on the plane, they wont count 'em as luggage if you use 'em durin' the flight. That'll leave you room enough for checking the two big suitcases you have in back."

She nodded, looking at the passes in the little envelope. She'd only mentioned in passing once, on their way to the rodeo in North Dakota that the kids still had their father's name and not her maiden one and how she longed to change them but couldn't afford it. He'd remembered when requesting the tickets.

He left her in the truck, still staring at the tickets, and returned a few minutes later with a room key. Kelli looked around the area. She spotted only convenience store and gas station not more than half a mile down the road as she pulled the limp baby from his car seat. The area was otherwise surrounded by airport parking and gated tarmac. Clay didn't trust his strength and balance to carry Ruby in, So he instead focused on using his one good arm to haul out Kelli's two big suitcases from under the cover of the truck bed. He was still wrestling them into the ground floor room as she carried the little girl in and tucked her into one of the beds.

Clay locked the door behind them with finality. They both crashed into the other bed. Kelli didn't care about what was right for the kids in the moment, should they happen to stir and find her in his bed. They were exhausted and fast asleep in their own bed. So she crawled under the covers with Clay and tangled herself up with him as best she could around his injuries. All her fears melted away as he pulled her close.

"I'm worried about you, Darlin'." He said quietly, his stubbly face scratching the pillowcase beside her. "You're not tellin' me somethin."

"I'll be alright. When you get home I'll be alright." She was too tired to talk about anything anymore. She only dreaded leaving him in the morning.

He sighed and then his breath caught with pain as he shifted a little. His good arm was wrapped around her shoulders and his fingers combed through her hair. She wanted to taste his mouth, to feel the weight of him on her. But she settled for feeling small in his arms and drifted off to sleep, lulled there by his breathing and the smell of dusty leather and Old Spice.

-CHAPTER NINE-

After the flight, unexpected lay over, and the drive home it was past dinner time when Kelli finally pulled into town. The late summer heat had begun to brown the prairie grass and yards in the month they'd been gone. Everything smelled crisped and tired in the late day sun. She drove through downtown to the shopping area outside of the city limits. Although her and the kids were flat-out exhausted she dragged them in to pick up a few groceries and most importantly a pregnancy test. Clay had emptied his wallet of all its cash and given it to her at the airport, knowing they would need food.

"It ain't much. I'll mail you a check in a few days." He had assured her, giving her his money. It was a little over a hundred dollars. Just enough to buy gas for the drive and a few groceries. "Rent'll be due on your place here in a little over a week. It'll be there by then."

His hot mouth on hers lingered in her memory even now. The look of sadness and something like anger had crossed his brow as he watched them shuffle through airport security. Eventually he'd smiled one last time before waving and dragging himself out to his truck. He'd be halfway to Memphis by now, and although it was closer to Dixson than South Carolina she still felt as if he were on the other side of the world. Her mind had played tricks on her all day. She'd been certain she'd heard him call her name twice on the plane. And even now she caught little whiffs of Old Spice and leather even though there was nothing around to explain it. Six weeks felt like a life time, and November loomed impossibly far on the horizon.

Her phone jingled and she pulled it out and answered it. "Hey, Girl. Where you at?" Clay's smooth voice poured over her. The distance between them was suddenly magnified. It seemed cruel and impossible, cutting her to the quick.

"Just stopping at the grocery."

"You made it in alright?" She could hear the rush of his truck engine in the background and traitorously wished she was riding with him still, even if there was relief that the kids were spared the stress of constantly being on the road.

"Yeah."

"How's your stomach?" He grunted a little as he struggled to shift gears with one hand and a bum leg.

"I had to get sick on the plane." She tried not to sound worried.

"Sorry, Honey." He took a deep breath and sighed, "I miss you somethin' horrible."

"I really miss you, too. I wish you'd just come home." She turned the car into the store parking lot and slipped it into a space.

"I didn't take off that dirty shirt from the rodeo. It smells like you from sleepin' beside you all night. I don't think I have it in me to wash it."

"I swear I heard your voice today on the plane." She said, sounding regretful.

"Darlin', why don't you go out to the ranch, huh?"

"I don't think I can handle being there without you..."

"I'll be back in the area in a week, I'll come pick you up and we can spend those couple days together down at the ranch. Maybe get you settled in there."

"I'd like that. Though, I wish it was sooner." She started unbuckling the kids, "I'm at the store now, I'll call you back tonight, okay?"

"Alright, Girl." The phone scuffed against his face a little and his breath huffed noisily as he drove, "I love you, Kelli."

The tender sincerity in his voice made tears well in her eyes. "I love you, too, Clay." She managed.

Hanging up felt like severing something vital in her heart. She wished he'd come home. It felt terrible being alone in Dixson again. She wasn't even halfway through the store before she completely regretted her decision to leave him on the road. She started second guessing if it had really been too hard on the kids. They seemed to love him so much, maybe it was worse for them to be away from him entirely. Her churning stomach soon reminded her, though, that she needed to be home. Home and laying down. Hurriedly she completed her shopping task and scurried back to the waiting trailer.

The place had grown even sadder and lonelier while they were gone. She shooed the kids ahead of her as she unlocked it and hauled the bags into the kitchen with barely enough time to close the door before vomiting into a nearby trash bag. Wiping her mouth with a paper towel she rummaged through the bags on the floor. In the last one she located the little box containing a single white pregnancy test. She trotted off down the hall to the bathroom, forgetting all else in the house.

After peeing she laid it on the sink counter and exited the bathroom. She'd look at it later. After she fed the kids and put them to bed. Maybe after she called Clay. She wondered how she'd tell him. Wondered how he'd take it if she were pregnant. She feared what would become of them if she was pregnant and he was seriously harmed during a ride. Or worse, killed. At least if he did leave her she could rest assured that their child would know him. She couldn't imagine a scenario where he'd shut out his own child. A cold sweat ran like electric down her spine and she pushed the thoughts away. She was rapidly growing weary from the constant torment or worry.

In the kitchen she put the groceries away and made the kids some mac and cheese for dinner. To her horror she had found that in the time they'd been away long legged cellar spiders had moved into almost every corner along the ceiling and floor. She stared at them with disgust as she mixed up the noodles and made plates. There was no vacuum for her to suck them up with, and she was not looking forward to climbing chairs and chasing them all down with paper towels. Thinking of it made her queasy.

"I miss cowboy." Ruby whined at her plate as Kelli sat it before her.

"Cowboy. Me too." Joshua nodded.

Kelli sighed, "But it was too scary to see him get hurt. And its hard work being on the road all the time. Here you kids can play all day. Clay will be home soon. In a few weeks." She assured all three of them.

"I like cowboy better than Daddy." Ruby poked some noodles with her fork and pouted.

Kelli chuckled, "Me too, Baby."

"Cowboy's buying me boots mommy. Just like his. Only with pretties in them." She stuffed her mouth and Kelli watched her little legs kick as she talked excitedly, remembering every detail of his promise. "Then I'll be a cowgirl. Cowboy said I'll be the prettiest one. Its true mommy. He said so. And our boots will be the same."

"Well, he's not a liar so it must be true." She said, quoting him with a smile.

Kelli heard the familiar sound of Marty's truck pulling into the driveway outside. She hopped up and went outside to catch him on his way into the house next door. His hair was disheveled and he reached back into his truck before walking away to grab his lunch box and thermos, a huge wad of chewing tobacco distorting his face.

"Whatchya want, Woman?" He called to her without looking her direction.

"We're home." She said, walking to his porch ahead of him.

"I can see that. Without your man." He started muttering, "Damn bull riding bullsh..."

"Marty, I have to return this car to the rental place here in town... Can you pick us up and bring us back home?" She interrupted as he crossed in front of her to climb the stairs.

He stopped and glanced at her. His lip curled in one corner as he pretended to look disgusted. Kelli was not impressed, but his antics brought a smile to her face. He growled a little and spit off the porch beside him. He was part of Clay, and she had grown to love that about him.

"You can drive my car, we don't have to take your truck." She glowered at him a little, matching his scowl. "I will make you a big dinner for your fridge." She finally offered.

"Pot roast." He pushed his lips into a smooch as he thought about his order, his stained facial hair enveloping his mouth. "With red potatoes and sweet potatoes and carrots. And nothing funny or green."

"Alright, I can do that." He was not hard to figure out, he liked quiet, food, and beer. It wasn't a complex equation, and she'd solved it long before hitting the road with Clay.

He turned on his heel and shuffled to his door. "What time tomorrow?"

"Some time in the morning."

"Darn it, woman. You know I'm sleeping in the morning."

"How would I know that? All you ever do is growl at me." She felt a wave of nausea threatening as she raced back to the trailer, "We'll have to stop at the store so I can pick up your food."

She only heard him make gravely sounds in his throat before his door shut behind him. Her face hovered over the garbage in the kitchen a moment later as she tried to mentally calm her stomach. The kids stared at her, concerned, their forks poised midair. She willed herself not to throw up and took deep breaths as a cold sweat prickled her sides and arms. It passed. She was thankful, she'd need to eat something before she could vomit any more.

A little later, when she felt somewhat able, she hauled their suitcases in and set about unpacking them. It was good to hear the kids running about in play. They were taking turns riding "bulls" on the kitchen chairs. Kelli hoped it would be a fascination that would pass when Clay quit the rodeo and came home. The thought of Joshua riding the angry beasts threatened to make her throw up again.

Eventually Kelli tucked the kids into bed without any argument. They were indeed exhausted from travel and worry; compounded by the flight. They were asleep before she could turn off the bedroom light. On her way past she ducked into the bathroom. Curiosity was growing. She took a few deep breaths and picked up the white stick on the sink. At length she forced herself to look at it.

Two very positive lines looked back at her.

She felt sick. Sick and excited. Kelli left the spinning room and glaring test and stumbled out to the sofa to lay down. Halfway there she changed direction for the kitchen and grabbed up her cell phone and switched off everything but the stove light.

She tried to picture what a baby with Clay would look like. His strong jaw and thin lips. His brown hair and wide cleft chin. Her babies had been born with flaming red locks, this one would likely not be a redhead. It was a foreign thought. Two hours ticked by as she considered everything. It was exciting. She loved being pregnant and the knowledge of giving Clay a child of his own, even though he seemed to naturally to slip into the role of dad with her children, felt like the greatest gift she had to offer him. She still worried for him though. She'd be utterly alone without him, she cursed him and his rodeo under her breath and said a prayer for his safe return. She made herself believe that he'd never leave her, surely he was nothing like her past.

She bolstered her confidence and dialed Clay's phone number. It rang a few times before he finally answered.

"Hey, Girl." His voice was thick and satiny and instantly all her fears fled.

"Hey." She sighed a little. "Did you make it in yet?"

"Nah. Stopped to rest for a few hours. I got about another five or so to drive yet." She heard him grunt a little as he shifted in his seat. "Truck sure feels empty without you and the kids."

"This whole state feels empty without you." She cleared her throat a little and started to talk a few times but stopped. Finally she found the right words, "Clay, we gotta talk."

"Oh yeah?" She heard him sit up in his seat. "You leavin' me again? You know I'll just track you down, Girl." He was joking, but there was a level of uncertain seriousness in his tone.

"No, I'm not leaving you."

"That's a relief." He laid back down and his whiskers whooshed against the phone noisily. "What you want to talk about, Honey?"

"Babies."

"What about 'em." The words were, passive, indulging what he assumed was her simple conversation.

"Well... I did the math before I left and I was really late. So I took a test." She gathered herself, "It was positive."

There was silence on the other line for a few long minutes. She heard him draw in a long shuddering breath and exhale it out.

"Clay?" She asked quietly. His breath shuddered again, "Clay, are you crying?"

"No." He said with finality, then quietly, "Yes."

"Don't be upset. It'll all work out. We'll get married for real and I won't tell anyone until then. Although this is the third time around and likely I'll be the size of a hippo by November, I'm sure people will assume..." She trailed off.

"Upset? Not tell anyone?" He swore quietly under his breath, "This is the best damn news I've ever gotten. If I weren't stuck in this truck I'd be screamin' it all over this rest stop."

"Really?"

"Hell yes. Lemme see here. I can fly home in three days if I double time it to Colorado, I might be able to get away for an extra day or so." He said excitedly. "Why'd you have to go and leave me, Girl? Huh?"

"How's your knee? And your shoulder?" She changed the subject.

"Better now. Everything is better now." He sighed, "I just wish you were here so I could love on you."

Kelli sat up and took the phone away from her ear. She thought she heard a car door outside and listened intently for a few moments, but heard nothing further.

"You there? Kelli?" She could hear Clay as she picked the phone back up to her face.

"Yeah. I thought I heard someone outside." She listened again but still heard nothing. "It's nothing. I must have heard someone down the lot."

"Is my uncle home?"

"Yeah, he's taking us in the morning to return the rental car."

"I don't like you being so far away on your own." He fussed, "It took me all this time just to get you with me and now you've gone run off again."

"I know. I wish you were here." She said sincerely.

"Me, too, Girl. I wish you were at the ranch, though. Season'll be over before you know it." As he spoke his voice disappeared for a moment; she'd yawned and the pressure change in her ears deafened her. "You better head to bed, you sound tired. Don't want to over do yourself." He cautioned.

"Yeah, I am pretty beat." She stretched a little on the sofa. "But first tell me all the wonderful things about our life when you get home. I just want to hear your voice for a little while."

He chuckled a little bit and took a thoughtful breath "Well, we'll start out with some serious love makin'."

"Naturally." She smiled.

"And then I'll walk you all over the prairie back home and you can pick a place to build your house."

"You really want to build something? I feel like I am rapidly becoming a very expensive hobby for you."

"I've been roaming around collecting prize money ride'n bulls for nearly two decades and never had no one to spend it on besides the ranch and Momma. I've been waiting for a girl like you to come along. And you are not a hobby. You're everything to me, Kelli." He winced as he shifted his sore body again, "I mean that."

"I wish you'd just come home now."

"I gotta finish this circuit. I said I would. My yes is yes, Girl."

"Well, dead men have no babies."

"I'm not argue'n with you, woman. I ain't die'n either."

"I'm not arguing either, Clay. Just stating the facts, I can't raise this baby alone. Not with two others and no job."

"I'm gonna be right there beside you through every bit of it. Don't worry so much. Now you get some sleep. I'll call you in the morning, okay? Take care of yourself, little momma."

"Okay." She sighed sadly, let down that he refused to take her concern about him seriously.

"You're gonna be alright, Girl, didn't I tell ya?"

She laughed a little. "Yeah. Then you went and knocked me up."

He chuckled at her, "A man's defenses are only so strong against a woman like you."

"I suppose I am dangerous."

"Like a little tornado."

She cleared her throat. "Please be careful, Clay."

"I will, Darlin'. Don't fuss. Just relax. I'll send some money tomorrow, alright? You just relax and rest. I'll have Momma come check on you this week, too."

"Okay. Thanks Clay."

"Anything for you, Kelli. I'll be there as soon as I can get away." His scruff rustled against the phone again, "Call you in the morning."

The bedroom was quiet and lonely as she laid in it a little later. And the trailer felt spooky to her for the first time. She'd become so accustomed to Clay in the room with her that it was near impossible to fall asleep alone. Her mind began to wonder over the last couple days, and eventually recounted the uneasy words from Tim's last call. She shied from them quickly and thought instead about the baby, and about a new life, at home, on the ranch with Clay. Eventually her thoughts settled and she was able to fall asleep. She drifted into a dream about Clay and tall prairie grasses and cattle. The wind that blew through the grass smelled of dusty leather and Old Spice and she was warm and carefree.

Kelli started with a gasp at the sound of the kitchen door unlocking and opening. Her mind raced as she shooed the groggy cobwebs from her mind. Surely Ruby was too small to try to open the door. She ran from the bed and poked her head in the kids' bedroom. They were both asleep in their little tent beds, making tiny sleeping noises in the dark.

She stepped down the hall and reached into the living area for the light switch on the wall. Her hand flailed about in the dark searching for the light. White patches of city lights were cast on the dark floor of the space. Out of the corner of her eye, at the nearby kitchen island, she saw movement. The next thing she saw was red. A fist smashed into her eye socket and sent her reeling.

"I've been waiting for you to get home." Tim's voice sounded strange and thick and his words slurred. "I got pretty damn sick of driving by here every day this past month. And that damn motel room was getting expensive."

Kelli fell down, tears streaming from her eyes as she held her throbbing face. Tim reached down and picked her up by the neck of her shirt, choking her.

"Where have you been? Huh?" He kneed her hard in her stomach and she fell to her hands and knees coughing.

She raised her hands and tried to push him away, "Tim don't. Please, I'm pregnant." She gasped as his big hands wrapped around her upper arms and shook her.

"Did that dog get you pregnant? Eh?" He shook her harder. "Well I guess that'll make it a little son of a bitch then. You whore."

He cast her aside forcefully into the wall, sending her elbow straight through the flimsy particle board material. He moved down the hall to the kid's room and kicked the door hard, disappearing into the darkness inside.

Kelli scrambled to her knees, crawling down the hall after him. She met him in there, one of the kids tucked under each of his arms. Ruby's hair hung down over her face and she cried in unison with Joshua, clawing and pulling as they tried to free themselves.

"Ouch! Daddy! Ow!" Ruby sobbed as Joshua just screamed in terror.

Kelli reached for them but her side met with Tim's heavy shoe. He took a step after her and paused to kicked her again.

"Guess you wont be needing these anymore, now that you got a new one." He bent down and jostled the kids a little at her. His breath smelled like like liquor and cigarette smoke.

"Tim, no!" She screamed, crawling and clawing for the children as he walked away. She coughed and spat up bile, forcing herself to stand. "Stop! You can't take them! No!"

Tim stopped short and tossed the kids into a pile on the floor. He doubled back and pushed her into the kitchen wall. "You shut up. You damned little bitch. You ruined *everything*. These are *my* children. That damn dirty dog can make his own with my sloppy seconds, but *these* ones are mine." He slammed his fist into her face again after cutting her an evil look in the dark.

She gasped and fought the enclosing darkness around her peripheral vision. Her hearing collapsed into a single ringing tone. As her sight faded she saw the children reaching for her as Tim hauled them out the door. And then she passed out.

All track of time was lost in the black. And her memory was hazy when she came back to herself. Kelli looked around at the dark ceiling over her and wondered how she'd got there. Soon the pain in her face and stomach jogged her memory. She scrambled to her feet and ran to the door which was still ajar. The driveway was emptied of Tim's vehicle and the warm night was treacherously quiet. She fell on the floor inside the kitchen door. The muscles in her middle burned and throbbed sharply with pain.

Great sobs rose up in her throat. She kicked the door open and screamed Marty's name. Begging him for help before searching for her phone in the kitchen, only able to stand for a few seconds at a time. She knocked things off the counter as her hands searched clumsily. Things clattered and smashed. Finally she found it and fell to the floor. She dialed 911 and heard Marty's door tear open outside simultaneously.

"He stole my children!" She screamed at the phone and Marty who staggered sleepily through her door, his jeans not even buttoned and his feet bare.

"Calm down ma'am" The operator soothed, "Who stole your children. Where are you?"

Kelli gave the man her address and recounted the story to him. "Please, I'm afraid he'll hurt them."

She hung up, hearing the scream of sirens in the far distance and dialed Clay's phone. She watched Marty pace the floor before her. It rang to voice mail and she hung up. She dialed again but there was no answer. Again she tried. Finally he answered, groggy with sleep.

"Hey, Girl." He said, rubbing his face and jostling the phone.

"He took them! Oh God, Clay! He took the kids!" Her voice seethed and gasped so much she hardly understood herself.

"What? Kelli! Clam down, I can't hear what you're sayin'." His voice grew tight with concern.

Kelli breathed in whistling gasps, "Tim! He broke into the house and took the kids."

"Where is he?"

"I don't know!" She shrieked, "He knocked me out, I don't even know how long they've been gone!" She sobbed hysterically into the phone.

"I'll kill 'em. I'm gonna kill 'em." He seethed. She

heard him shuffling around; heard doors open and shut and his truck engine roar to life. "Go get my uncle, have Marty stay with you."

"He's here already..." She cried.

Marty stomped over and tore the phone from her, "You get your ass home NOW boy. You hear me? Enough of this bullshit. Be a man." She could hear Clay screaming at his uncle from the distance between them, "You just get yourself on a plane. I will pick you up. I ought to beat the shit out of your useless candy ass. Chasing those damn belt buckles, you're as useless as your father was." He had to stop himself from throwing the phone at Kelli in disgust.

Clay was spitting angry on the phone when she put it to her ear, obviously unaware that Marty was no longer there.

"Clay?" He stopped short.

"Are you okay, Girl? Are you hurt bad?" His voice caught with emotion.

She sobbed quietly for a few minutes, "He kicked my stomach a bunch. It really hurts."

The truck engine roared over the phone line as Clay punched the gas. "I'll be there in a few hours, Baby. Hang on." His voice sounded different, it was laced with something she'd never known him to express before.

Fear.

Screaming sirens pulled into the park and skidded to a stop outside her trailer. "The police are here." She cried. "I have to go. Please come home, Clay."

"I'm comin', Kelli. It's gonna be alright." He growled before hanging up the phone. But this time she knew he was assuring himself just as much as her.

Paramedics crowded in behind the police officers as they entered. Kelli recognized the taller officer from the last time the police had come out. The sight of her made him shake his head.

"I told you." He said, kneeling down beside her on the floor where she sat, recalling his advice to her earlier that summer. "I'm so sorry, ma'am. Everyone is already out, we will find them." He assured her.

"Please!" Kelli sobbed until she had to throw up, but she only racked with dry heaves.

She retold the account again to the officer as the paramedics helped her to the ambulance. They insisted she come to the hospital, doubling their pressure after she confessed she was newly pregnant.

"We'll find him. We already have a code blue across the area. He wont get far." The tall officer reassured her again as the paramedics shut the doors to the back of the ambulance and drove off.

She watched Marty and the policemen grow smaller as they stood talking at the end of the drive. She curled onto her side and cried. The EMT beside her patted her shoulder and tried his best to sooth her between asking her different questions about her health and how she was feeling.

Kelli felt like she was dying. She prayed the tiny seed within her had escaped unharmed. She prayed that her children would be found quickly. A glint of morning light was burning the horizon as they neared the hospital. People were driving to their jobs and doing every day things like stopping for coffee. But she felt no recognition or connection to the everyday. She was locked in a bad dream.

"How will I hear from them?" She asked the man sitting beside her as the vehicle slowed. "How will I know when they've found my babies?"

She tried to keep from thinking about news stories she'd heard over the years. Stories of insane spouses killing themselves and their children. Abandoned children found besides their parent's bodies. Children drowned in tubs. She tried to block them out. But the nightmarish thoughts overwhelmed her.

"There will be an officer here. The one on duty at the hospital. We'll have him stay outside your room."

"Really?" She felt a little calmer.

"Really." He assured her as her gurney bumped out of the vehicle.

-CHAPTER TEN-

Kelli had drifted to sleep after many tests and a dose of pain killers and light sedatives. The hospital doctor had insisted on an MRI scan of her head after looking at her swollen face and reddened eye. He also ordered an ultrasound to confirm her pregnancy. The whole process was unnerving. She felt like a ghost watching foreign events happen around her. Without her children she was nothing.

The scan had revealed a very thin crack in her left eye socket, and the bridge of her nose had been broken. Neither were very bad and aside from the swelling and pain they were fine. Their main concern was her eye. The organ itself was full of blood and swollen slightly. Neither were good signs, but the doctor was confident that since the retina was firmly attached still it would be alright. Kelli didn't care either way, she just wanted to hear Ruby's little voice and feel Joshua in her arms. Everything the doctor said sounded like water in a tin can to her.

The ultrasound had been the only thing of interest to her. The black snowy screen had focused on a tiny figure-eight- shaped mass within her innermost being. The technician pointed to one half of the eight and explained that it was the yolk sac. She had pressed some buttons and shifted the view to the other side of the mass. It flickered with pulsating movements. The tiny heart thrived within the undefinable mass. The woman kindly pointed out the hard to detect features. The tiny head, the spine which ended in a tail still, and four little nubbins that would soon grow into limbs. The baby was alive and healthy. Kelli wept with joy as they wheeled her out of radiology and back to her room.

She dozed fitfully through the rest of the morning. She

roused herself twice to call the officer on the chair in the hall outside her room and ask him if he'd heard anything yet. Both times he regretfully said no. Depression squashed her into the yucky plastic-smelling hospital mattress and threatened to stifle her breath completely. She drifted back to sleep trying to escape it and the sounds of beeping and whooshing machinery.

When she awoke again the doctor was standing at the bed beside her.

"Ma'am. I am going to sign your release papers. Everything looks good at this point, but you're going to need to follow up in the morning with your doctor." He autographed some papers on the clipboard in his hand. "Unfortunately there's nothing we can do if you should experience any vaginal bleeding or cramping. But the pregnancy and baby look good. Your body has done this before and that tends to help a lot in these situations. I want you to come back into the ER if you start to feel dizzy, or start vomiting uncontrollably, or if your vision blurs. Muscle weakness, loss of coordination; these are all signs of complications from a concussion. Those hits to your face are pretty serious."

"I don't have a car." She said blankly, unable to process anything.

"Oh, you can't drive. Not for a week at least. No, you'll have to call for a ride. Or a taxi."

She nodded. "Where are my things?"

The officer outside her room came in and helped the doctor rummage around for her cell phone and clothes. She felt more alone than any one person should ever be able to feel. Where would she go? She couldn't bear the thought of going back to the trailer. She could hardly consider anything except sitting her car and waiting for something to happen. Or someone to come wake her from this terrible dream and rescue her. She wanted to go sit at the police station, but knew they'd only send her away.

"I can give you a ride Ma'am." The officer said. He was short and Latino and his face was soft and friendly looking.

"Okay. Just let me get dressed and tell people where I am." The men left her alone and she eased herself out of the bed. Her body screamed in pain with every movement. Her head throbbed. And even through the medication her stomach rolled angrily.

The door flung open again almost instantly as she was struggling into her shirt. Clay stumbled into the room, looking around wildly. He rushed to her in a flash, grabbing her up against him gingerly. His hands hovered over her bruised face, unable to find a safe place to hold. Tears welled up in his eyes as he looked her over.

"I'm done. No more. Not ever." His voice was tearful. "Damn the sponsors and the circuit. I'm not leavin' you alone for even another hour so long as I live." He promised apologetically.

"They still haven't found him." Kelli said, sobs choking out the words as she laid her head carefully on his chest.

He wasn't wearing his sling or his knee brace. He stood on his good leg and held her with both arms, but more strongly with the left one. "He's a darn coward Kelli, he wont hurt 'em. They'll find him. He better hope they find him before I do. I'll kill 'em." He held her away from him a little and looked her all over. "Are you okay?"

She nodded. "They thought at first that I was going to lose my eye, but it look worse than it is. It'll be okay in a week or so. The baby is alive and everything looks good with the pregnancy."

Relief fell across his whole person and again tears threatened his eyes. He towered over her protectively, carefully laying his arms around her bruised body again.

"Never again, Kelli. Never." He whispered into her

hair. "I am so sorry."

"I want my children." She said through sobs and hiccups.

"They will be found, and they will be alright." He stated steadfastly, as if he were commanding the universe to produce it.

Kelli nodded, trying desperately to believe him. He sounded so terrible she thought fate wouldn't even dare make a liar of him. They stood for a long while holding each other. Clay muttered whatever promises or exclamations he thought might ease any of her suffering. And when that failed he held her and let her cry.

"Excuse me?" The police officer knocked on the door and called to her quietly, interrupting their thoughts.

"Yes?" Kelli wiped her eyes and looked around Clay to the door.

"Ma'am, they found him. They just picked them up at a convenience store in Bismark. The children are fine."

Kelli fell to her knees sobbing. Clay knelt down with her and held her close as, new, thankful tears shook her body. She gasped and laughed and wrapped her arm around her sore middle.

"You can wait for them to send them home after the paper work is filed, or you can drive out to the station in Bismark and bring them home yourself." The radio on his shoulder buzzed as she began shaking with relief. It had only been less than eight hours, but it had felt like an eternity for her.

"Oh! Oh, we'll leave right now! Just tell me where to go!" Clay helped her to her feet.

"I told them you'd be down there." The officer laughed a little. "I'm glad this worked out well. These situations so often can end in tragedy." They followed him as he talked, leading them out to the main doors.

Clay had driven to the hospital in the small rental

car he'd gotten her. Marty had dropped him off at it after picking him up from the Bismark airport. Kelli did not want to know about their time spent together. The snapping anger in Marty's usually kind eyes had made his rough face look terrifying when she'd been hauled away that morning. She didn't want to know about the berating she was certain Clay has taken.

Her legs shook and she pressed her feet into the floorboard as the car tore down the freeway towards Bismark. Clay held her hand the whole way, rubbing the rough callous of his thumb over the smooth back of her hand. He raised it to his lips countless times and kissed her fingers, or just held her hand against his mouth and breathed in the smell of her skin. She knew he still had to be in pain from his injuries that were only two days old, but if he was he hid it from her completely. Aside from a gimpy walk he acted and moved strong, like his normal self.

The doctor at the hospital had sent her on her way with some anti-nausea medication that was working wonders. He had cautioned her about her weight and as they left he encouraged her to eat freely and relax more. It had floated in one ear and out the other, her only concern was getting her arms around her children.

The highway slipped away under them, and little towns and countryside flew by. The sun shined from nearer the horizon behind them. But she hardly noticed anything except the slowest moving clock she'd ever endured.

It felt like an eternity before the little rental car pulled into the parking lot of the single story brick police station. Black squad cars were parked in rows behind chain link fences and a pair of officers in their black uniforms stood outside smoking and talking. They stared at her bewilderingly as she jogged towards the entrance. Clay tried to keep up behind her, but his own injuries made it difficult. No doubt they were taken aback by her swollen face and blood-red eye and his broken gate.

Kelli flew through the doors and up to the glass window inside the waiting area. She caught the reflection of her face in the glass and felt a little embarrassed. She looked horrible. Her cheeks were swollen and her lip had a huge knot in it. Her eye was still swollen almost shut and the whole area was a bright purple color. The officer behind the window looked up at her and started slightly.

"You have my children!" She panted as Clay finally caught up to her and placed his hand across her back reassuringly. "Ruby and Joshua Nevins, they were kidnapped by their father, Timothy Nevins."

"They said you'd be coming. The children are with some FBI agents right now, you can come right in and see them Ma'am." He handed her some papers, "Mister Nevins the one that did this to your face?" The man behind the glass eyed her, shaking his head.

Kelli nodded and signed the papers before sliding them back under the glass to him. He pressed a button under the counter and the heavy metal door to the right of them buzzed. Kelli raced to it and Clay opened it around her. Inside were various offices and desks. People in handcuffs sat in chairs, and some looked up at them with blank expressions as they entered.

An officer met them and walked them towards the back rooms. They passed a throng of criminals in the holding area and a half dozen officers that milled about doing paper work.

Clay's reassuring hand suddenly left her back and she turned just in time to see him hop over the short divider railing between the hall and the chairs full of arrestees. She spotted Tim sitting in a chair in the back row near a desk. He looked up into the end of Clay's fist, without any time to move.

Clay pounded him with such ferocity that it took a

team of six men to pull him off.

"You coward! Beatin' on a pregnant woman! Stealin' children!" Clay struggled against the men that held him with his elbows high behind him. He broke free and tore into him again, "I'll kill you, you son of a bitch!"

Even the biggest thugs in the holding area jumped aside. They exclaimed and winced as the beating continued nearby. They huddled at the length of the handcuffs that tied them to their chairs.

Clay grabbed Tim's head and held it in a tight grip, forcing him to look at Kelli, "Look what you did! You bastard!" He threw him loose.

His boots lashed out at where Tim had crumpled onto the floor between the toppled chair and desk. He stopped only to shove the police away from him before snatching Tim up another time. He threw a few more punches, both of them losing their balance.

Officers pulled him away again. Others rushed to gain control of the group of handcuffed men that hissed and jeered at their brother-in-cuffs that would be cast to the lowest standing behind bars for the nature of his crimes.

"I oughta bust your head open on that floor!" Clay's voice was terrible, and his body coiled tight against the men holding him.

Tim made no attempt to argue. His hands were cuffed before him and he laid on his side looking up at Clay. Clay struggled harder against the officers and nearly freed himself from their grasp a few times before yet another police officer tackled him to the floor.

"Clay!" Kelli yelled at him as the pile of men produced a very ruffled Clay, in hand cuffs.

An aged, fat, officer accompanied by a middle aged man in a black suit looked on as he was finally subdued and quieted. Kelli remained where she was as they dragged him by his elbows out of the holding area and back into the hall.

"Ma'am?" The man in the suit asked her, stealing her attention away from Clay. She nodded at him. "I'm agent Jefferson with the FBI. Is this your..."

"Husband. Clayton Tackett" She informed him.

Clay was still seething, his lip curled up baring his teeth as he breathed in big puffs and stared at Tim on the floor a small distance away. Tim could only look at the other prisoners who leered at him and growled suggestive obscenities at him.

"Oh, this must be 'Cowboy' that your kids spoke of." He turned to Clay who was standing with his hands behind him.

They both paused and watched as Tim was hoisted back up into his chair. Huge red welts were rising on his face and a steady stream of blood trickled from his nose and over his lips and chin. The agent walked over and slapped Clay's shoulder.

"I don't know about you, Sergeant, but I didn't see anything here. In fact, so long as Mr. Tackett can find some restraint I'd venture to guess Mr. Nevins fell right out of his chair without any cause or provocation. That's what the rest of you saw, isn't it? That man falling right out of his chair by himself?" he pointed at Tim, glancing around the room at the other prisoners.

Many of them nodded and a few made whooping sounds.

Some mumbled 'Yes, Sir'.

Clay seethed. Huge breaths of air rushed through his flared nostrils and mouth. He looked between the officer and Tim. Finally he spoke.

"Yessir." He said, calming himself down.

The officers slowly loosened their grip on him. Clay turned away from Tim and focused on Agent Jefferson and Kelli.

"I hope everything is okay." Jefferson asked, indicating her wounded face and bloodied eye.

"It will be when I have my babies back." Then she asked, "What about Tim?"

"Mr. Nevins has committed a federal crime, ma'am. On top of a slew of other charges, he'll be going to prison after a simple trial."

Kelli smiled with relief. "Are the children okay?" She asked, "When can I see them?"

"They're shaken up, and tired, but aside from some bruises they are not injured." The squat little police sergeant behind Agent Jefferson answered.

A female officer emerged from around a distant hallway corner, almost on cue. Kelli caught immediate sight of them, even with her swollen eyes. The officer held Ruby and Joshua's hands, guiding them reassuringly. The children had bags under their eyes and walked solemnly and obediently with the strange woman.

Joshua caught sight of Kelli first, and despite her swollen and tattered appearance he wrenched his hand loose and ran for her. Kelli jogged to him forgetting all the pain in her body. The sound of his little shoes beating the floor was joined by cries of Ruby calling for mommy. Kelli sank to her knees and wrapped them both in a bear hug. Her body ached and stabbed like knives as they snuggled against her, but she didn't care. They were hers and they were in her arms.

She kissed them until she couldn't anymore. And then she held them so close she could feel them breathe. Cries of joy and relief spilled from all three of them and echoed through the entire place that had grown quiet at the sight of them.

"Cowboy!" Ruby shouted, tearing free of Kelli after a few moments. The little girl's tear filled eyes locked on his. She ran to him and he lifted her up and hugged her. "I missed you! Where were you?"

"I don't know!" He crooned, "But I ain't leavin' again." He petted her poofy red locks and pressed her head against his shoulder. Joshua let loose of his mother and ran to Clay also, wrapping himself around his leg, sitting his little diapered bottom on his big boot. He looked up at him and grinned widely.

"Hey buckaroo." Clay said looking down at him. He reached down and pulled him up and set him on his other arm, across from Ruby. He looked at Kelli as she pulled herself up from the floor. "Lets get out of here, huh?"

Kelli walked to him and wrapped her arm around his waist, leaning her bruised head against his arm. Everything was together, everything she wanted was right here. The sweet smell of her children and dusty leather and Old Spice filled her senses. She smiled and nodded.

"Who wants to go ride a Strawberry pony?" Clay asked the kids, bouncing them a little in his arms.

They both replied with excited squeals, throwing off the terrible trouble of the night.

"Ma'am, we'll need you to fill out some paperwork for the investigation and indictment." Agent Jefferson informed her as they turned to leave.

"You'll find her at my place, sir. I'm takin' my family home." Clay handed Joshua to Kelli and placed his wide hand across her back possessively, guiding her down the hall away from her awful old life and into a new one.

Kelli smiled deeply, "Home." She repeated dreamily, hanging on his arm.

-EPILOGUE-

"The place suits you." Clay pointed out.

His wrists rested on the saddle horn of the big roan he worked on daily. He'd shown up for his usual midday visit from the pastures.

Kelli looked down at him from the deck, then across the prairie behind him. It stretched out, unbroken, 180 degrees before her. Huge clouds, white as bleached linens, sailed by in slow motion. The grasses nodded and rolled like waves. Birds called from the tree tops where the creek flowed through its deep gully. In the far distance long bands of black cattle seemed to flow like a constant stream through the hills.

Their new house surveyed it all with her from the hill where it was perched. It was painted a soft yellow and the four sided roof squatted low above the walls and banks of windows. It provided a roof over the deck. And it smelled like raw, bruised, wood and paint; the scents wafting out through the open windows and screen door.

"I love this house." She stated, again, for what had to have been the millionth time since they moved in. Her hands smoothed back and forth along the top deck railing as she thought about it.

"Stop it." Clay said, low.

"Stop what?" She asked, grinning; snapping back from her revelry.

"Stop touchin' the darn railing like that. It's makin' me jealous." He took his hat off and watched her devilishly. "Where's the kids?"

"Your mom came and got them again while you were running fence. She wanted to spend some time with them. The baby is inside sleeping though, I just laid him down." She traced her finger along the top of the railing purposefully, biting her lip. "It's just me, here. All by my lonesome, Cowboy."

"Girl." He said, lowering his eyes at her while stuffing his hat on and pulling the brim down low, "You better run, cause if I catch you..."

"Maybe I wanna be caught." She interrupted, leaning over the railing at him.

He hopped off the horse so fast it danced sideways and he accidentally jerked the reigns tying it to the deck post. Kelli squealed excitedly at the sound of his boots clamoring up the porch steps.

They ran through the sliding door laughing, and she dodged his grasps as he neared. She deftly danced and leaped through the kitchen and living room, always just a fraction of an inch ahead of him. Her shrieks and his laughter echoed through the place.

Finally, Clay caught her around the waist as she scooted around the recliner in the living room and spun her around to him, planting hot kisses on her face and neck. They both laughed, exchanging kisses, through puffs of breath from the exertion of the chase. Kelli pulled his hat off and threw it on the sofa as he lifted her into his arms and carried her down the hall; his spurs chiming and muddy boots thumping.

"You better not wake the baby." She chided, her face burrowed in his neck.

"Speak for yourself." He chuckled, laying her out on their big canopy bed and kicking out of his boots and jeans.

She did the same, only faster, and they laughed at the race of it.

"You can't keep doing this every day." Kelli warned, her silk shirt bouncing off him as he made his way to her.

Clay paused kissing her just long enough to look at her questioningly.

"Your uncle is going to get royally ticked off that he has to send someone to come find you nearly every afternoon." She explained.

"Why, Missus..." He sat up, taking in the sight of her warm naked skin under his fingers, "You sound like you're complainin'."

He laughed when she yanked him back down to her by his shoulders, "I'm only complaining if its an eight second ride."

"You little tornado." He growled, smiling against her mouth.

A long while later they lay together in a beam of summer sun that spilled in from the double windows beside the bed. Kelli drank in the vision of him gleaming in the sun; his tan body slick with sweat and bulging with testosterone inflamed muscles. His thin upper lip curled near the corners as he smiled at her, tracing the hills and valley of her hip, waist and side. Their trance was broken by the urgent crying of a waking baby down the hall.

Kelli pulled his shirt on and snapped the buttons quickly as she padded along the hardwood floor to the baby's room and returned a moment later, laying their little creation on the bed between them. Clay offered him a finger and then kissed his little hand when he grabbed onto it.

"He's so perfect." Clay said dreamily.

"He looks so much like you." She noted the baby's long legs and straight mouth. Already, at just over three months of age, he had his father's slightly cleft chin.

"Did you know my daddy's sisters were all red heads." He said in passing, "My grandmother too."

"Really?"

"Oh yeah. Even my great aunt had hair as red as fire and it stood out on all sides if she didn't keep it wrapped up." He smoothed the baby's brown locks, "Momma can show you pictures some time. Hair as red as Ruby's and Joshua's, even on the day they died."

"Clay..."

He turned from the baby, loosening his grip from him before taking a hold of her face. He kissed her slowly, his lips transferring silent information like a telegraph wire. Kelli felt as if she were melting as slow as molasses, like a Dali portrait.

"It's like ya'll were mine all along." He said against the corner of her mouth. "I shoulda come found you sooner."

"We'll make up for it, I'm sure." She said, laying her head on his shoulder.

"I'll make up for it. I'll make up for all of it, Kelli." He promised her.

The warm breeze of late spring billowed the white curtains. Clay smoothed her hair and sighed with contentment. From the bed she could see into the room the baby shared with his brother, and also into Ruby's bedroom. They were also cast in the soft glow of a sunny day, and were warm with soft carpet and rich paint and furniture. And everywhere everything spoke of their love. Everything was right with the world. Kelli was amazed at how healing 'okay' felt to her, and to the children.

Tim was little more than a strange word that drifted through her memories. Cowboy remained the biggest man in her children's lives. And all of it built into the explosive crescendo of a happily cooing newborn; the physical expression of all they were.

"Well, this is a great start." Kelli said, watching their smiling infant with him.

It *was* a perfect start. And inside a thankful prayer welled up from her heart for all distance between her old life and this bright new world beside Clay. Because once again life was free and new and pure.

COMING SOON!

TYLER
BY P.C. ROGERS

Joanna's stubborn resourcefulness is no match for fate...

Joanna hates no one half so much as Tyler McCollister. The annoying neighbor boy who hunted her across their Wyoming ranch lands, the school kid who picked on her mercilessly, and the judgmental ass who questioned her every adult decision. As if circumstances couldn't get worse she learns at the reading of her father's will that he sold her beloved, ailing, ranch- all but the house and barns- to none other than McCollister's modernized operation. Now she's forced to deal with him nearly every day. She wont give up though, she'd rather work herself to death than touch that money, even with a newborn in tow. That's just what it comes down to, and its only after severing ties with Tyler that she begins to realize that the noises he'd been making all her life hadn't been meant as cruel, they'd been his awkward, desperate, love song. Joanna finds herself adrift in a sinister, murderous plot to acquire her money. Has her hurtful pride made Tyler blind to her silent cries for help? Can the man who's loved her for a lifetime save her and Baby Henry, or is it too late?

STAY UP TO DATE AT: WWW.PCROGERS.COM

Made in the USA
Middletown, DE
15 January 2023